THE LAST STAR WARDEN
VOLUME II:
The Un Quan Saga

Written and Illustrated by
Jason J. McCuiston

From
Dark Owl Publishing, LLC

Praise for

THE LAST STAR WARDEN
VOLUME II:
The Un Quan Saga

"In the tales of the Last Star Warden, Jason J. McCuiston didn't just take sword-and-planet space-fantasy, half a dozen other sub-genres of science fiction, the classic Western, superhero comics, the long tradition of pulp adventure stories, and real world concerns and throw them in a blender, he carefully deconstructed them and reassembled them into something as fresh as it is exciting. He did it. He made science fiction fun again!"

~ Philip Athans,
Author of *Writing Monsters* and *The Best of Fantasy Authors Handbook*

"Filled with adventure and danger, *The Last Star Warden – The Un Quan Saga* by Jason J. McCuiston is retro sci-fi at its best. After entering a void-spanning wormhole, The Warden crashes his vessel on an alien planet at the edge of Uncharted Space. The Warden's newest galactic journey features a Forbidden City, robots, clones, smoking blasters, and attacking carnivores on a world divided by gender. A sense of wonder permeates McCuiston's novel and makes readers long for The Last Star Warden's next perilous mission."

~ Vonnie Winslow Crist,
award-winning author of *Dragon Rain*, *Murder on Marawa Prime*, and other books

"A non-stop thrill ride of nostalgic science fiction with aliens, planets, ship and gun fights. Intrigue and suspense are woven into the action and revolve around the classic hero, The Last Star Warden. Fans of throwback sci-fi and Star Trek will love it."

~ R.M. Schultz,
Author of *The Forgotten Sky*

Praise for

THE LAST STAR WARDEN:
Tales of ADVENTURE and MYSTERY
from Frontier Space
Volume I

"...Jason J. McCuiston's *The Last Star Warden* is about an actual hero... the titular Star Warden. The stories have everything that one could want in science fiction action/adventure. There's dastardly villains, shootouts, space battles, mysterious space stations, and an indomitable sense of right and wrong... The Star Warden is a straightforward hero—no deconstruction, no metanarrative, no satirization. He's an unapologetic Good Guy. He's a rarity in his world, and in this one as well..."

~ Carl R. Jennings,
Reviewer for *Phantasmagoria Magazine* and author of *Just About Anyone*

"*The Last Star Warden* is exactly what it looks like: a rollicking collection of space western stories. McCuiston delivers big with plenty of imagination and thrills. He pays homage to a western classic formula while injecting enough delightful alien weirdness to justify the intergalactic setting. The Warden and Quantum are unashamedly heroic heroes doing what's right in an unforgiving universe. Highly recommended."

~ Bryce Beattie,
Editor of *StoryHack Action & Adventure* and author of *Swordcrossed Frostbite*

"The Last Star Warden—a.k.a. 'The Phantom Lawman' or 'The Ghost of the Frontier'—finds himself displaced a hundred years into his future and facing off against numerous foes and dangers he never dreamed possible: a derelict space station haunted by vengeful ghosts, a behemoth corporate-built machine that feasts on entire stars, and a merciless prison ship among them. Armed only with his twin Comet pistols and his former-enemy-turned-sidekick Quantum for backup, the Last Star Warden meets all with steely grace and nobility—and a rare and refreshing level of pure, pulpy fun. Jason McCuiston's excellent book of adventures reads like a time warp back to boyhood Saturdays when classic Science Fiction played all afternoon on UHF. A fantastic experience!"

~ Gregory L. Norris,
Author of the *Gerry Anderson's Into Infinity* novels by Anderson Entertainment

Also From
Dark Owl Publishing

Anthologies
A Celebration of Storytelling
The anthological festival of tales

Something Wicked This Way Rides
Where genre fiction meets the Wild West

Collections
The Dark Walk Forward
A harrowing collection of frightful stories from John S. McFarland

The Last Star Warden:
Tales of Adventure and Mystery from Frontier Space, Volume I
The first in the series of the Star Warden's adventures from
Jason J. McCuiston

No Lesser Angels, No Greater Devils
Beautiful and haunting stories collected from Laura J. Campbell

Novels
The Keeper of Tales
An epic fantasy adventure by Jonathon Mast

Just About Anyone
High fantasy comedy from the twisted mind of Carl R. Jennings

The Black Garden
An atmospheric gothic historical fiction novel from John S. McFarland

Young Readers Novels
(Coming December 1, 2021)

Dragons of the Ashfall
Book One of the War of Leaves and Scales
An epic steampunk fantasy story by Jonathon Mast

Grayson North: Frost-Keeper of the Windy City
A totally cool urban fantasy adventure from Kevin M. Folliard

Buy the books for Kindle and in paperback
www.darkowlpublishing/the-bookstore

For Kim.

Table of Contents

PART I

i.

The Last Star Warden ducked behind a stack of PlaSteel crates as blaster fire zipped through the artificial air. The Silver Knuckles were determined not to let him escape the pirate base alive.

"We have reached the Einstein-Rosen bridge." Quantum's emotionless voice sounded from the earbuds in the Warden's cowl. "I will get the refugees to the nearest Star Cav outpost and come back for you as soon as is practicable."

The Warden's twin Comet blasters dropped another pirate. A dozen more rakishly garbed and heavily armed men seemed to take the dead freebooter's place. If the Warden gave the gang enough time, poorly disciplined as they were, they could still trap him in a lethal crossfire.

The Warden spoke into his chrono. "Don't worry about me. I think I see another way out." He scanned the three-engine, silver-and-black corvette on the landing platform with his multi-spectrum visor. It wasn't armed, but it was fully fueled. "Just make sure those people don't become slaves again."

Not waiting for a response from his alien friend, the Warden charged from cover. Both pistols led with a barrage of fiery bolts. Pirates scattered or fell before the supercharged plasma salvo from the blue-and-silver clad phantom.

The buccaneers guarding the ship understood they faced a living legend, but now they saw firsthand the skill and courage which had engendered that legend. The Star Wardens had died out decades before, but this man was the embodiment of the heyday of those fabled peacekeepers. Criminals accustomed to preying on the weak and outnumbered were simply no match for the so-called "Phantom Lawman."

The Warden leapt aboard the ship, firing at the rallying pirates as he sealed the hatch. A few moments later, under a hail of blaster fire, the commandeered spacecraft took flight. The corvette rocketed away from the slaver space station hidden deep in the heart of the Seti Omega asteroid belt.

The Warden lay in a course for the system's single Einstein-Rosen bridge, wishing he had been able to finish off the slave market and the pirate gang. He consoled himself in knowing that he and Quantum had rescued over two dozen people, now crammed aboard the *Ranger VII* and on their way to freedom. They had also wrecked the pirate fleet's flagship in drydock. If the Silver Knuckles weren't done for, they were certainly on their last leg.

The Warden hoped he would have the opportunity to finish the job someday soon.

That hope seemed more than a little optimistic when proximity alerts sounded from the corvette's control panel. The Warden scanned the instruments, noting six gunships moving to intercept. If he had been at the helm of his beloved *Ranger VII*, the long-range assault scout he had flown since the days before the Continuum War, six pirate fighters would be little more than an annoyance. Instead, he was aboard a stolen corvette that, while well-armored, had been on the landing pad for weapons maintenance. Maintenance yet to be carried out, space pirates not being among the most conscientious of workers.

"I guess we'll have to do this the hard way." The Warden throttled the engines to maximum and raced directly for the ERB. He wouldn't attempt evasive action unless absolutely necessary. He was counting on his bigger ship's hull plating to outlast the poor marksmanship exhibited by the typical pirate flyer. He knew if he could reach the bridge, the gunships would break off their attack. They would not dare follow him into what could be a Star Cav stronghold.

When the first fighter made its pass, the Warden almost laughed. The pirate went wide, spraying blaster-cannon fire over a hundred meters off the mark. The second and third ships did no better. Which was when the Warden realized he might be in trouble.

"Not even drunken pirates are that consistently bad shots."

They were intentionally trying to draw him into an engagement, trying to draw his attention. Tapping in a wide-spectrum scan, he understood why. Another ship, a larger, faster corsair-class had just emerged from the asteroid belt. The Silver Knuckles on the station had needed just enough time to get this hunter into the chase.

Alarms blared and the Warden pushed the corvette into a starboard spiral as a barrage of rockets streamed past the hull. The fighters formed up on the corsair in something resembling a military formation. He would have to take evasive action after all.

"Or maybe not." The Warden pulled back on the yoke with all his strength, forcing the corvette into a hard bank. Back toward his enemies.

Pushing his borrowed craft into a dive straight for the corsair, the Warden locked on the enemy ship with the targeting controls. Blaster fire raked the corvette's armored hull but did little damage. The Warden had no missiles, but the corsair's crew did not necessarily know that.

They did as he'd expected. The larger ship fired retrorockets, banked hard to port, and jettisoned a cloud of chaff to confuse guidance systems. The problem with this tactic was that the corsair's six wingmen were not notified first.

Two of the gunships were shredded as they flew through the clouds of exploding metal chaff like hitting a debris field at supersonic speeds. Another pair spiraled into explosive collisions with asteroids after being clipped by the corsair's large dorsal fin. Seeing the carnage wrought by their own ally, the last two fighters broke off and headed for the station.

The Warden made use of the confusion, putting the corvette back on its original heading at maximum speed. He was halfway to the Einstein-Rosen bridge before the corsair regained a pursuit vector. By the way the ship closed the gap, the Warden guessed the corsair was burning in the red, risking a reactor meltdown. The pirate captain must have been embarrassed by losing the unexpected game of chicken and was not willing to let his opponent get away unpunished.

An alarm signaled a weapons lock. The Warden checked the countermeasures, noted they had also not been restocked. He swung the corvette hard to port, then cut just as hard to starboard. He skimmed a rolling asteroid, putting the giant rock between himself and the launched missile. The asteroid exploded and the sound of shrapnel pounding the armored hull echoed through the cockpit. The ship stuttered as a cloud of irradiated dust enveloped the engine ports.

The Warden pushed the throttle into the red as fiery plasma bolts zipped past the corvette. Several hit the ship, ricocheting harmlessly off the armored plating but jarring just the same. Blaring alarms announced that the corsair had scored a hit on one of the corvette's three engines.

The Warden activated the emergency jettison protocol, sending the damaged cell hurtling back at his pursuing enemy.

Just a few hundred kilometers separated him from the huge glowing rectangle gateway of the Einstein-Rosen bridge.

"If I'm lucky and time this right, the shockwave will carry me into the ERB before he can get another lock."

The Warden was half lucky.

The atomic drive in the damaged cell exploded, but not before it had passed the missile already heading his way. The shockwave sent both the warhead and the damaged corvette careening into the yawning mouth of the opened Einstein-Rosen bridge. Worse, the substandard shielding on the pirate craft did not protect the controls and instruments from the ensuing electromagnetic pulse.

The Warden flew a dead ship into the void-spanning wormhole. Without an active control beacon to communicate with the ERB network, he was again at the mercy of the Cosmos and its infinite unpredictability. Just as he and Quantum had been when they had fallen into the biggest black hole in Frontier Space a century before.

He could wind up anywhere there was an open ERB, or he could ride the wormhole forever.

The ghost of a wish crossed his mind. Maybe he could return to his own time when everyone he knew and loved was still alive and the galaxy still made sense. He shook that hopeful thought away. He could not live with himself even if he did somehow make it back. He might be a man out of time, but Quantum—being one of the interdimensional aliens who had invaded this reality in the Continuum War—was the last of his kind in this galaxy. The Warden knew that if they got back to their rightful places, it would be together, as a team. As friends.

The pirate ship's systems cycled back to life.

The Warden had been dozing in the command chair, an emergency tank of Ox strapped at his side, its GlasSteel helmet ready to don as soon as the dead ship's atmosphere became toxic. He was surprised, however, when the controls lit up and the overhead illumination panels filled the darkened bridge with a dull white glow. He took a deep breath, testing the life support.

Apparently environmentals had come back online as well.

He was about to check in with the ERB network and set new coordinates for his exit when he remembered the pirate missile that had followed him into the gate.

He remembered because it exploded beneath the corvette's hull.

The shimmering phantasmagorical lighting of the wormhole rippled and flashed in a nauseating rhythm. If the Warden had not been strapped into his chair, he would most certainly have been killed by the violence of the ship's ejection into real space. He had only a moment to comprehend the coalescing infinity of light and shadow breaking open into endless night. Then the corvette's crumbling wing clipped the DuraSteel edge of the ERB, exploding in a shower of sparks and flame.

The next moments held no sense of up or down, speed or position as the damaged ship cartwheeled away from the ruptured portal. Only his rigorous training allowed the Warden to get the crippled corvette back under any semblance of control without losing consciousness. After engaging the retrorockets to stabilize the craft, he made a scan of the system and the ERB. He tried to pinpoint his relative location in the galaxy.

"What in the Sam Hill…?"

The damaged Einstein-Rosen bridge was offline, its construction and maintenance bot drifting in so many pieces as a wide arc of debris. A shame, really, as—unknown to the Warden—the robot had just concluded construction of the bridge in this isolated star system after a seventy-six year sojourn through normal space. Because of the manner of his arrival, based on what the readouts told him, the Warden was the first—and quite possibly the last—person to pass through this particular ERB.

"I'm in Uncharted Space."

In his day, the golden age of Earth's space exploration, mankind had traveled deeper and deeper into the Milky Way, charting new worlds, discovering new beings, forging new alliances, and ever increasing the technology that made it all possible. Eventually, the core of the galaxy was reached and the Tuatha had been discovered. Though in gradual decline, the Tuatha were the most ancient, advanced, and powerful of species. Wars were fought and treaties signed, and the core became known as Frontier Space. And it had been the Star Wardens' responsibility to patrol that frontier, to ensure that the treaties were not violated, that Star Law was upheld.

But everything beyond the core, beyond the Frontier, all those other spiraling arms of the Milky Way became Uncharted Space. The Warden had never imagined an ERB bot could make it this far from the Civilized Worlds. "Someone must have sent it from deep within the Frontier. But who? And why?"

These questions would have to wait. According to the diagnostics he'd just run on the corvette, the ship was in a very bad way. The fuel compartment had been damaged in the collision with the ERB and over half of the energy rods had spilled out into space. The atmospheric maneuvering engines were operational, but the chemical fuel upon which they ran was also in short supply. With the damaged wing, this would make planetary entry dicey to say the least. But worst of all, one of the ship's two remaining engines had suffered a reactor core breach and was leaking radiation. It would have to be jettisoned soon.

The Warden needed to find a safe place to land and hopefully find a way to make repairs. Once the craft was space-worthy again, he would see about getting the ERB back online. Failing that, he could at least send a deep-space communication that might reach Quantum and tell him what happened. Of course, even if the transmission reached his friend, the Warden knew he'd probably be in his grave decades before anyone ever heard the message.

Eight planets orbited a pair of twin stars in the binary system. The first five of these worlds, according to long-range scans, were desert wastelands. The sixth proved even more uninhabitable as it was a worldwide ocean of liquid mercury. The outermost was a gas giant, the "comet catcher" that all systems needed to enable an inner world to sustain life.

Fortunately, the seventh seemed to be just such a world with an oxygen- and nitrogen-rich atmosphere. The green planet had three small moons and temperate climate zones not too dissimilar from Earth. Though a few scattered large-scale structures were detected, the humanoid population registered was surprisingly small, the balance of the world's ecosystems constituted by vast swaths of flora and large numbers of various types of fauna.

"Home sweet home," the Warden muttered as he strapped into the command chair and checked the countdown sequence. He had spent the last two hours sealing off the irradiated engine cell and making minor repairs on the interior bulkheads damaged in the crash. He had the ship's computer plot a landing trajectory to the green planet. He would jettison the damaged engine, detonate it, and use the shockwave to propel him into the approach just as he had used the first damaged engine to enter the ERB. Even with the added propulsion and using the last of his fuel in the single engine at maximum burn, it would take another two days to reach the planet's orbit.

Two days of hoping life support held out. Two days of hoping the heat shields worked when he hit the atmosphere. Two days of thinking about being stranded on the far side of the galaxy for the rest of his life. And he hadn't checked to see if the pirates had stocked the galley.

"I just wish Quantum were here. I'd trust his calculations a heck of a lot more than those of a pirate-plundered nav computer..."

The Warden activated the jettison protocol.

The ship hit the planet's atmosphere like a ball of fire. With less grace.

The heat shielding held, keeping the Warden from being charred to a crisp in the first fatal seconds. But that was the extent of the damaged corvette's cooperation. The retrorockets refused to fire, and the jet engines would not come online. The ship dropped from the hazy orange sky like a burning rock.

The Warden's spacesuit and his training kept him conscious as he battled crushing g-forces. The edges of his vision clouded grey and black. His lungs ached and his head felt like it might pop off his shoulders. He could not feel anything below his hips. His arms threatened to snap like twigs as he wrestled the ship's yoke, trying to keep the burning nose up just long enough for something, anything to kick in and slow the descent.

Moving his left hand with the speed of an inchworm against a monsoon wind, the Warden managed to hit the retrorocket controls four, five times. A vast green continent grew from the size of a place setting to a conference table in a couple of seconds. The next moment it filled the forward viewport.

He hit the retrorockets button a sixth time.

The hull shuddered and groaned as the roar of rockets filled the thinning air. The ship seemed to stop and for a moment there was no gravity at all, just complete weightlessness. Then the crushing descent resumed, but with a noticeable lessening of g-force. The Warden had enough time to try the atmospheric engines again.

They fired.

Blood slowly returned to his extremities as his suit sensed the change in inertia, and the Warden guided the crippled ship across the dense canopy of a continent-spanning jungle. He tried to get as close as he could to a kilometers-wide scatter of relatively large structures, but the chemical fuel tanks were running dry. He was forced to put the corvette down at the mouth of a large river delta, hoping the muddy soil would cushion the impact.

If it did, he couldn't tell by the way his bones and teeth hurt after the smoking ship finally came to a stop in a tangle of churned up riverbed, twisted and torn trees and vines. Steaming muck and clumps of vegetation coated the viewport. The control panels flashed angry and irrelevant alerts and beeping warnings. The cabin ticked and groaned with the sound of the ship's superheated hull cooling in the humid air. The jet engines whined as they lost power and gradually came to a stop.

The Warden unstrapped, switched off the alarms, and managed to get the ship's computer to pull up a diagnostic routine. He ran another scan on the immediate surroundings to ensure habitability, then decided to examine the damage from outside.

Exiting the hatch, the Warden realized he hadn't tasted real, unfiltered air in quite some time. The planet's atmosphere was hot and humid but filled with a bouquet of sweet floral aromas and pungent earthy odors. Above the hissing and groaning of the cooling spaceship, he could hear the melodious calls of strange avian life and the constant rhythmic buzz of flying insects.

It reminded him of his childhood home in summer. The thought brought a smile.

The smile faded as soon as he waded through the steaming brown shallows to reach a muddy bank from where he could see the extent of the corvette's damage. He shook his head and drove his gloved fist into the soft bark of a felled tree. Even without donning his cowl-mounted multi-spectrum visor, the Warden knew his poor technological skills would be an enormous detriment if he ever hoped to see space again. The ship was a total wreck.

"Task Sergeant Athans always said I'd eventually end up wishing I'd paid better attention in tech class…"

A thunderous roar followed by a high-pitched scream sounded to the east. A screeching flight of bright pink, long-winged birds erupted from the canopy in that direction.

The Warden drew one of his Comet blasters and ran toward the apparent danger. He charged through the thick undergrowth, razored fronds slashing his spacesuit, his boots sinking into squelching mud, then spongy moss. Towering black boles rose like obelisks into the emerald canopy. These were crisscrossed and wrapped in leaf-covered vines that seemed to writhe and move with the flashing rays of orange-gold light lancing through the treetops. Something large and vaguely amphibian bounded away to his left, vanishing into the rustling underbrush of blue and yellow flowers.

The roar sounded again, louder and more menacing. Closer.

The scream faded into a low whimpering gibberish.

The Warden redoubled his speed, leaping a fast-moving rill of surprisingly clear water filled with silvery shapes. Ducking through a web of thick black vines laced with hanging green moss, he reached a rocky crag overlooking a narrow defile. In that pebble-strewn depression he saw the horror which had uttered the two unearthly roars as it raised its saurian head and gave voice to a deafening third.

Chimera was the word that came to mind as the Warden tried to make sense of the seemingly unnatural thing beneath him. The name was that of a mythological creature given to an amalgamation of species that should not exist outside of an unscrupulous laboratory.

The behemoth was larger than the mastodons of Yig, but rather than being covered with a thick coat of shaggy red fur, its hide was a camouflaged panoply of grey, green, yellow, and black scales similar to the pattern of a king snake from Earth. The lashing tail and undulating body gave the impression of something serpentine. However, it stood on eight articulated and chitinous legs like a giant spider or crustacean, its head resembling nothing so much as a carnivorous dinosaur.

The Warden assessed this all in an instant, his attention drawn to the slender golden figure cowering in the eave of a shallow rock outcropping. The monster—the "spider-saur" —was moments away from devouring its intended prey.

The beast recoiled as a barrage of fiery bolts rained down upon it, its gigantic pincer-tipped legs scrabbling in the rocky soil. It raised its fang-filled maw at this new threat and roared in surprised rage more than in agony.

Now that he had the thing's attention, the Warden realized it would not be so easy to kill. The spider-saur's hide was surprisingly resistant to blaster fire. Running along the edge of the defile, the Warden pulled on his cowl to make use of the visor's targeting program.

The thing had to have a weakness somewhere.

The spider-saur launched from the gravel pit, landing a few meters in front of the Warden with a crash of felled trees and tumbling boulders. He hadn't expected the monster to be so nimble. The Warden staggered, almost plummeted into the ravine in surprise. Caught off balance, one of the spider-saur's forelegs struck him.

The blow knocked the wind from his lungs and sent sharp pain rocketing through his chest and back as he crashed into the trunk of one of the tall black trees. Dazed, he managed to duck just before one of the massive pincers turned the wood above his head to pulp. Rolling away from the falling tree, the Warden opened fire on the spider-saur's underbelly with both pistols.

His gratification at the sight of bright violet blood spraying the green foliage was short-lived when the thing's tail whipped across his vision. He hurtled through the air and landed on the sharp rocks in the defile. Again, his spacesuit saved him from the worst of the impact, but he knew his body would be tattooed with bruises for days.

If he survived the next few seconds.

Scrambling to his feet, the Warden recovered one of his dropped Comets. The roaring monstrosity pounced down upon him. The targeting system in his visor had just enough time to spot the soft palate in the spider-saur's yawning maw.

The Warden fired.

The roaring beast went silent a second before its writhing, lashing body collapsed into the dust-filled pit a meter from where the Warden knelt, smoking blaster in hand. He put another bolt into the spider-saur's brain for good measure, then turned his attention to the monster's intended meal.

The Warden holstered his weapon, surprised to see a short, slender young man with bright yellow skin, long golden hair, and flashing hazel eyes standing before him. The youth wore a crimson garment that resembled a cross between a toga and a jumpsuit with lace-up sandals. Golden jewelry adorned his neck and wrists, a gold-studded leather belt encircled his narrow waist. From this hung a curved short sword in a gold-paneled leather sheathe. In his left hand he held a large leather backpack, apparently stuffed with provisions for a lengthy journey.

The young man wiped tears from his eyes and spoke in a gibbering language that resembled nothing the Warden had ever heard. He did recognize the expression of wonder, relief, and gratitude, however. Raising his hands in a gesture of peace, the Warden activated the translator on his wrist chrono. With any luck, the computer could build a rudimentary database from the youth's babbled words and eventually make sense of the language.

"I am the Warden." He touched his chest several times. "Warden. Me." He pointed at the youth with an open palm. "You? What is your name?"

The youth smiled and nodded, touching his own chest. "Andres." This was followed by a few garbled noises and the repeated word, "Un Quan." Andres waved around in all directions when he said this, indicating that Un Quan was the name of their current location, if not the world itself.

The Warden nodded with a smile as he recovered his other pistol. "Well met, Andres of Un Quan... Now if we can just figure out how to communicate, we can get you back to your family."

At this Andres frowned and shook his head. The Warden glanced at his chrono, noting that it had already made progress in translation. Apparently, the language had an antecedent somewhere else in the known galaxy.

"No," Andres said. "I... not wish... family."

The Warden stretched his aching back and sighed. "Okay. Why not? On second thought, why don't we continue this conversation away from the carcass? I imagine the jungle is filled with scavengers who would kill to get a crack at this much meat."

Andres glanced at the dead spider-saur and nodded. "Come... camp."

The Warden followed the youth up a trail out of the defile. He checked his blasters as they went. Both Comets were low on charges and he only had a pair of spare cells on his belt. He certainly hoped they would not run into any more trouble before he could replenish his ammo from the wrecked corvette's dynamo. "Of course, when was hope ever a strategy—"

"What?" Andres looked back at him as they entered a clearing. "Did you say something, Warden?"

"Never mind. Can you tell me why you don't want to go home?" The translator was working better now.

Andres led him through the clearing to a rather tidy campsite. A red, one-man tent and a fire pit sat in the center of a ring of improvised post alarms, tripwires connected to metal noisemakers. The youth invited him to sit on a small, moss-covered boulder near the fire pit as he drew a long copper-colored carafe from inside the tent.

"My father is King Mascos III." Andres poured the Warden a cup of cold water. "He wants me to marry in order to secure the throne's lineage and the continued unity of the tribes. I do not approve of his choice of suitor, and so I have decided to seek my fate in the Forbidden City."

The Warden sipped the water, trusting his immune-boosters to protect him from any foreign pathogens or parasites. "*Forbidden City?* That doesn't sound like the best place for a prince to find his 'fate.' Not unless by fate you mean death."

Andres shrugged and stared to the north as he sipped his own water. "The Forbidden City was home to the Ancients. It is said that they were masters of all manner of magic, like the fire wands you used to kill the secalaur."

The Warden perked up at this. If by magic Andres meant science and technology, there might be a chance that the Forbidden City held the key to his escape from this world.

Andres turned, his face lit by a wistful smile. "There is a prophecy—"

The Warden stood, his hands dropping to his sides, centimeters from the grips of his pistols. He heard approaching feet. A moment later, he saw them. Two dozen yellow-skinned men in gilded helmets and crimson cloaks. They wore bronze breastplates and greaves and carried swords and spears.

"Prince Andres!" The apparent leader, a hulking bearded man, gave a slight bow of his crested helmet. "We have come to take you back to Castle Vear." The warrior's pale amber eyes scanned the Warden like those of a hungry owl. "And... what is *this*?"

"You can call me Warden. Who in Sam Hill are you supposed to be?"

The man's hand rested on his belted sword hilt. "I am Hurm, Captain of the Royal Guard and sworn protector of the crown prince. Stand aside, stranger, or prepare to die."

"Please," Andres said, stepping in front of the Warden. "He saved me from a secalaur. He is a... friend."

Hurm sneered. "Friend, eh? Then why does he wear the color of the enemy?"

The armored men began to fan out, encircling the camp.

The Warden's lip twitched. None of this was really any of his business. Andres had run away from home, and it only made sense that a worried father would send people looking for his son. But the Warden had just rescued the prince from a monster and felt responsible for the lad's life. And if Andres could show him the way to this Forbidden City, then he might find what he needed to repair the ship.

But aside from all that, there was something about Hurm's manner, his arrogance and obvious aggression that just rubbed the Warden the wrong way.

"Maybe I'll accompany you and speak with your king."

Hurm drew his sword. "And maybe you are an assassin slave sent by Marajin. Maybe we should just kill you now."

The Warden bared his teeth. "You're welcome to try, but I advise against it." His hands rested on the hilts of his pistols.

The air sizzled, a volley of arrows erupting from the bush. Half of Hurm's men went down with long, feathered shafts jutting from their necks and faces. Other projectiles bounced off helms and breastplates, stunning their wearers in surprise.

A high-pitched howl rose from nearly a hundred throats as the jungle came alive with tall, blue-skinned warriors. They wore pale green linen cuirasses and brandished bows and spears. Their arrival scattered the surviving yellow men.

The Warden stood rooted to the spot. The attackers were all women.

Raising his hands in a gesture of peace, the Warden saw that he was alone in the ring of serrated spears. Hurm had thankfully gotten Andres safely away.

A pair of muscular women stalked into the circle to face the Warden. Both were tall, one taller than himself with shoulders nearly as broad. Their skin was the same shade of shimmering blue as his spacesuit. Their hair was so dark and lustrous it contained the hues of a midnight sky, and their eyes sparkled like sapphires on snow.

The taller woman stabbed him with her spear.

The Warden collapsed in as much surprise as pain, the serrated blade withdrawing in a gush of blood. He clamped his hand over the wound in his side before the shock hit him. Struggling to remain conscious and alert, he saw the shorter woman grab the weapon and wrest it from his attacker's hand.

"What are you doing, Sappoc?" the younger woman demanded. "I gave no order to kill the stranger."

Sappoc bridled, face hardening as her icy eyes flicked from her challenger to the Warden who knelt in the grass. "Look at him, Princess! He is clearly one of them. If you don't want him dead, let me geld him and take him to the slave camps."

"No." The younger woman, the princess, tossed the bloody spear to the ground and turned to look at the Warden. "Look at his skin. It is not the color of gold, it is like nothing I have seen before, a darker shade of the *singerwing*, perhaps. But he wears the colors of the Matriarchy. We should take him to see my mother."

Sappoc scoffed as she retrieved her spear. "I disagree. I think your head is full of children's tales reawakened by that fire in the sky. But I am captain of your troop and will do as you bid, Princess Jynnessa." Turning to the surrounding warriors, Sappoc ordered, "Dress his wound and bind him. We return to Castle Sarquis."

The Warden was lifted, his wound girded with a strong-smelling bandage before he was wrapped in thin but heavy chains. After taking his gun belt, two women carried him through the jungle on their shoulders. Whether from the loss of blood or the medicine in the bandage, the Warden found himself drifting into unconsciousness. The rhythmic sway of his bearers' strides beneath the green and gold canopy, the heat of the day, and the gentle murmuring song of the jungle soon carried him into oblivion.

ii.

It was dark when he woke.

Two silvery crescent moons hung against the glowing dust-swirl of the Cosmos in a blue-black sky. The Warden stared at those stars, admiring how they looked from a completely different perspective. Despite his predicament, he smiled at the knowledge that he was, in all likelihood, the very first Earthman to see the galaxy from this side of the core. It was for just this sort of thrill that he had joined the Star Wardens in his youth—the unyielding desire to explore, to discover, and to push his own limits as well as those of the known universe.

Shifting his head, he saw the entourage of women warriors marching up a rocky crag jutting above the jungle. At the pinnacle of this black rock stood an imposing fortress of stone and metal. Even at a distance, the Warden acknowledged the impressive craftsmanship of the castle. Its construction far exceeded what he believed achievable by his captors' technology and acumen. He hoped this fact meant that somewhere on Un Quan he might find the means of repairing the crashed corvette, and one day return to his own side of the Milky Way.

The cortege was challenged from the battlements by torch-bearing sentinels. The Warden recognized Captain Sappoc's harsh response, heard a loud groan as ancient machinery opened the towering metal gates. The troop passed quickly through these and into a crowded courtyard filled with the fortress's inhabitants, come to see their princess's return.

The Warden studied this torch-lit gathering of some several hundred. There were many warriors, clad like the women who had captured him. But there were many more dressed in long, diaphanous gowns of various colors, all with brilliant blue skin and eyes with slight variations in shade. There were children in the crowd, running about or clinging to their mothers' skirts.

It struck the Warden as odd that there were no men or boys to be seen. The enclave was populated exclusively by females. This revelation made him more nervous than anything he had yet seen since his arrival on Un Quan.

He had heard far too many lonely spacefarer fantasies that began with this very scenario. And he had never been lonelier in his life than at this moment…

Presently he was brought into the castle's throne room. This was a long, high-ceilinged chamber of polished white marble illuminated by large silvery braziers filled with burning blue crystals. Here, according to a silver-clad herald, he was presented to Marajin XVI, Matriarch of Un Quan, and her council of noble advisors. The Warden was led chained into the chamber by a pair of guards behind Captain Sappoc and Princess Jynnessa. When they reached the dais, the warriors bowed and forced him to his knees.

The queen rose from her silver throne, a warm smile breaking the cool expression of her beautiful face. "Welcome home, my daughter. What strange gift have you brought me?"

She stood taller than Sappoc and though still fit, Queen Marajin displayed more womanly curves than toned muscle. Her long, dark tresses were crowned by an ornate silver headdress encrusted with sparkling diamonds and sapphires, her supple limbs encircled by bands of gleaming silver. A long cloth of shimmering scales hung from the gem-studded belt encircling her shapely hips, and a pair of silver-studded sandals adorned her graceful feet and lower legs.

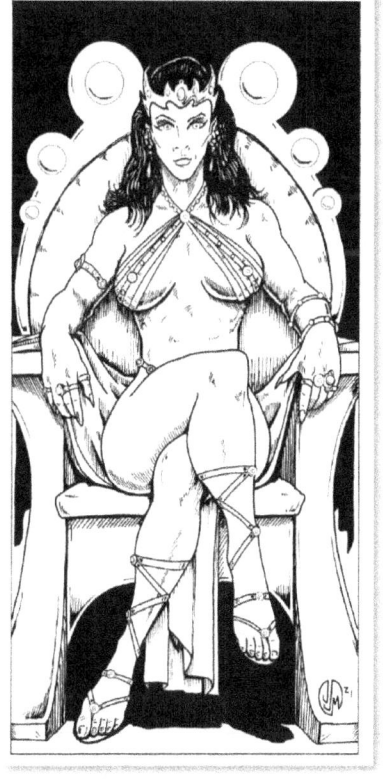

The Warden was distracted from the woman's unearthly beauty by the presence of two gold-skinned men standing behind the throne. Though a more accurate description of their complexion would be sallow. Wearing only black leather masks that bound their eyes and mouths, the men were shackled to a pair of large, green-feathered fans which they used in service to the enthroned queen. This dearth of attire displayed the cruelty of their mutilation. The

Warden grimaced, recalling Captain Sappoc's words: *"...let me geld him and take him to the slave camps."*

For the first time in a very long while, the Warden's belly filled with warm water.

He tensed, waiting for an opportunity, any opportunity to attempt an escape.

The Princess Jynnessa handed his belted Comets to the queen. "I saw him use these to kill a secalaur. They release blades of fire, but we can't make them work." The princess paused and glanced at him. "I think he came here from the sky, in the falling star. I believe he could be the fulfillment of the prophecy."

Queen Marajin clucked her tongue and handed the weapons to one of her noblewomen. "Oh, my daughter. The prophecy is just so much foolishness passed down by our ancestors during the Dark Times to keep up their spirits... There were no Ancients, no miracles, and no prophecy. They are all simply legends."

The queen's eyes roved over the Warden. "But he is certainly an *unusual* prize... I see that he is damaged. Take him to a guest room and summon a healer. When he is up to it... I will speak with him."

The Warden relaxed somewhat. He had seen that look before. He wasn't in trouble for the moment, but if he didn't play his cards right, he would be. He spared the eunuch slaves another look as he was hauled away, reminding himself what was at stake.

After being led from the throne room, the Warden found himself ensconced in a surprisingly lavish suite. This occupied a tall tower overlooking the jungle and the winding, moons-speckled river to the south. A cool night breeze flitted through the white gossamer curtains hung across the opened balcony, guttering in the wall-mounted torches illuminating the ivory-paneled rooms. The chambers were furnished with heaps of overstuffed pillows and cushions, short-legged furniture of polished darkwood, and long-fronded green plants in silver pots. Goblets, bowls, chargers, and pitchers of silver stood on one of the low tables, filled with brightly colored fruits, dark wine, fresh water, and a savory cheese.

The Warden's chains were removed and an old woman in long black robes came in, ordered him to remove his filthy spacesuit, and to get into the large, floor-set tub. This had been filled with steaming water and the dried petals of some indigenous flower which filled the suite with a honeyed, aromatic scent. When the Warden had eased his aching body into the blessedly warm water, the black-clad woman added several splashes of some viscous green fluid from a stoppered vial. She uttered a guttural dialect that completely stumped his wrist chrono's translator. The effect of this medicinal additive was almost immediate. The Warden felt the pain of his wounds flow out of him as if by magic.

He looked to his side to find that the hole made by Sappoc's spear had already knit shut and the skin was forming a puffy pink scar. When he returned his attention to the old woman, she was gone. He had the sensation of being alone for some time though the water was still warm. Rising from the tub, clean and refreshed, the Warden donned a blue silken robe and inspected his quarters.

Pouring himself a glass of surprisingly cold water, he picked up a fruit that bore a passing resemblance to an apple from Earth. "As prisons go, I've definitely been in worse."

The alien apple and fresh water eased his hunger and thirst but not his anxiety at the discovery of his missing spacesuit. His chrono was now the only link to his existence before entering Uncharted Space. An odd feeling of freedom and excitement washed over him. He wondered if it was a result of whatever the old woman had put in the bath. He stepped onto the balcony to clear his head with a breath of fresh air.

The Warden could not resist a smile as he stared out over the unending expanse of benighted virgin wilderness. The planet was untouched by the restrictive modern ways of the Civilized Worlds and the rampant lawlessness of Frontier Space.

"An entire world free of galaxy-spanning bureaucracies, corporate greed, interplanetary criminal syndicates, mechanical monstrosities, mad scientists, and power-hungry politicians. Truly something to behold."

After a moment of quiet thought, he sensed someone entering the room behind him. He turned to see the tall figure of the queen standing in the glow of the chamber's torches. She had come alone, wearing a hooded green cloak rather than her sparkling regalia. He stepped past the diaphanous curtains and gave a solemn bow. "Your Majesty."

Queen Marajin lowered her hood and raised an imperious brow, a small smile twitching at the corner of her perfect blue lips. He got the impression she was not wearing much, if anything, beneath the cloak.

"What is your name, stranger? Where do you come from?"

"I guess you can call me Warden. As your daughter told you, I come from *up there.*"

For a heartbeat he had toyed with the idea of telling her his real name. What would it matter this far from where he belonged? But he recalled the only other person he had been tempted to tell, and now she was gone. The Warden had no superstitious notion that it had been bad luck. Rather he understood that the feelings he had had for Ramirez, or at least thought he had, had come from a different place than the feelings this powerful woman now inspired in him.

The queen scoffed and walked to the low table where the wine and goblets were set. She moved with the languid grace of a predatory cat. The Warden understood she thought of him as prey. "Warden, eh? As in a guardian or sentinel?"

"Something like that." He could not take his eyes off her and hated himself for that weakness. "I used to protect those." He waved at the stars in the night sky. "Before I came here."

Marajin poured two goblets of wine, deftly keeping her cloak closed as she did so. With a smile she held one of the silver goblets out to him. "Really? And how did you manage such a miraculous feat? That seems like an impossible task for a single... *man.*"

The Warden accepted the goblet, not to drink but only to be closer to her. Even barefoot, she stood several centimeters taller than he. "Once upon a time there were many of us, thousands. Now I am the last... though I did—*do* have a friend who helps me continue in my mission. He is still out there somewhere, hopefully looking for me."

The queen took a long sip, studying him with her bright sapphire eyes. The Warden could see the resemblance between her and the princess, but the youthful fire in Jynnessa's eyes had been replaced with a cold and uncanny shrewdness in Marajin's.

"Fascinating. And how do you move between those?" She flicked her long lashes at the starry sky. "How did you come here?"

"In a ship. Mine was damaged and I crashed in the delta. If you send someone to check, they will find it. It's hard to miss."

Marajin nodded, stepped to a large pile of cushions and gracefully melted into them, one long, shapely leg slipping from the folds of the green robe. "Come and sit beside me, Warden."

He set the untouched wine on the table and did as he was told.

She smiled, studying him over the rim of the goblet playfully for a moment. Extending her arm to place the empty chalice on the table, she exposed her naked torso as if by accident. "You fascinate me. You are the first male I have ever seen who did not immediately inspire revulsion, anger, and hatred... In fact, I feel something altogether different when I look at you... Your pinkish skin... but your eyes and hair so much like my own..."

She stroked the muscles of his forearm as if petting an unfamiliar animal. The Warden felt his pulse race and drew in a long, deep breath. He cleared his throat. "I need your help, Your Majesty. My ship is badly damaged, as is the gate through which I came. But from what I have seen of your fortress, and based on what I have heard from your daughter and Prince Andres—"

Marajin stiffened and rose from the cushions, the cloak flaring about her as she spun. "He is no prince! And his father is no king! I am the only true power here!" She stabbed a thumb between her breasts. "I am the Matriarch, and we are the rightful inheritors of Un Quan. The males are nothing more than barbaric abominations. As soon as we are strong enough, we will destroy or enslave them, and then we will reign in peace and prosperity for a thousand years!"

The Warden blinked as he got to his feet, thankful for her sudden change of mood as it allowed him to regain his own bearings. "I am sorry, Your Majesty. I do not wish to offend, and I am certain I don't understand the details of the political situation here. I just want to fix my ship and get back to my side of the galaxy."

Marajin's nostrils flared as she stroked her throat, calming herself. She had thrown the cloak back from her shoulders, studying his reaction to her revealed beauty. It took all his willpower to keep his eyes focused on hers, his hands clenched at his sides.

They stood staring at one another in that manner for some time.

"Tell me, Warden, do you know how to please a female?"

The Warden swallowed. There it was, the reason she had come to his chamber, the reason she hadn't had him killed or gelded at first sight. He was a curiosity, a new toy to assuage the boredom of perceived absolute power. He could tell by the look on her face what her next words would be and he sighed in disappointment.

He *was* in one of those lonely spacefarer stories.

"If you can satisfy me, Warden, I may help you with this ship of yours. We have caches of things left from before the Dark Times, things you may find useful. But first, you must satisfy me, and then you must agree to help me destroy Mascos and his brood of warlike mutants."

The Warden looked up at the frescoed ceiling, knowing he would never see home again. "I cannot do that, Your Majesty. Setting aside the fact that I'm not a hired killer, where I come from, men and women loving each other isn't all that uncommon. And… *satisfying* each other is an expression of that love. Flattered as I am, I'm not the kind of guy who does it just for the heck of it."

Her face broke into a feral snarl before she regained control. Pulling her cloak around her, she gave him a cold, hateful glare. "Guards!"

When four spear-wielding women entered the chamber, the Warden knew he would not be sleeping in the posh suite, alone or otherwise.

"Take him to the dungeon." Marajin stared at him. "I will decide what to do with you at my leisure. Rest assured there will be some form of torture, Warden. No man insults the Queen of Un Quan without living to regret the day he was spawned."

The use of that word, "spawned," triggered a thought in the Warden's mind. He glanced at the exposed midriffs of the women now snapping chains on his wrists. He noticed something he had overlooked while trying not to ogle the queen's nude body. Though obviously mammalian in nature, the women of Un Quan had no navels.

"You're clones," he murmured as he was led away. "You're all clones."

The dungeon proved to be an oubliette, from an ancient Earth word for "to forget." It was a hole in the stone floor on the lowest level of the castle, covered by a lid of iron bars. The hole was deeper than the Warden was tall and just wide enough for him to sit, but not lie down, though he preferred to lean against the smooth stone walls as the floor was a sluice of ankle-deep and foul-smelling mud. At least his chrono told him it was mud. If it wasn't, he didn't trust even his immune-boosters to keep him healthy for very long.

"Well, this is a pickle."

He stood with his back against the cold wet stone for hours according to his chrono, watching the dim, reflected moonlight glimmer and shift in the near total blackness. He was honestly surprised they had not taken the chrono, but being of dull PlaSteel construction it probably appeared to be worthless when compared to the silver, gold, and gem-crusted jewelry he had seen since his arrival. And as neither Un Quan's men nor women seemed to be of a particularly technologically-advanced society, they would not understand that the chrono was a rather useful device instead of a simple piece of ornamentation.

Useful in translating alien languages, certainly. Useful with adapting to local functions of time in relation to the Universal Clock, obviously. Useful in accessing, processing, displaying, and transferring data with nearby computer systems, absolutely. Useful in getting one's self out of an oubliette in an ancient mountaintop castle on a primitive planet in Uncharted Space, not so much.

The Warden blindly tested the rock walls for any sign of a finger-hold, but without any luck. Next, he tried to find a section of stone which might be broken off and fashioned into a primitive weapon. Again, no dice.

When the moons set and the cell plunged into complete and utter darkness, the Warden took a long, deep breath. He could feel frustration creeping into his mind, threatening to unleash all the anger, fear, and uncertainty which he'd carefully put away since his arrival in the system. His training had prepared him for these sorts of situations, conditioned him to stay optimistic, to be observant, to be prepared when any opportunity presented itself, no matter how small. Worry, doubt, and fear were the harbingers of defeat and it was foolish to give them the slightest foothold.

"Warden!"

He jerked awake, having wedged himself upright into a corner. He wondered if he had imagined the whisper as he could see and hear nothing. His world was a tiny black void filled with stinking mud.

"Warden." The whisper was louder. "Can you hear me?"

"Princess Jynnessa?"

"Yes. Quiet now… I'm going to get you out."

The Warden almost laughed as a wave of relief washed over him, driving the fatigue from his body like asteroids before a supernova. When he heard the iron grate creak painfully loud in its hinges, he held his breath, but no alarm sounded. A second later, he felt something rough and slender brush his face and glance off his shoulder.

"Take the rope and climb up."

Escaping the oubliette felt like being reborn. The dungeon level was dark, but nothing like the hole. Princess Jynnessa had brought a small horn lantern which painted her figure in shades of cobalt and teal. She wore a hooded cloak and carried a large leather pack along with her unstrung bow and quiver of arrows. A short sword was belted at her side.

"Here." She pressed a canvas bag into his hands. Through the thick material the Warden felt the familiar shapes of his spacesuit, boots, and even his gun belt. "I imagine you'll need these if you are going to get me to the Forbidden City."

The Warden nodded and gave her a smile. "Get me out of here and I'll get you to the other side of the galaxy if you want."

They crept out of the dungeon and slipped into the darkened courtyard. Jynnessa led him through shadowed corridors and past patrolling guards until they reached a secret hatch near the outer wall. Slipping through this, she closed and locked the door behind them.

"I discovered these tunnels as a child. I'm not certain if any adult even knows they're here. They've never been patrolled, and they exit further down the mountain."

"You spoke of a prophecy," the Warden said as he opened the bag and began to don his gear. "Before you ambushed the males and captured me, Prince Andres used the same word. Care to tell me what all this is about?"

In answer, Jynnessa pulled an aged parchment from her pack. By the dim light of the lantern, she unrolled the page and held it up to his view. The Warden glanced at the arcane symbols and strange pictograms. He shook his head. "Sorry. Can't read it."

Jynnessa frowned, cleared her throat. "…Given the nature of all things, the Un Quan must unite and become one people or forever pass from existence to be replaced by a new—and hopefully wiser species…"

The Warden raised an eyebrow as he buckled on his Comets. "That doesn't sound like a prophecy to me. More like the summation of an academic article or something…"

Jynnessa inhaled sharply and put the scroll away. "No one believes in the prophecy. No one believes in the Ancients but me. But I know the answers are in the Forbidden City, and we must go there and find them."

The Warden smiled. "You know, I think you and Prince Andres would get along just fine. He told me pretty much the exact same thing. That's where he was headed when he ran afoul of that spider-saur."

Jynnessa rolled her eyes. "Come."

She led the Warden deeper into the tunnel. "I do not know how a barbaric male could have such high-minded thoughts. All they care about is food, fornicating, and fighting. They are like a plague that has to infect everyone and everything."

The Warden shrugged. "Suit yourself, but you sound like your mother when you say things like that."

She spared him a cutting look over her shoulder but said nothing.

"Speaking of which," he continued. "I wouldn't say that nobody believes in the Ancients. In fact, I think your mother does. She as much as admitted to it when she tried to… hire me to fight Mascos for her tonight."

This brought Jynnessa to a halt. "What did she say?"

"She said she has a store of things from before the Dark Times that I could use to repair my ship. That tells me that she's got technology that she doesn't understand but believes was built by your 'Ancients.' If she believes in them, maybe she believes your prophecy as well. But maybe she can't bring herself to want to see it fulfilled. She hates the males quite a bit."

Jynnessa resumed the march. "If you had seen what the males have done to us in the past, you would understand."

The Warden didn't ask. He could well imagine. He'd seen all manner of evil perpetrated in his years of service. Not all of it committed by men, but a goodly portion all the same.

With no further discussion they made good their escape from Castle Sarquis.

iii.

The twin suns were rising in the north when they exited the tunnel at the foot of the ridgeline. The morning air was humid but not yet hot. A heavy mist clung to the ground, dew sparkling on every surface of rock, leaf, frond, and trunk. The thick air reverberated with the songs of a hundred different species: croaking amphibians, chirping and trilling avians, thrumming and chittering insects. Somewhere in the distance to the east an aggressive roar challenged the serenity of the jungle, reminding the Warden that dangerous predators called this world home.

"This way." Jynnessa set off in the direction of the rising suns. "We have many days' travel ahead of us and it won't take long for my mother and Sappoc to discover that we are missing."

The Warden followed the determined princess, impressed by the pace she set. If his Star Warden training hadn't honed him to the peak of human physical condition, he would have had a hard time keeping up with her. Even in his rugged boots, designed to deal with every foreseeable interplanetary terrain, his steps were not as sure as those of her sandaled feet.

They traveled without stopping until both suns were lost high in the canopy and the temperature had risen to a sweltering degree. His spacesuit was equipped with body-temp regulating sensors, but the Warden still felt the jungle heat as rivulets of sweat ran down his face, chest, and back. When they came to a towering waterfall above a crystal-clear pool, he sighed with relief. The fall's spray cooled the air around the pool only a few degrees but it may as well have been air-conditioned atmosphere on a spaceship as far as the Warden was concerned.

Jynnessa knelt at the pool's edge to refill the canteens. "This water is pure. Drink as much as you can now. The closer we get to the Forbidden City, the less likely we are to find uncorrupted water."

The Warden splashed his face and hair, took a mouthful of cool water in his palm. "Uncorrupted? What does that mean? Radiation?"

Jynnessa looked at him with a wrinkled brow. "I do not know that word. Only that those who drink from the waters near the Forbidden City grow violently ill and most die."

The Warden rubbed water from his chin. "Sounds like radiation. If you're right and the Ancients did dabble in advanced technology, atomic energy could be the source of your so-called Dark Times. Maybe this isn't such a good idea…"

The princess frowned and rose to her feet. "It is the only idea. Come, we had a deal."

The Warden followed her from the pool, shaking his head. Yes, he had promised to take her to the Forbidden City in exchange for his freedom. But that was before he knew he might be escorting her into fallout which could kill her in the most agonizing way imaginable. His suit would protect him for a short while, but lightly clad as Jynnessa was, she would succumb almost instantly, depending on the amount of radiation exposure.

"And cities don't become 'forbidden' for no reason…"

Several hours later they came to a vine-covered rope bridge over a narrow but fast-moving river. The Warden spotted several scaly forms surfacing and snapping at low-flying birds in the brown-white water. Jynnessa hurried across the swinging bridge with the practiced grace of an acrobat. The Warden took a bit longer to cross the span as the bridge had obviously not been designed for the extra mass of an adult male.

Each shaking step caused the ropes to creak and groan, but he eventually reached the opposite bank.

As soon as the Warden's feet sank into the mud, Jynnessa drew her sword and hacked the bridge's mooring. The ropes coiled and sank into the roaring water. She flashed a smile. "That should buy us a little more time. If I'm right, Sappoc and her troops are already on our trail."

"Then we should keep going."

That night they camped in the cleared-out den of a creature resembling a six-legged boar. Jynnessa had spotted the thing's tracks as the twin suns began to descend in the south. They had tracked it to its lair and with the skill and accuracy of a lifelong archer and hunter, the princess had lured out the *barghru*—as she named the squealing, snarling beast—and dropped it with a single arrow to the left eye. After clearing the animal's filth from the rather spacious den, she set to skinning and preparing the barghru for dinner.

The Warden was surprised at how tasty fire-roasted barghru proved to be.

"Aren't you worried the campfire will draw Sappoc's attention?" They sat in the wide-mouthed den, the fire at one end, most of the smoke drifting through a hollowed-out stump. "Even if she can't see the flame, surely the smell of the smoke and cooking meat will carry."

Jynnessa shrugged as she cut another hank from the roasting barghru. "I am confident that she is on the other side of the river. The next nearest crossing is a day's walk to the east. If she tried to rebuild the bridge, it would have taken her the better part of the day. Besides, the fire and smoke will keep the animals and insects away. Most of them, at any rate."

"Most?"

The princess wiped grease from her chin and frowned. "The males are on this side of the river. If they have night patrols, they could come upon us. As soon as I have eaten, I will set traps outside the den. That should give us ample warning of their approach, and as they can only come at us from one direction, I am confident that my bow and your fire blades can make short work of them, no matter their number."

The Warden studied the young woman. During the course of the day he had watched her smile and revel in the beauty of the jungle as they traveled, he had seen a purity of spirit and innocence he had not seen in a very long time. Yet now, sitting in the glow of a smoky campfire, he saw the unquestioning loathing and hatred he had seen on her mother's face.

"What happened in your past? Why do you despise the males so much?"

Jynnessa dropped a bone into the pit she had dug for disposal. "It happened before the Dark Times. We females once ruled Un Quan in peace and prosperity. But somehow the males came to power. They enslaved us and treated us as property and beasts of burden, our only purpose to be their broodmares and servants."

The Warden nodded, trying to sift the truth from the obviously one-sided history.

"But one courageous woman, the first Matriarch, the first Marajin, escaped and braved the perils of the Forbidden City. When she returned, she had knowledge and weapons, and she freed a great many females before leading them to the Ancient-built Castle Sarquis. Since then, we have grown in strength of body and in number, and in time, we will again reclaim Un Quan as our own."

"I imagine that was quite some time ago. How have you grown in numbers without… without the males?" The Warden suspected the answer, but wondered how much the princess understood.

Jynnessa's face wrinkled in disgust. "The first Matriarch also brought the secret of birth from the Forbidden City. With that secret, we no longer require the male and can create progeny stronger than ourselves."

"Cloning technology. I'm guessing the males also recovered this 'secret,' otherwise they would have perished long ago as well. Or at least be green-skinned rather than yellow from breeding with captured females."

Jynnessa's disgust grew to open revulsion, driving her from the den. "Get some rest. I'll set the traps."

The Warden could not understand how the two factions had become so gender fixated. After all, the power of designer clones should have allowed the males to make amenable female clones and vice versa for the females in order to continue the species. There had to be so much more to this story, but he imagined the root of it was lost to antiquity.

Unless that truth lay buried somewhere in the Forbidden City.

They travelled in relative silence for the next two days. Every night they camped and ate from their rations and the leftover barghru, and every morning they were off again before suns-up. Jynnessa led the way with a torch taken from the dwindling campfire, the Warden using his multi-spectrum visor to keep an eye out for nocturnal predators looking for a last-minute meal. By the time the two suns broke the northern horizon, they had already covered six kilometers, on average.

Around noon on the fourth day of travel, they came to something that caught the Warden's eye. A brown obelisk jutted out of the jungle's undergrowth like a giant exclamation point. He used the machete Jynnessa had provided to cut a path to the ancient artifact.

Jynnessa called after him, anxious. "That is an Ancient's stone! A grave marker, haunted by evil spirits!"

"That's not stone and there's no such thing as evil spirits." The Warden climbed the gentle rise surrounding the pillar. Using the edge of his blade, he scraped a thick layer of rust away to reveal pitted steel. He smiled and looked at the structure's crown. "This is a signal pylon. Probably part of a network of some kind. Communications or travel guidance would be my guess."

The discovery gave him more hope of finding a means of escape in the Forbidden City. Apparently the Ancients' technology was not limited to genetics and biosciences. If they had an advanced means of telecommunication and/or guided transportation, they might have the equipment he would need to repair the corvette and the ERB.

The obelisk hummed. The hair stood up on the back of the Warden's neck.

"I told you!" Jynnessa knocked an arrow to her bow, scanning their surroundings. Bright plumed birds took flight, speeding away from the shuddering pylon. "Evil spirits!"

A mechanical voice croaked something from deep within the ancient structure. The Warden's chrono could not decipher it, but he suspected it was a warning of some kind. Springing away from the metal tower, he drew his Comets. "It's not evil spirits, but I've got the feeling we need to get away from here."

The obelisk creaked and groaned, then a section of it flew open in a cloud of aerated rust.

"Too late."

A flash of green fire sizzled past him, kicking up a chunk of black dirt and disintegrating a clump of undergrowth. A shiny metallic orb about a meter in diameter emerged from the pylon, hovering on a jet of blue flame and bristling with six segmented arms. Two of these arms fired more green bolts.

The Warden dived for cover as a plasma blast slashed across the back of his left thigh. The pain was sudden and fierce, but quickly went numb. Rolling across the thick undergrowth, he returned fire. His bolts took off one of the segmented arms and exploded in a shower of fiery sparks against the signal tower.

Jynnessa loosed an arrow that glanced off the thing's metallic hull.

The attack drew the robot's attention.

The Warden watched in horror as the automaton's red eye swiveled and locked onto the princess.

Jynnessa knocked another arrow.

The Warden raised his Comets to fire, but both were empty.

He had forgotten to reload after the fight with the spider-saur.

"No…"

A spear sailed out of the tree line, striking the bot's central eye. The glass lens shattered and the green bolts went wide, burning swaths on either side of Jynnessa. Standing her ground, the princess sighted her bow and sent another shaft into the robot. The arrow struck beside the jutting spear, burying itself in the inner workings of the ancient machine.

The robot hummed, jittered, its spidery arms flailing and blue fire sputtering. It fell back against the pylon, uttered a command in the forgotten tongue, and collapsed to the jungle floor in a puff of sparks and white smoke.

The Warden reloaded his pistols with his last charges and limped to where Jynnessa stood. She had knocked another arrow and crouched, scanning the tree line. "Are you all right?"

"Get down," she whispered. "That spear is of male make."

The Warden glanced at the shaft as it caught fire in the downed bot's torso. "Well, either they're a very bad throw or they weren't aiming for you." He stepped past her and called into the wood. "Thanks for the help! If you come in peace, we can talk. Come on out!"

"What are you doing, Warden? There could be a company of them!"

"I'm guessing there's just one, and I'm guessing I know who that one is. Come on out, Andres! We won't hurt you."

The Warden smiled when he saw the lithe young man emerge from cover, a sheepish grin on his golden face and an atlatl in his hand. "Well met, Warden. Well met, female companion of the Warden."

Jynnessa drew back on the bow. "I am Princess Jynnessa, heir to Queen Marajin XVI, the Matriarch of Un Quan, and sworn enemy of all males. Especially the vile spawn of Mascos the Pretender."

The Warden stepped between the broad head arrow and the young prince. "He just kept you from being incinerated, Jynnessa. Where I come from, killing someone for saving your life is considered bad form... Besides, I gave him my word we wouldn't hurt him. Don't make a liar out of me."

Jynnessa's hardened face twitched, and in that moment she looked very much like her mother. In that moment, the Warden thought she might kill him in order to kill Andres. The generations-old hatred was that strong. She drew back on the bow, then spun away with a guttural growl as she released the tension on the string.

The Warden turned to Andres. "I guess you ran away from home again."

Andres smiled. "Yes, only this time I am better prepared, having spent a few days in the jungle before Hurm caught me last time. I am confident that I will reach the Forbidden City on this expedition."

Jynnessa turned from where she had retrieved her errant arrow. "He's not coming with us! I know you are not from our world, Warden, but it is bad enough traveling in the company of one male. I refuse to do so with two."

Andres gave a condescending laugh. "As if I would deign to travel with a female. The only reason I intervened here is because I recognized the Warden. I had to repay my life debt to him. I can assure you that had you been alone, Princess, I would have been more than happy to watch the Ancient's sentinel burn you to a crisp."

The Warden rolled his eyes. "All right, you two. Enough. Let's have a look at this thing and the inner workings of this pylon."

"It is just the metal corpse of one of the Ancients' magical playthings," Jynnessa said with the air of someone who knew everything on the topic. "We should move on."

Andres knelt beside the Warden as he inspected the bot. "Calling something 'magic' is just another way of not dealing with it, Princess. There is a system at play within each and every thing in the universe. It only takes will and effort to discover what that system is and how it works."

The Warden grinned at Jynnessa. "He's not wrong. Look, this is a robot. An electronic machine designed by your Ancients. It was programmed to guard this pylon and to maintain and repair it. However, when the Dark Times came, whatever they were, the network went down and the bot went offline. Somehow when I fiddled with the thing, the bot reactivated."

The Warden initiated the data scanner on his chrono. The device probed the inner workings of the bot and the pylon, trying to access and process any information contained in the ancient machinery. After a few moments, the tiny display screen told him all it could.

Standing with a wince at the dull ache in his left thigh, the Warden said, "Looks like your Ancients were on par with my world's technology of roughly the late twenty-first century, give or take. Not great news, but good enough."

Jynnessa looked back to the south. "We should be going. The sounds of battle would have carried. Sappoc may be close."

Andres looked to the southwest. "As could Hurm."

The Warden rubbed the cauterized wound on the back of his leg. "That settles it, we go on together. You two will just have to learn to get along."

Jynnessa scowled. "I refuse."

The Warden snapped a dark look at both of them before Andres could protest as well. "Look, all three of us want something from this Forbidden City of yours. And all three of us are being hunted, and if we fall into the hands of the wrong faction, we will most likely be killed—and worse, besides. So it only makes sense for the three of us to pool our efforts and resources. If we can do that and work together, we might just come out of this alive and with the answers we seek. Got it?"

The prince and princess glared at each other, but both gave terse nods. Without another word, they gathered their gear and resumed the trek north.

The Warden made use of the caustic silence to order his thoughts. His limp would slow their progress unless one of his two companions had brought something akin to the woman in black's healing salve. If not, he reckoned that one or both of the pursuing groups would overtake them within the next day or two. He knew he only had enough power in his Comets for another two dozen shots. He also knew he'd burn through those in a hurry if they came across another spider-saur, another guardian bot, or something even worse.

A part of him wanted to work on the logistics of getting machinery from this Forbidden City back to his crash site and repair the damaged ship, but he refused to think about it. There was no point building castles in the sky as they had not yet reached the city, and there was absolutely no guarantee that the technology would be there when and if they did. He had to remain focused on the problems at hand, not the least of which was making sure his two traveling companions didn't kill each other along the way.

That night they set camp between the bulging roots of a tree taller than some rocket ships the Warden had known. By using both Andres's and Jynnessa's tents, they made a spacious bivouac in a hollow between the roots. The Warden helped the princess set up the perimeter traps while Andres arranged the tents and hung sprigs of dried herbs to keep the multitude of swarming insects at bay. He also produced an unguent to ease the pain in the Warden's leg, claiming it would heal the burn before dawn.

As their pursuers could be close, they did not build a fire.

Afterward, while the three of them sat in silence, eating cold barghru meat, the Warden studied his empty blaster cells. He wondered if there might be a way to transfer the power from his suit to give him a few more shots.

"What are you staring at?"

The Warden looked up to see Jynnessa glaring at Andres, who sat surprisingly close to her. The prince smiled and tilted his head. "You are very attractive. Are all females so comely?"

Jynnessa's face turned a shade of purple. Jumping to her feet, she huffed out of the tent. "I'm going to check the traps."

The Warden raised an eyebrow at Andres.

"Well, she is."

"Yes. But what *exactly* does that mean to you?" He was mindful of the things Jynnessa had told him about the history of male-female "relations" on this planet.

Andres watched the princess stalk along the edge of the clearing. With a sigh, he said, "It means I don't think I hate her." His brow furrowed as he turned to the Warden. "And I don't want her to hate me. Is that wrong?"

The Warden smiled. "No. In fact, I think that is about the furthest thing from wrong I can imagine. Just be nice to her. Maybe she'll come around."

Andres returned his gaze to the blue-skinned warrior moving through the tall grass. "Be nice…"

The Warden shook his head and put the useless cells away. This planet was an Eden, so why shouldn't it have its own Adam and Eve? Though, as he thought on it, the whole thing felt more like *Romeo and Juliet*.

"But then, neither couple had the happiest of endings…"

The Warden woke in total darkness. It took a moment to realize his instincts had warned him of danger. His eyes adjusting to the pale glimmer of starshine merely hinting at shapes, he eased across the campsite to quietly wake Andres. Jynnessa was already buckling on her sword belt. A moment later one of the alarm traps made a dull, rattling clang that echoed through the still night.

A deep voice cursed in the darkness.

Pulling on his multi-spectrum visor, the Warden adjusted the view to night vision. In shades of emerald and jade, he saw half a dozen armed men fanning out along the far edge of the camp. By their movements, using free hands and spear butts to feel the way ahead of their steps, he knew they were as night blind as his companions.

"Sh," he whispered. "Get as much as you can carry. I think we can sneak away from them without a fight."

It only took a few moments to gather the travel packs, machetes, and weapons, and then the Warden led the two youths in a slow belly crawl out of the great tree's root system. The men closed in on the campsite, but the Warden used his night vision to maneuver the trio around the approaching soldiers. By the time the six men had discovered the abandoned tents, he and his charges were out of the clearing. Linking hands, they hurried as quietly as possible into the benighted jungle.

They didn't stop to rest until the north-rising suns melted the pitch black of night into muted shades of blue and grey.

"That was close!" Andres grinned at Jynnessa as if they had played an exhilarating game.

The princess scowled. "And costly! We no longer have tents, bedrolls, or perimeter traps. We are now completely at the mercy of the jungle and its predators. And it is *your* fault!"

Andres blinked, the smile falling from his face. "*My* fault?"

"Yes. Those were your father's men looking for you! If you had stayed at home, they would not have found our camp."

Andres took a deep breath, but did not raise his voice. "And if I had stayed at home, Princess, that robot would have killed you yesterday. Ergo you are correct, they would not have found your camp, because you would not have been alive to make it."

Jynnessa clinched her fists and growled. She turned on the Warden. "That is only because you awakened the roh-but! Why am I surrounded by stupid males?"

The Warden scratched the back of his thigh. Andres's medicine had worked, though some native bug had decided to take advantage of the exposed skin and have a feast. "You know, Your Highness, you are not the first woman I've heard say something to that effect, and I daresay you'll not be the last. But this bickering is not solving any problems."

"And what is your solution, Warden? Do we double back and try to collect our gear?"

The Warden shook his head and started walking north. "Nope. We continue the mission. Look at it this way, maybe now that we're traveling lighter it means we can travel faster."

He didn't have to look back to know that the two youths exchanged frustrated looks before falling in behind him. They marched on, cutting a trail through the underbrush that a blind man could follow. The Warden hoped to find a way to lose their pursuers before they caught up with them. He also hoped they weren't walking straight into a radioactive hell.

But hope was never a strategy.

After a while, the suns' green-gold rays falling through the high canopy, they came to a grove of short, spindly, white-barked fruit trees. A family of purple-furred simians screeched and howled as they fled at the trio's approach. Jynnessa plucked one of the golden fruits from a low-hanging branch and tapped it with her dagger.

"*Josco*," she said, handing it to the Warden. "Drink the juice before you eat the flesh. Hydration helps the digestion. One fruit will keep you on your feet for days."

Andres grimaced and shook his head when the princess held a fruit out to him. "No, thank you. My father says they are good for... stamina."

The way Andres turned a shade of orange and looked away when he said it told the Warden all he needed to know. He drank the sweet, sticky juice but did not eat the fruit.

Jynnessa laughed as she devoured a josco and led them out of the grove. "Males are so silly. How you even came to know of the prophecy, much less understand it is beyond me."

Andres quickened his stride to catch up to her, excitement in his voice. "It was not easy, I assure you. My father has had the archives sealed for longer than I have been alive. But I learned a secret way in and have devoted my life to studying the Ancients." He cleared his throat and quoted the prophecy in a somber voice. "Given the nature of all things, the Un Quan must reunite or forever pass from existence to be replaced by a new and wiser species."

The Warden raised an eyebrow at the slightly different wording of this version.

Jynnessa scoffed as she tossed the josco rind into the brush. "You don't even have the prophecy right! And you say you have devoted your life to its study? Perhaps you should choose another endeavor. You are too puny to make a proper warrior, but maybe one of them might choose you as his catamite."

Andres stiffened and walked ahead in silence.

Jynnessa, still laughing, dropped back to match the Warden's stride. "Maybe it is the josco talking, but there is something appealing about him when he gets so serious like that. For some reason I want to tickle him instead of stab him, and squeeze him instead of strangle him. Isn't that strange?"

The Warden glanced at her and shook his head. He couldn't decide if his companions' furtive and unorthodox attempts at courtship made him feel young or very, very old. "No. Not strange at all."

iv.

Sometime after midday they came to a rift in the canopy. The patch of open sky was the result of a large crater in the jungle floor, this being filled with deep water. Drawing closer, the Warden spotted a dim shape at the pool's bottom, the object that had caused the ancient crater.

"That looks like a plane or a ship of some kind."

"It is another cursed place, Warden." Jynnessa stopped walking several meters before reaching the crater's lip. "Evil lurks in those waters. They are not uncorrupted."

Andres looked at her, then to the Warden. "Perhaps she is right."

The Warden frowned but checked his chrono. It detected a slightly elevated rad count, but nothing too harmful. He scanned the water for any dangerous bacteria or parasites, detecting none. The ancient craft at the bottom still emitted a low energy signature which disrupted complete analysis. "Well, that's a mixed bag. There may be something useful onboard, but then again the energy output may be masking something dangerous in the water."

"Leave it. Let us continue."

"Yes. We seek the city, not whatever is down there. Why risk it, Warden?"

The Warden looked at his two charges. "Because if there's protective gear aboard that craft, it might keep us safe when we reach the city. And let's face it, there's probably going to be far more dangerous things in that city than a hulk at the bottom of some foul water."

Jynnessa and Andres looked at one another but said nothing.

The Warden unbuckled his gun belt, handed it to Andres. He wasn't worried about the young man hurting himself or anyone else with the weapons. As Jynnessa had discovered when she captured him, Quantum had installed ID recognition failsafe software on the blasters. "Let me have your knife."

"Are you seriously going in there?" Jynnessa's jaw dropped.

"You two stay here and watch your backs. If you hear anyone coming, head north as fast as you can. I'll catch up with you." With that, the Warden took a deep, deep breath and dove into the black water.

Having been trained to function in the worst-case scenarios offered by space travel, the Warden could hold his breath considerably longer than most athletes. And thanks to his visor, he was able to see clearly in the murky depths. Nothing more sinister than some deep-dwelling amphibians appeared to have made a home in the crater since the ancient aircraft's crash.

The vehicle was short and cylindrical with an array of four wings crumpled and twisted around the central fuselage. The engine appeared to be some form of anti-gravity ring positioned at the craft's rear, this being the source of the energy reading.

A long shadow uncoiled from beneath the ring. This shadow rapidly took the form of an aquatic serpent at least four meters in length and thicker than the Warden's thigh. Three ridged fins encircled its arrow-shaped head. The snake's mouth opened, exposing a pair of long white fangs. It darted forward.

Still holding his breath, the Warden moved to the side at the last second, slashing out with his borrowed blade. The weapon glanced across oily scales before biting into flesh.

Black blood spilled from the wound as the serpent recoiled and swam for the depths.

Certain the creature had fled for good, the Warden gained access to the craft's flooded cabin by swimming through the cockpit's shattered windscreen. Noting three skeletons in rotting uniforms, he hurried to search the plane's interior for anything useful. His lungs began to ache and his head to throb. In a closed compartment near the rear he found several mechanical valises. Opening one, he recognized a first-aid kit and what resembled a hazmat suit. Grabbing three of the cases he hurried back to the cockpit. He snagged the dead pilot's sidearm before swimming for the surface.

Climbing from the crater with his salvaged treasures, the Warden gulped in the jungle's humid air. The relief he felt at being able to breathe again vanished in a heartbeat.

Andres and Jynnessa were gone, his blasters with them.

One of Jynnessa's arrows jutted from a tree on the northern edge of the clearing. There was blood on the grass.

"Sam Hill."

Before the Warden could fully assess the situation, a cacophony of bird calls sounded to the south, and the air filled with the flutter and hum of wings. Above this noise, he heard the telltale sounds of marching feet. By the level of racket, he guessed at least twenty or thirty men were headed straight for the clearing, possibly more.

Clutching the recovered valises and the primitive pistol, he bolted to the tree impaled by Jynnessa's arrow on the northern edge. Grabbing the shaft, he wrenched the marker from the trunk and hurled it as far as he could to the east. Then, tapping his visor, the Warden switched his vision to thermal and followed the glowing blood trail deeper into the jungle.

The trail died a hundred meters from the clearing. Using every spectrum available to the visor, the Warden could not detect the sign of anyone's passing further into the jungle. He did pick up an unusual energy reading not too dissimilar to that of the downed craft in the flooded crater. The grass was crushed in a spiral pattern where the reading was strongest. The Warden looked up, judging that there was maybe just enough room between the towering trees for a small antigravity vehicle to maneuver.

"Looks like the 'Ancients' aren't completely gone after all." He set his visor to follow the energy trail.

Hearing the sounds of pursuit growing closer, the Warden tossed two of the large valises. He then took off as fast as he could with the last container and the primitive pistol. The bug bite on his leg had grown from an itchy annoyance to a swelling inconvenience. Each step sent a nagging stab of pain up his backside. He pushed this from his mind, trying to put as much distance as possible between himself and the male warriors.

He knew it had to be the males behind him. When Jynnessa and Sappoc had launched their ambush, the entire troop of women had been silent as the wind. This in stark contrast to the blundering approach exhibited by Hurm and his mere score of soldiers.

From the sound of it, the Warden guessed close to a hundred armed males now marched at his heels. Overwhelming odds even if he still carried his Comets.

A sensor flashed red on his visor, alerting him to a dangerous shift in his body temperature. The sweat pouring off him in spite of his suit's thermal equilibrium and his recent swim in the cool waters had already confirmed his worst fear. The bug bite was infected if not poisonous, and he was in danger of succumbing to fever.

Sprinting through the underbrush, the Warden scanned the trees for any that might be climbable. Not spotting any, he looked for anything that could provide sufficient concealment on the ground. The fact that the waist-high grass left a trail in his wake made this search all but futile. There simply was nowhere to hide before the male army caught up with him.

Shaking with a sudden chill and gasping for air, the Warden stopped and placed his back against a tree trunk. Dropping the valise at his feet, he checked the ancient pistol. It appeared to be a composite structure similar to the chemical propellant firearms still in use by some spacers. With a few quivering gestures, he cleared the action and checked the pommel-housed magazine to find a mere twenty metal projectiles. Given that the weapon was not linked to the targeting feature of his visor, he would have to wait for the warriors to get close.

Close enough to throw their serrated spears.

Sliding down the trunk to a kneeling position, the Warden placed the heavy valise in front of him, more to steady his aim than for protection. He could hear the soldiers getting closer, the steady tramp-tramp-tramp of sandaled feet on the jungle floor. Birds and bat-like things fluttered and darted beneath the canopy, fleeing the persistent approach of these invaders.

The Warden wiped sweat from his eyes a moment before a shard of sunlight glinted on a bronzed helmet in the distance. Blinking away more sweat, he saw a wall of yellow and red moving through the blue-green haze at the limit of his vision. He enhanced the magnification on his visor until he recognized the tall, armored figure of Captain Hurm. The man was flanked by a quartet of warriors carrying something that looked like crossbows or perhaps even primitive firearms. These would be lethal at greater distances than thrown spears.

The Warden took a deep breath and shivered, waiting for the enemy to spot him. He hoped it would not be before they were in range of the pistol. He knew he was about to die, but he wasn't about to make it easy for them.

His teeth chattered. His vision blurred. His stomach roiled.

A now-familiar high, keening wail sounded from behind the approaching host.

A moment later the jungle filled with the sounds of battle—angry shouts, frightened cries, and surprised screams—as arrows and spears cut through the humid air, piercing blue and yellow flesh. Spilling red blood.

The females had ambushed the rear of the male column.

The Warden didn't waste a moment on this lucky break. Snatching up the valise containing the first aid kit and hazmat suit, he turned and ran north. By the time he had escaped the echoing sounds of war, both suns were on the decline. He found himself at the foot of an outcropping of black granite, jutting up into the canopy. He stuffed the pistol into his boot and used the valise's straps to lash the case to his back.

Though his muscles felt like sacks of lead and his belly threatened to crawl up his windpipe, the Warden began to climb.

Struggling up this rocky formation, he sought a defensible position in which to hole up for the night. If he could have just enough time to make use of the valise's first-aid kit and get a little rest, he trusted his own reserves would kick in and he would be able to resume the trek come suns-up. Provided, of course, that the medicines in the kit were still viable and not toxic to his physiology.

He was halfway up the outcropping, some twenty meters, when he spied a glimmer to the north. Hugging the side of the rocky prominence, he used his visor to magnify his view. Beyond the northern edge of the primordial forest, the waning, pink slanting rays of daylight cast pale purple shadows against the base of a sprawling city. Its silvery towers shimmered like a mirage in the distant haze.

A cold breeze tugged at the Warden, threatening to pluck him from his precarious hold. An immense shadow fell across the jungle a mere second before it began to rain.

It was not a slow, gentle rain. More like some malicious deity had picked up a lake or small sea, carried it high above the Warden's head, and simply let go. The rocky surface became slick as oil beneath the sudden deluge and the Warden's shaking fingers lost their grip. He slid down the sheer wall as if propelled by a rocket. The valise's straps snapped and the medicine and hazmat suit sailed far out into the jungle.

Scrabbling for purchase, the Warden's left hand found a crevice, his fingers locking in like desperate talons. His momentum stopped with such force that he felt something pop in his left shoulder, sending flames of pain rippling through his neck and torso. But he held on and managed to scramble up to a slender outcropping where he could perch.

Taking a deep breath and shivering against another body-wracking chill, he opened his eyes to see that he sat only five meters above the undergrowth. Even using the magnification of his visor, the Warden could not tell where the valise had landed in the torrential downpour. He shook his head and reached into his right boot for the pistol. It was gone.

He closed his eyes as the jungle descended into waves of rain-swept darkness. His teeth chattered and he rocked violently against the wet stone wall, his insides twisting into a cold knot.

"This looks like a good spot for the night. Give it another go in the morning..."

Her eyes were flames of ice and her cool breath burned his flesh. His body ached, every cell straining and twisting for the want of her. She smelled of summer rain and a sea of flowers, her long dark hair enveloping him like a shroud. His hands shook, clenching as they reached out to take hold of her blue curves, yearning to feel her warmth against his freezing skin...

"Marajin..." His cracked and muffled voice stirred him from the fever dream. He had a moment's recrimination before slipping back into maddening illusion.

At some point before dawn, Quantum found him. The Warden opened his eyes to see his tall, blue-skinned friend hovering above the rock ledge. A pale glow surrounded the alien's lithe frame, sparkling in his big black eyes and silhouetting his

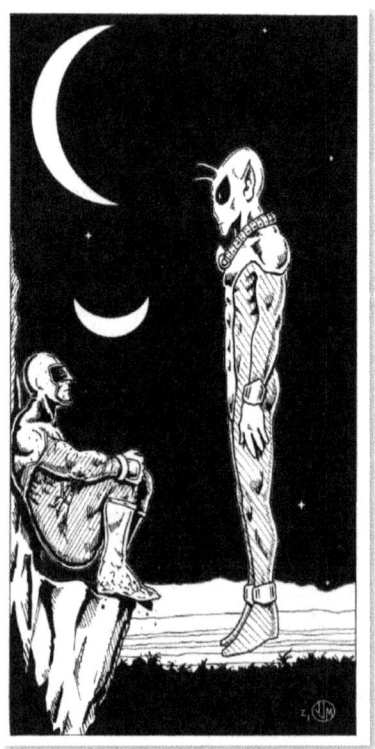

wriggling antennae. Quantum rarely showed emotion. But his undersized mouth always seemed to have a childlike smile playing across it, as if silently judging or mocking this dimension.

"Boy am I glad to see you." The Warden's voice sounded like a rusty gate in his ears. His thirst was terrible. He regretted not taking advantage of the deluge to drink fresh rainwater. "How'd you find me?"

Quantum tilted his head. "I have not. You are hallucinating. If you do not come to your senses very soon, you will die."

The Warden laughed and tried to convince himself it wasn't maniacal. "Leave it to you to be completely calm and logical even in a fever dream."

"You are falling."

The Warden gulped in a mouthful of air, his eyes going wide behind his visor. He *was* falling. He tried to grab hold of the rock. Pain exploded across his left side, numbing his mind and body.

He hit the ground with bone-jarring force and tasted blood.

He lay in the wet grass for some time, gathering his strength and conquering the fear to move. He knew movement meant pain as he learned the extent of his injuries, but it also meant survival. Taking a deep breath, he moved his arms under his chest and pushed up against the agony rippling through his shoulders and back. A chorus of aches in his hips, knees, and ankles joined in as he got to his feet.

Plucking a handful of dew-laden grass and sucking the moisture into his mouth, the Warden started walking north. It felt like things were moving inside him that had stayed put his whole life. Swaying like a drunken man, he could only hope that the city he'd seen hadn't also been a figment of his fevered imagination.

He'd taken a dozen wobbly steps before recalling his hunters. He shrugged. "Nothing I can do if they come for me now... No need to worry about them anymore..."

He blinked, tasting dirt and grass.

He lay face down on the ground. Coughing, he pulled himself back to his feet and stumbled forward. Four, five steps later he fell again. The Warden stayed down longer this time, sucking as much air into his lungs as he could, but again he got up and continued his trek. He no longer sought the Forbidden City. His goal was the next tree where he could catch his breath before moving on.

He made it to the third tree before the flies found him.

He didn't know if it had taken hours or days to reach the edge of the forest. All the Warden knew was that if he had a drop of blood left in his body it must have been indigestible to the swarms of biting insects that had plagued him on his hellish walk. Leaning against the bole of one of the last trees overlooking a steep ridge and rolling valley, the Warden realized he had not imagined the silvery city after all.

A warning beep from his chrono drew his attention. He glanced at the readout, noting the elevated levels of radiation. He was still in a relatively safe proximity to the source, which he determined to be the frothing green river separating this edge of the jungle from the plateau upon which the hidden metropolis perched. Still, the readings did not indicate the radioactive hell he had feared to find at the Forbidden City.

Watching the sunlight play along the distant steel spires and glass towers, he smiled. After a while, he spotted a shining object rise up from the city and move steadily in his direction. The Ancients were coming to get him. He nodded in satisfaction at the realization, then slumped at the base of the tree to wait for his ride.

V.

The Warden felt disappointment more than surprise when the hovercraft's pilot turned out to be a robot rather than an "Ancient." And not just because of his personal distrust of AIs. He understood that his hallucination of Quantum had not only been a manifestation of missing his friend, but also of missing interaction with a more technically advanced people. As much as he had come to admire the primitive beauty of Un Quan—and its inhabitants—the Warden understood that he belonged not only to another part of the galaxy, but also another epoch of civilization.

"The Masters wish to speak with you. Do not resist." The robot, more anthropomorphic than the pylon guardian, was as silver as its vehicle and the city gleaming in the distance. The mechanical man held a modern blaster pistol in one shining hand. It extended the other to the opened gullwing door of the hovercraft.

"I'll take the carrot." The Warden grunted as he got to his feet. The pain had settled in his bones and the fever made him lightheaded. "Lead the way, Jeeves."

Strapping into the safety harness of the vehicle's passenger seat, the Warden noticed green lasers passing over his body. His robot chauffeur took the controls and the craft rose into the air on a pad of antigravity. Without acknowledging the Warden's questioning look, the faceless bot said, "You are unwell. The Masters are conducting a diagnostic analysis of your body to determine if you pose a biological threat to the population."

The Warden shrugged. "Makes sense... Can you tell me anything about my travelling companions? Do you know what happened to them?"

The robot did not answer. The flying car drew quietly closer to the city.

From this altitude, the Warden saw that the Forbidden City sat on a plateau surrounded on three sides by the irradiated river, the entire kilometers-wide clearing situated in the midst of the continent-spanning jungle. Clearly this was one of the clusters of advanced structures he had first detected upon entering the system. Seeing the scale of the forest at this distance, he had to admit just how miraculous it was that he and his young companions had ever gotten this close on foot.

As the bot guided the vehicle into the city, gracefully maneuvering between the gleaming spires and mirrored towers, the Warden felt a strange sense of homesickness. A very long time ago, when he had first joined the Star Wardens, Earth had looked similar: great sprawling metropolises separated by vast swaths of environmentally protected forests, grasslands, mountains, marshes, agricultural preserves, and river valleys. Unlike those memories of home, however, this city appeared to be all but dead. The flying car was the only moving vehicle in sight, and there were no visible signs of population.

For a moment the Warden worried that these so-called Masters were no more than an advanced line of bots who had risen up and replaced the city's organic inhabitants, Andres's and Jynnessa's "Ancients."

This frightening thought was alleviated, however, when he spotted a flash of bright colors on a rooftop landing pad. A group of nine, elegantly garbed people stood awaiting the hovercraft's arrival. Nine people of both genders with green skin.

When the vehicle came to rest, the Warden was struck by the uniform baldness and apparent age of the Masters. If they had been humans, he would have judged them all to be senior citizens ranging between their early seventies and mid-nineties.

"Ancients, indeed."

Exiting the vehicle, the Warden breathed in the fresh, high-altitude air of the rooftop and nodded at the nine Masters. Most of them were smiling.

"Welcome to Quan City," a tall thin man said. He wore golden hoops in his ears and a flowing robe of red, green, blue, and yellow geometric patterns. A gold chain of office hung around his neck and more gold adorned his wrists. "I am Thede, the Administrator. These are the Masters of Science, Technology, and Industry." Thede made the introductions, ending with a hard-faced woman named "Dr. Gamela, Master of Biology."

Like the other female members of the Masters, Dr. Gamela's bald head was wrapped in a multicolor cloth that matched her robes. "You are an interesting specimen, stranger," she said, her emerald eyes studying him as if he were on a microscope slide. "Once you are well, you should prove ideal for our needs."

The Warden leaned on the hovercraft as his head spun. "Slow down, Doctor. Where I come from, it's polite to get to know somebody before you go asking them for favors. And you can call me Warden seeing as how we're *all* strangers right now."

Thede the Administrator flashed a conciliatory smile. "Quite right. We will get you well and then we can discuss the other matters. Please, Warden, come along."

The Warden didn't budge. "First, I want to know about my travelling companions. Where are Jynnessa and Andres? What have you done with them?"

Dr. Gamela bridled. "The natives? They are unharmed, though if they had been injured it would have been their own fault. The female attacked the members of our society, sent to fetch the lot of you, injuring one of them. If the others had not used stun weapons, your two companions would have perished. That is why we sent the robot after you. We cannot risk the life of a single member of our society, and we have assessed you to pose a far greater threat than the two natives."

The Warden shrugged. On any other given day that might have been true, but he was fairly certain that an irritable kitten could have taken him with ease at the moment. "I want to see them, then you can do with me as you will."

Thede the Administrator gave Dr. Gamela an assuring gesture. "Very well."

The Warden accompanied the nine Masters and their silver guardian into a large elevator. This sped them deep into the towering building's foundation. A low sound emanated from unseen speakers and it took the Warden a moment or two to realize it was music. The realization or the fever made him smile, wondering if "The Girl from Ipanema" was on the playlist.

"You lot don't seem too interested in my differing appearance."

"We know you come from off-world," one of the male Masters said. "We tracked your arrival in our star system and observed your crash landing. We wanted—"

Gamela cleared her throat. "There will be time enough for answers when our... guest is feeling better, Dr. Hydrax. For now, Warden, please conserve your strength."

Scratching the festering bug bite on the back of his leg, the Warden nodded. He knew there would be some kind of *quid pro quo* at the end of this encounter, and by Gamela's demeanor he got the sense it would be quite a hefty one. But seeing as how the Masters were the only viable means of returning to his side of the galaxy, it was a price he would simply have to pay. He just hoped he could afford it when the time came.

Exiting the elevator, the Warden found himself in a long, winding corridor running between broad observation panels. These windows opened onto cells or displays akin to some zoos he had visited. Each spacious chamber contained a simulated biosphere and a mated pair or small family of some kind of native animal, though he did not see any spider-saurs in the collection. The Warden had never been fond of zoos, even as a child. Something deep within him recoiled at the deprivation of freedom, even in non-sentient beings.

He slammed his palms into the glass when they brought him to a particularly large display. He wiped sweat from his eyes to make sure they were not betraying him, though he supposed it could be another hallucination. Below the window, beside an idyllic waterfall scene, Jynnessa and Andres laughed and ate a picnic feast on a flower-studded lawn.

"You've got them in a cage? What manner of people are you?"

"The civilized kind," Thede sniffed. "We do have holding cells more in line with keeping criminals and prisoners, Warden. However, we thought the subjects might enjoy the menagerie better. Based on their expressions and body language, I would have to say we were right."

The Warden couldn't deny that. The last time he had seen the youths they had barely gotten over the ingrained urge to kill each other. Now, here in this artificial paradise, they appeared to be in the opening phases of an active courtship. "I want to speak with them."

"Out of the question," Dr. Gamela said. "The experiment has begun and we cannot risk you contaminating it."

"Experiment?" The Warden turned on her, swayed uncertainly.

Thede put a gentle hand on the Warden's shoulder to steady him. "I assure you, we will explain everything later. Now come along, you are almost dead on your feet, young man."

The Warden nodded. He was in no condition to make demands, but he promised himself that once he was back in fighting trim, he would have his answers. As he was led away, he gave the youths another look to reassure himself that they were real and in no immediate danger.

The Warden stood on the balcony of his luxurious hi-tech suite, staring out at the gleaming skyscrapers and the tangerine sky reflected in their mirrored windows. Wearing a flowing robe of silvery silk, he breathed in the cool fresh air of a clean, modern city. That sense of homesickness washed over him again. He fought against the thought that he could, if need be, make a life for himself here.

The notion that Queen Marajin might be included in that life surprised him, but not unpleasantly. He realized he had allowed the woman's beautiful image to occupy his idle thoughts ever since he had laid eyes on her...

As remarkable as the healing skills of Jynnessa's and Andres's people were, those of the Ancients, or Masters, proved even more efficient. Before being brought to his new quarters, the Warden had been taken to a med lab in the same building as the menagerie—the Office of Bio-sciences, he was told. There, Dr. Gamela had given him a single pill and a glass of cold water before ordering him into a steam shower. By the time he had emerged with the jungle's grime washed away, his fever and the bug bite were gone. The blaster scar left by the pylon bot had all but vanished, as had several from older wounds.

A chirp at the front door alerted him to the arrival of Thede and Dr. Gamela. He stepped back into the suite's living room to meet them.

"Beautiful isn't it?" Thede smiled, staring past the Warden at the city beyond. "The last bastion of a once-thriving and advanced civilization."

The Warden nodded. "What happened here?"

Gamela poured three goblets of wine. "*We* happened. Our ancestors learned what I'm sure you already know. Affluent societies can become stagnant societies, and that stagnancy breeds discontent and unrest."

The Administrator stepped to the balcony and stared out at his beloved city. "There rose a generation at the pinnacle of our species' achievements with no great challenges set before them: no great wars, no great causes with which to test themselves. Their forebears had faced all the challenges, fought all the wars, and marched for all the causes with the hope of leaving their descendants a perfect world." He turned and looked at the Warden with profound sadness. "And for this unforgivable crime, those forebears were despised."

The Warden sipped the dry wine, but said nothing. Earth had faced a similar crisis of civilization nearly eight hundred years before he was born. The human race had been saved from a new Dark Age brought on by apathy and disunity by reaching to the stars. Clearly Un Quan had not embraced space travel as the new challenge which could have broken their race's destructive ennui.

"The generation of malcontents, having no enemy save themselves, made war on history. Identity, or rather the illusion of identity predicated upon biology, was the preferred weapon." Doctor Gamela frowned as she set her goblet on the table. "Reopening old wounds that had long since healed, they factionalized along new ideologies and so-called 'communities,' turning differences into divisions, words into weapons, and opinions into crimes.

"It was not long before a planet-spanning civilization of individuals once united behind the idea of a mutually beneficial society crumbled into a plethora of warring agencies, subversive cabals, and rebellious organizations. Global, regional, and local governments were compromised or failed altogether until civil war swept the planet and anarchy prevailed."

The Warden raised his chin. "And the genders?"

Gamela shook her head. "We never reached out to the stars as your civilization obviously has, Warden. But our ancestors were true masters of biology, chemistry, and genetics. With the perfection of cloning technology, the traditional means of reproduction became… superfluous. And during the era of unrest, the Great Decline leading up to the so-called Agenda Wars, the act eventually came to be despised as a barbaric practice of oppression. Women became increasingly resentful of men and men more and more suspicious of women…"

Thede rolled his goblet in his hands, staring at the tiled floor. "We have found records which indicate that a secret experiment was undertaken by one of the old factions. By introducing certain additives into common foods, they hoped to make male and female body chemistry as close to one another as possible. The thought being that with similar hormones, men and women would think more alike, thus fostering harmony."

"Not only that," Gamela added. "Another group had an entire organization dedicated to engineering society through manipulation of popular entertainment. Male characteristics, being considered too aggressive and dangerous, were subverted and replaced with feminine traits while encouraging women to espouse these very same 'problematic' male characteristics."

The Warden nodded. "And these… plots were discovered."

Thede ran a hand over his bald head. "That discovery was the first piece of the puzzle that led to civil war. Fortunately for us, this city became a haven for all the free-thinkers and moderates: those who had rebelled against the propaganda and the partisanship, refusing to take part in the Agenda Wars. Using powerful ray-shielding generators, these founders, our ancestors, protected Quan City against the ensuing centuries of war, famine, disease, and cultural decline."

Dr. Gamela fixed the Warden with her emerald eyes. "Unfortunately, those very generators which protected us for generations may have proved our ultimate undoing. Until recently, they emitted a very specific type of radiation resulting in gradual sterility. By the time our great-grandparents discovered this, it was already too late. The genetic markers had been irreversibly damaged."

Thede added, "No children have been born to our society in over forty years, Warden. We are slowly dying out."

"Not so slowly anymore," Gamela corrected. "Last month we numbered over three hundred souls. But a… lab accident has reduced that number significantly."

"But you said you have cloning technology—"

"We have destroyed the cloning facilities as well as the files containing the secrets of the process." Both Masters frowned and shook their heads as Gamela spoke. "It was the cloning which enabled and encouraged the divide in our species and fostered the hatred…

"Some time ago, our ancestors tried an experiment with the savage survivors in the jungle. They brought prime specimens of the male and female war bands into the city and tried to reeducate them, to civilize them. The barbarians killed and looted, taking the cloning technology back to their kin to continue their uncouth lines. You have seen for yourself the fruition of this failure. The brutes have made use of that technology for generations and it has brought them no happiness, no peace."

The Warden saw their point, then realization dawned on him. "*Your* experiment! With Andres and Jynnessa. You are trying to see if they can still produce offspring in the… traditional way."

Gamela nodded. "We have harvested the necessary cells from other subjects, but in vitro fertilization has not proven successful thus far. We believe it has something to do with the cloned genetic material itself. If our species is to survive, it must be through natural fertilization and gestation."

Thede poured himself another goblet of wine. "Yes. They are not the first with whom we have tried. Their predecessors either killed each other or found the prospect of mammalian reproduction so abhorrent that they let themselves waste away."

"And you let them. You just stood behind your glass walls and watched them murder each other or give in to self-destruction." He placed his goblet on the table with a loud thump and walked to the balcony.

"We couldn't very well let them return to their tribes, Warden." Gamela joined him at the rail. "Our records tell us what those warlike monsters can do with the technology we have. We cannot make the same mistake our ancestors did. That is why we have spent centuries cultivating this city's security, both with science and with mystique."

"The irradiated river." The Warden was angry now. "You've been poisoning them as well. And what about the other hapless lifeforms of this world? How many mutations have you created? How many species have gone extinct? How much damage have you done to the biosphere?"

Thede shook his head, frustrated. "No, no, no. What you see as an ecological travesty is in fact one of our greatest triumphs, Warden. The river now houses *all* the residual fallout left behind by the Agenda Wars. We of Quan City have spent generations using our technology to not only draw it out of the planet's atmosphere and water tables, but also to rapidly reduce the radiation's half-life. Yes, we do use it as a passive deterrent against the jungle tribes, but we have placed sensors that warn the indigenous fauna away from the water's perimeter."

Gamela elaborated. "The tribes have used the stolen cloning technology to grow in numbers. The males alone number in the tens of thousands and we suspect the females number even more. If either faction assaulted us *en masse*, we would be forced to defend ourselves tooth-and-claw, thereby only hastening our own extinction."

"You can't justify this. They are still people and you're treating them like animals. Worse than animals, apparently. Don't you see that by doing this, you are becoming the very things that those 'malcontents and subversives' claimed their forebears were?" The Warden frowned. He recalled Marajin's veiled reference to devices from before the Dark Times. "Besides, they may already have technologies other than the cloning devices."

Thede waved the criticisms away as he joined them on the balcony. "We have closely monitored them. They may have a few relics hidden away in the vaults of their strongholds, but thankfully they have so built up their own superstitions that they fear to use them. I doubt they ever will."

"Jynnessa and Andres might when they come to power. They don't seem to share their parents' blind adherence to tradition. They both spoke of a prophecy..."

Gamela rolled her eyes. "Prophecy! That word alone shows how degenerate these people are. What they call 'prophecy' was actually the summation of a scientific paper published by Dr. Janos Kitatma, the Minister of Sciences during the days of the Great Decline: 'Given the nature of all things, the Un Quan must reunite and again become one people or forever pass from existence. If we fail in this, I can only hope that we will be replaced by a new, and hopefully wiser, species.'"

The doctor cracked a rueful smile as she studied the empty city. "Her words have indeed proved prophetic, I'll grant you. When she wrote them, she was speaking philosophically. Centuries later, the warning has become a physical reality. We are so very close to passing from existence... We cannot afford to take any more chances."

The Warden knew she was getting to the point where he fit into this history lesson, so he waited.

Gamela's eyes flashed back to him. "We've told you how few we are, Warden, but we've not told you the worst of it. The city's operational mechanisms must be recharged on a monthly basis. Unfortunately, something has happened recently and we cannot enter the foundations to begin the recharging process."

"Let me guess. This is where I come in. Well, I hate to tell you this, but you've got the wrong guy. I'm about as handy with technology as one of those folks out in that jungle. In fact, I'd be willing to bet my spacesuit that Andres has more technological knowhow than I do."

"You misunderstand, Warden." Thede gave him a politician's smile. "From what your companions have said, you are a mighty warrior. That is what we need, not a technician or scientist."

The Warden raised an eyebrow. "I've fought in a war, but my role is that of a peace officer. I prefer to disarm hostile situations, not engage in them."

Gamela laughed, surprising the Warden. "Do not worry. We don't want you to fight anyone. In truth, you would be more of a hunter than a warrior. Remember the lab accident I mentioned...?"

The Warden placed the three-meter long vibro spear against the wall before entering the menagerie habitat. He wore his cleaned and repaired spacesuit, its visored cowl flipped back to hang between his shoulders, and his reloaded Comets belted at his hips. The Masters had captured them along with Andres and Jynnessa, and though they had been unable to activate the weapons, they did have the technology to recharge the blaster cells.

"I want it on record that I disapprove of this." Dr. Gamela didn't need to repeat this statement, but she did not let that stop her.

Thede shrugged. "What harm can it do? From what I can tell, I'm guessing it was his influence on the subjects that has allowed these two to show such promise."

The Warden ignored them as the holographic shield closed off the outer corridor from the inner paradise. He didn't care about their "experiment." Considering what they wanted him to do, seeing Jynnessa and Andres one more time was not too big a thing to ask. He knew he was risking the possibility of the Masters helping him repair the spaceship by making such a demand, but the Warden would not go into the city's bowels without speaking to his erstwhile traveling companions. He had something important to tell them in case he didn't make it back.

He watched as both youths stopped splashing playfully in the pool at the base of the falls, their faces filled with joy. He couldn't help but return their smiles as they tumbled out of the water and ran to embrace him.

"Warden! You're alive!" Andres shouted, snatching up his crimson toga from the grass.

"I knew you were too strong to die!" The Warden felt his face and ears go hot with embarrassment when Jynnessa didn't bother donning what little attire she wore before grabbing him in a crushing hug.

Clearing his throat and allowing himself a paternal glance at her sparkling eyes, the

Warden eased out of the embrace and nodded to Andres. "Well, you two seem to have done all right for yourselves. Looks like you didn't need me after all."

"That's not true and you know it." Andres grasped his hand and clapped his shoulder.

"Isn't it wonderful here?" Jynnessa pulled on her tunic with no inkling of shame. "The Ancients and their marvels are everything I've always imagined."

"And they've convinced you not to kill each another?"

Jynnessa and Andres exchanged sheepish smiles. The prince cleared his throat. "Well, not exactly…"

The princess laughed. "Actually, we were about to kill each other while you were in the pool of black water. We each blamed the other for not stopping you. If the Ancients hadn't arrived when they did, we may have come to blows."

"A common threat united you." The Warden had seen that story play out before.

"More than that," Andres said, his face solemn. "When we saw their green skin, the males and females working together… we realized that we are both descended from one people. And they explained the prophecy to us."

Jynnessa slid her hand into Andres's. "It was like a door being opened in a hot room, letting out all the stifling air. We saw each other… differently."

Andres blushed orange. "And I think we liked what we saw."

"I'm glad that you did." The Warden sat on a moss-covered boulder and indicated they join him. "I came to tell you something before I go."

Jynnessa frowned. "Where are you going? We'll go with you."

The Warden shook his head. "No, that won't be necessary. I'm going on a… on a hunt. It may take a long time, so you may be gone when I get back. If that's the case, I want the two of you to do something for me."

"You saved my life, Warden." Andres stared at him with a firm jaw. "Whatever you ask, I will do it or die trying."

The Warden smiled. "Nothing so dramatic as that, though it may prove even more difficult."

"What is it?" Jynnessa asked.

"I want you to convince your parents that peace is the only way for your race to survive. Take to heart what the Masters, the Ancients, have shown you here. At one time, you were one people, one species, one society." He gestured at the amazing chamber around them. "You see what that kind of unity can accomplish. Now it's up to you to lead the way back from the brink of extinction, back to... well, all this."

Andres shook his head with a bitter chuckle. "You are right. That will be more difficult than dying."

Jynnessa put her blue hand on the prince's yellow arm, both green in the shadows of the simulated Eden. "But it will be worth it."

"Good." The Warden stood and smiled. "Now, I've got to go. In case I don't see you again, safe travels and happy landings to you both."

Jynnessa caught his wrist. "What are you going to hunt, Warden?"

"Oh, just the biggest and meanest spider-saur our hosts ever managed to build."

vi.

The entrance to the city's subterranean workings was a ten-meter-diameter, meter-thick metal door set into a massive concrete tunnel. A robotic maintenance crew worked with torches to reopen the sealed portal as the Warden leaned on the vibro spear beside Thede and Dr. Gamela.

"Any idea what it's been eating since it went down there?"

Dr. Gamela shrugged. "No idea. The plan was to release it into the jungle with a preprogrammed patrol route. We knew the thing would immediately become the apex predator of the biosphere, and thus there was the danger of it overhunting the designated territory. Which in turn would cause it to eventually increase its hunting grounds beyond the desired scope. Thus, we designed it to have a slow digestive cycle to offset this possibility."

"So, it's hungry. Great." The Warden grunted, then looked at the tip of the deactivated vibro blade. "And you're sure this thing will pierce its hide? I'm going to have to get pretty dang close to use it."

Thede patted the weapon's haft with pride. "Oh, it will cut through almost anything, Warden. And once you've pierced the beast, don't forget to activate the electromagnetic pulse. This will shut down the creature's cybernetic systems and nanobot regeneration."

The Warden gave the man a wry smile. It seemed no matter where he went in the galaxy, he was bound to find mad scientists or the technological terrors that were their legacy. "Sure. I won't forget."

The work crew turned off their torches. The bot foreman announced, "We are through. As soon as you are inside, we will seal the door behind you."

The Warden hefted the spear. "Then let's get this show on the road."

"And don't forget to turn on the generators in Sector 12," Thede added. "That will be the signal for us to come get you."

The Warden glanced at his chrono, the Masters having uploaded the vault's schematics to the device. "Will do."

A moment later, he walked into immense darkness, the sound of the welding torches sealing the door behind him. He switched his visor to night vision and began the hunt.

The Warden hadn't traveled far before understanding why the entrance to the underground power center was so large. The walls of the cavernous chambers were lined with titanic machinery that hummed with a low electric malevolence. A quick scan with his chrono indicated that the metallic monoliths were storehouses for the city's energy. Most of these batteries showed between ten and fifteen percent capacity. A few were completely dormant.

The Forbidden City was dying, and with it all hope of Un Quan ever regaining its former glory. And any chance of the Warden returning to his side of the galaxy.

Crossing from the first chamber into a corridor lined with power cables and utility tubes, pipes, and wires, the Warden discovered the remains of the Masters' first attempts to hunt down their rogue experiment. The floor of the corridor was littered with shattered and shredded metal carapaces, limbs, and featureless heads. Thede had told him that the robots had been dispatched several times, but all had been destroyed.

After six such attempts, the Masters realized they were expending more of their dwindling resources manufacturing the bots than they could afford to lose. Thede's engineers had already designed and built the EMP vibro spear, but they had little

hope of its successful use until observing the Warden in his trek through the jungle. The city's aging populace had survived in an entirely non-confrontational lifestyle.

At the end of the corridor, the Warden paused. He caught the scent of something animal in this sterile, inorganic atmosphere. His instincts went to red-alert. He crouched, muscles taught, fists clamped on the hi-tech primitive weapon. He scanned the next chamber with his night vision, but saw no sign of the creature. Just more rows and rows of the towering batteries. If anything, this next room was even larger than the first.

The Warden crept into the cavernous space, keeping his back against the metal wall, his head on a swivel, ears straining for the slightest sound.

A clicking, rattling noise echoed from somewhere deep in the darkness.

He felt like he was being watched. Studied.

Hunted.

The Warden continued to move, circling the huge chamber filled with dead and dying machinery. He stepped over more robotic corpses.

A low, guttural growl rumbled like thunder. The acoustics of the room amplified and reverberated the sound so that the Warden could not discern its origin.

The floor shook. The click-clacking rattling sound echoed again.

The monster was on the move.

He still saw no sign of the thing. He considered switching his visor to thermal, but decided the room's machinery might radiate too much ambient heat to see the beast before it was too late.

He moved farther into the room.

His boot struck something at ankle level. He almost fell, but managed to right himself by using the spear shaft as a brace. His left foot was caught, trapped in some kind of cable or wire. Reaching down to remove it, his glove stuck to the thick strand, like metal to a super magnet.

"A web."

Realization struck him the same moment he heard the rattling, click-clacking noise again. Overhead.

He understood. The creature was not moving along the floor, but the ceiling. In the jungle, the spider-saur had acted like a reptilian hunter. In this dark interior space, this cyber spider-saur had adopted the role of a predatory arachnid.

The Warden threw himself to the floor and rolled.

A bone-ridged leg the size of a ship's landing gear struck where he had stood, punching a hole in the metal floor like a blaster bolt through foil. The creature's massive head lunged from the shadowy ceiling. Two-meter-long fangs spread wide as a primal roar battered the Warden with the force of a sonic boom. Thick ropes of foul-smelling saliva rained down, splattering him in slime.

His left boot and right glove still stuck in the webbing, the Warden clutched the spear with his left hand. An awkward lunge sent the glowing blade at the monster's face. It was a weak blow, but apparently caused enough pain for the thing to retreat for a moment in rage.

Tugging his hand free from his captured glove, the Warden grasped the spear with both hands and swung the blade at the cyber spider-saur's nearest leg. The blade bit deep into the chitinous member, carving an oozing wound that glowed purple in the darkness.

Again the creature howled, launching itself back into the looming shadows overhead.

The Warden took the reprieve to free himself from his immobilized boot. Bounding to his feet, he clutched the spear and ran. He watched for more spidery traps while keeping alert for the monster's next attack from above.

Glancing up, he maneuvered between two of the battery towers at a jog. He didn't see a strand of web until his visor struck it. It was like being clotheslined. His feet flew out from under him. His head snapped back like a shot.

The spear flew from his hands, clattering to the metallic floor somewhere in the darkness.

Hanging by his face from the obscuring web, the Warden heard the cybernetic monster pounce on top of a nearby battery with a metallic crash.

Disconnecting the visor from his cowl, the Warden dived to the side as slavering jaws chomped shut mere centimeters away.

He was free and alive, but now he was blind.

Drawing his Comets, the Warden opened fire on the void where he suspected the monster to be. By the flashing blaze of superheated plasma and exploding ricochets, he caught a glimpse of the thing's size for the first time. The beast's head alone was half as big as the spider-saur he had killed his first day on Un Quan.

The blaster bolts had proportionally less effect.

He also caught a glimpse of the dropped vibro spear.

Diving toward the weapon, the Warden felt a crushing pain explode across his left shoulder and back. The wind rushed from his lungs as he cartwheeled through darkness to slam into something hard and metallic.

He had lost one of his Comets, but still held the one in his right hand. Gasping for breath and praying the thing was not a moment away from devouring him, the Warden fired into the darkness. He knew the monster was impervious to blaster fire but hoped the battery opposite him was not. And he hoped it had enough juice to provide some light.

For once, his hopes were rewarded.

The colossal battery exploded in a blinding conflagration of white and blue electric flame. The cyber spider-saur was caught in this blast, shielding the Warden from the concussion with its titanic body. The chamber filled with the stench of scorched metal and burning hair and scales as heat boiled across the metal floor.

His eyes readjusting to the intense light, the Warden crawled to where the spear lay near the flames. He grasped the butt end of the weapon as the wounded monster scrambled back to face him, its slavering jaws only meters away.

Bellowing in hunger, pain, and rage, it lunged for the kill.

Unable to use his left arm, the Warden grabbed the spear and swung with all the power in his battered body.

The glowing blade entered the charging beast's left nostril, just above its opened maw. Sparks and flame carved along its scaly face as it impaled itself on the spear. The red left eye ruptured in an explosion as the spider-saur's fangs brushed the Warden's bare knuckles.

He hit the EMP trigger, felt the shockwave of energy ripple through him as it destroyed the thing's electronic brain and robotic immune system.

The monster collapsed with the force of a demolished building. The Warden coughed against the ensuing cloud of choking dust.

For a moment, he lay still in the fading glow of the burning power cell, trying to catch his breath. Carefully dragging himself to his feet, he made a brief catalogue of the parts of his body that had been replaced with pain. This included most of his left side above the waist. Grateful that his feet and legs still worked, he checked his chrono to find the quickest route to the generator in Sector 12.

He glanced at the battery he had destroyed. "I sure hope that wasn't integral to the system coming back online."

With that, he set off in the dark.

The extent of the Warden's injuries required more than a single pill and a steam shower this time around. When the Masters' work crew arrived at the generator, he lay slumped on the edge of unconsciousness at the control panels. Hurried back to the Office of Bio-sciences, he was rushed into a regeneration tube. There he spent the next three days while his body regrew the damaged tissue, reknit the shattered bones, and replenished blood lost in his battle with the rogue abomination. He spent another two days under the watchful eye of Dr. Gamela resting in his luxurious penthouse suite.

Though "resting" was not an easy thing for the Warden to do after so much forced inaction. By the end of the second day of seclusion in his rooms, he thought he might try to scale down the side of the tower just for a change of scenery. Noting his increased anxiety and frustration, Dr. Gamela surprised him by making an allowance for visitors.

"Warden!" Jynnessa said as she and Andres entered the suite. Both wore the flowing, multicolored robes typical of the Masters. "You're alive and well."

The Warden smiled as the youths drew near and embraced him. "Was there ever any doubt? I hope you haven't worried on my account."

Andres gave a rakish smile. "None whatsoever. I told her no secalaur in all of Un Quan was a match for you, no matter how big."

Jynnessa grinned as she punched the prince in the shoulder hard enough to make him flinch. "Liar. You were the one planning an 'escape' so we could go and rescue him."

The Warden laughed, though the tightness in his new ribs and shoulder reminded him just how close things had been. "And how are the two of you? I see your newfound friendship remains intact."

Andres placed his arm across Jynnessa's muscular shoulders. "I think we are more than friends now, Warden. I have asked the princess to be my spouse and she has honored me by accepting."

The Warden's smile grew wider. "Congratulations! And how have the King and Queen taken the news?"

They looked at each other with fading smiles. Jynnessa glanced at the floor. "We haven't told them yet. Technically, I believe we are still prisoners of the Ancients. They have not permitted us to leave the city."

This brought a scowl to the Warden's face. "I'll see about that. Your peoples were on the verge of a full-scale genocidal war just before I arrived. I had hoped that while I was out of the picture, the Masters might use their renewed energy to allow you to try and broker a peace."

Stalking to the wall console, the Warden tapped the intercom. "Could you please let the Administrator and the Doctor know I would like to see them at once."

The robotic guard's voice answered in the affirmative. While they waited, the Warden turned a fresh smile on his visitors. "Well, in the meantime I suppose you deserve a toast."

The youths glanced at one another. "A what?"

The Warden stepped to the table and poured three goblets of wine. "Where I come from it's customary for good news to be celebrated with a libation and a speech of some sort. I'm not great at speeches, but the Masters do make pretty good wine. If you're into that sort of thing."

Handing out the drinks, the Warden cleared his throat and raised his cup. "To the future King and Queen of Un Quan. To the future of the people of Un Quan. May you all live happily ever after."

The door buzzed a moment before Thede and Dr. Gamela entered the room. The doctor immediately scowled at the wine in the youths' hands. "They should not be drinking spirits. It could hamper the experiment."

The Warden waved the objection away. "I'd say your 'experiment' is as much a success as it need be for the moment. They've proven that the warring genders can be reunited in harmony. From what I've seen, your medical science can handle the rest if there's an issue."

Gamela sniffed. "You said yourself that you are not a man of science, Warden. You should leave such decisions to those—"

"That's right. I'm not a scientist. I'm a peace officer, intent on diffusing violent situations rather than participating in them. And I'm here to tell you that you've got one heck of a violent situation brewing out in that jungle right now. The day before you found me there was a major battle fought between the males and females who were no doubt looking for their respective heirs.

"Now the way I see it, your best chance of making sure this 'experiment' is more than just academic is to let these kids go back to their people and show them that there can be peace on this world. Otherwise, you'll be safe behind your walls, watching the final extinction of your species as those men and women eventually wipe each other out."

Gamela scowled, but Thede shook his head. "We can't take that chance, Warden. If the warring societies refuse to listen to these children, then the experiment will fail completely and our race will end."

Andres thumped his chest. "I'll die before I allow my father to separate me from Jynnessa."

The princess embraced the young man. "As will I."

The Warden sighed and looked at the ceiling tiles. "Romeo and Juliet…"

"You see," Gamela said. "They are our only hope of seeing our race reborn."

The Warden set his wine on the table and shook his head. "No. I'll take care of it. But I'm going to need one of your hover-cars, a couple of your bots, and a few things from your lab, Dr. Gamela."

vii.

The Warden hated what he was about to do. In his mind it still amounted to kidnapping, even if it was the best way he could think to prevent the complete self-eradication of a people. Of course, he also knew he was justifying his actions in the very way Dr. Gamela and Thede had justified their 'experiments' on the captured jungle dwellers.

He knew that Quantum would have come up with a better plan, though he also knew his alien friend might not see the necessity of doing so. The Mechtechan had invaded this universe over a hundred years ago with the intention of interdimensional conquest, and Quantum occasionally displayed his race's capacity for complete and utter sentimental detachment.

But Quantum wasn't here, so the Warden would have to make do with his own best judgement. Even if his "best" was the worst thing he could possibly imagine. Abducting an innocent person and depriving that individual of freedom and agency for any amount of time was abhorrent to him and everything in which he believed.

He checked the stun pistol holstered on his belt and the leather pouch containing the hypos filled with sedatives. He wore a dark jumpsuit favored by the Masters' work teams rather than his flashier blue-and-silver spacesuit. His benefactors had recovered and repaired his visor. This would prove invaluable to the operation. "Like a thief in the night…"

"Warden?" one of the two silver bots said in response to his mumbled observation.

He scowled at the metallic man. The Warden had never been fond of bots and didn't see his opinion on that changing any time soon. "You two stay here with the hoverer. Only come after me if I signal for help on my chrono. Understood?"

"Affirmative."

The Warden turned and jogged into the darkened jungle, his visor turning the world into a swirl of illuminated shades of green. He had a three kilometer hike to get to the male stronghold. Fortunately, Andres had told him the best way to get into Castle Vear without being seen, the prince having made use of these secret byways on his many escapes from custody. The Warden hoped that these hidden paths had not since been discovered and placed under guard.

Hope not being a strategy, he had brought the stun pistol.

Castle Vear was at once smaller and more imposing than the female fortress. Squat and hunched on an island in the midst of a broad marsh, its black walls crawled with thick, leafy vines and were caked with moss. Pale firelight glimmered from the narrow arrow loops in those walls and the jutting towers. Torches moved back and forth across the battlements, illuminating the helmed heads of sentries. A fortified guard tower secured the bridge that led to the main structure at the northern edge of the lake.

Just as he had bypassed the night patrols, the Warden avoided this bastion. Andres had told him there was another way. Hugging the tree line sixty meters from the outer banks of the mere, the Warden reached a small rocky outcropping that lined up with the southeastern tower. It was in this tower, he had been told, where King Mascos kept his private chambers.

The Warden touched the side of his visor, changing the spectrum of visible light. He almost smiled when he saw the flat grey shapes hidden beneath the black water's surface. Andres had been right. The castle's original builders had included a secret path across the lake, either as a means to launch sorties or for escape.

Lying on his belly, the Warden crawled through the long grass that separated the jungle from the water. Reaching the shallows, he remained prone and slid into the muck until he made contact with the camouflaged walkway. Crawling along this with just his nose and eyes above the surface, he made his way to the tower's base.

Still unseen, the Warden scaled the ancient, vine-shrouded stone. He climbed to the top level, some sixty meters above the jungle floor. Pausing at the balconied window, he took a moment to look out above the canopy, breathing in the sweet night air and listening to the melodious drone of the multitude of insects and animals singing in the darkness. Three crescent moons shed a pale, silvery light on the endless forest, glimmering on distant peaks and the towers of the not-so-distant Castle Sarquis.

The Warden could easily imagine Mascos standing on this balcony every night and staring with hatred and fear at that stronghold while Marajin did the exact same thing from a window in her own royal chambers. He wondered how many generations of men and women had done likewise, loathing and despising one another without ever knowing the joy of friendship and love that the two genders had found in so many other parts of the galaxy.

Thinking on this and on the happiness he had seen on Andres' and Jynnessa's faces the last time they had spoken, he knew he could not do what he had come here to do. At least not the way he had come to do it. Taking a deep breath, he hauled himself over the balcony and into the darkened bedchamber.

His night vision revealed the rugged splendor of the room. Polished weapons, shields, and armor hung on the plastered walls. The floor and the furnishings were of dark wood, and heavy drapes covered the windows as well as the four-poster bed dominating the space. This bed was occupied by a sleeping man.

"King Mascos."

The man jerked awake at the sound of the Warden's voice in the quiet room. Mascos held a curved dagger in his right fist. "Who is there? What do you want?"

Silhouetted against the night sky, the Warden cleared his throat. "You can call me Warden, Your Majesty. I've come to take you to your son."

Mascos rose from the bed, more concerned with the dagger than with donning nightclothes. He was tall and sinewy, still a warrior though at least a decade older than the Warden's apparent age. "You are the stranger, the pink skin. What have you done with Andres? I'll have you flayed alive if—"

"He is safe and well." The Warden raised his hands in appeasement. "Come with me and I'll take you to him."

Mascos turned to the door and opened his mouth to shout.

The Warden drew the stun gun before the first syllable could emerge. "Don't, Your Majesty. Just don't."

The king blinked in the darkness, trying to understand the strange weapon. "What is that? Andres said you had magic wands that spit fire strong enough to kill a secalaur. Would you kill me in my own bedchamber? Are you an assassin hired by the females? Were you sent to capture me by that harpy Marajin the Usurper?"

"No. I've been to the Forbidden City. The Masters—the Ancients are still there, but they are dying. They need your help if your race is to survive on this planet."

"Lies." Mascos hurled the dagger, diving for the closed door.

The Warden ducked, surprised by the sudden action. He pulled the pistol's trigger. The room filled with a white glow from the stun bolt, its intensity blinding the night vision visor.

"Guards! Hurm! I'm under attack!"

"Sam Hill." The Warden blinked the starbursts out of his eyes as the door flew open and three armed men rushed in. Tapping his visor to normal vision, he fired again, dropping the first guard beside Mascos. Apparently, the initial stun bolt had glanced the king's legs, rendering him inert but not unconscious.

A spear slashed past the Warden's side, narrowly missing his abdomen. Another blade forced him to take an awkward step back. The movement slammed his right wrist against the stone balcony, knocking the stun pistol from his grip. The weapon disappeared over the side as the room filled with more armored men.

The Warden caught the first soldier to reach him by the arm. Realizing it was Hurm, he launched the surprised captain of the guard over the balcony. The man bellowed an extended curse until he hit the lake below with a loud splash.

The next two spearmen charged face-first into jets from the hypos the Warden had intended to use to sedate his royal abductees. The soldiers dropped to the floor like sacks of lead.

Kicking one of the fallen spears into his hands, the Warden swung the weapon in a wide arc, forcing the five other guards back into the bedroom. Taking advantage of the temporary retreat, he charged in amongst them. He had to regain control of this situation in a hurry, or dive from the tower and hope the bots could pick up whatever was left of him.

Without his spacesuit to protect him, any blow from the guards' swords and spears could prove fatal. And yet, the Warden had not come here to kill anyone.

He just had to prove it.

Burying the spearhead in the floor, he kicked the weapon, snapping the shaft just below the socket, effectively turning the spear into a quarterstaff. Using this less-lethal instrument, he struck the clustered guards on their unprotected knees, elbows, and wrists before battering their helmed heads.

The Warden took a few minor cuts to his own arms and legs, but in a matter of minutes he had filled the bedchamber with groggy and unconscious men while moving steadily to the door. Reaching this, he was able to bolt the lock and use the spear shaft as a crossbar to keep more soldiers from entering.

"Now." He turned on the prostrate king, who had picked up a fallen sword. "If you'll put on some clothes, Your Majesty, I'll take you to your son."

Mascos narrowed his eyes and scanned the groaning men sprawled beside him. "You could have killed any of them."

The Warden stepped to the balcony and signaled the bots with his chrono. "That is not why I came here. I came on a mission of peace, to reunite a father with his son and future daughter-in-law."

Mascos's brow wrinkled. "What is a... *dotterinlow?*"

Though he knew his plan of capturing both the king and queen in the same evening was now ruined, the Warden laughed. Catching sight of moonlight glinting on the approaching hover car, he shook his head. "You'll find out soon enough. Now, please get dressed."

As difficult as it had been to convince Mascos to go to the Forbidden City, the Warden knew it would be nigh impossible to do the same with Marajin. The queen had vowed to enjoy torturing him until she was content to see him destroyed. And Sappoc had already acquired a taste for his blood. No, convincing Jynnessa's mother to attend the peace summit would definitely not be easy without some means of persuasion.

Added to this difficulty was the fact that, due to his botched attempt to secretly capture Mascos, the male camp was no doubt on the warpath. From what little the Warden knew of Hurm, he was certain the warrior would have the army of men on the march as soon as possible. Whether their target would be Castle Sarquis or the Forbidden City was even odds at this point. Either way, until a peace was reached, it meant more violence between the two genders.

The Warden was officially on the clock.

The morning after the raid on Castle Vear, the Warden and the two bots headed for Castle Sarquis. He had no intention of sneaking in this time.

Directing the pilot to set the hoverer down a good spear's-throw from the castle gates, the Warden and his artificial allies exited the shining craft. He wore his restored blue-and-silver spacesuit, his belted Comets and his eye-concealing visor. Using the vehicle's loudspeakers, he addressed the fortress's inhabitants.

"This is the Warden. I've come in peace to speak with Queen Marajin XVI." His amplified voice echoed off the castle walls and the hillside's rocky crags for several moments before fading away.

Silence prevailed for some time.

At length, the metal groan of machinery rent that silence. A moment later forty armed women rushed through the towering gates, Sappoc in the lead. Behind this host, a dozen chained, yellow-skinned eunuchs carried a heavy silver throne on their shoulders. Marajin, resplendent in all her glory, rode this opulent conveyance as if she were empress of the entire galaxy.

The Warden watched the warriors fan out in a semicircle around him, the bots, and the hoverer. The sight of the mechanical marvels kept them at bay for the moment, but he did not doubt that a word from either their queen or their captain would launch the women on a murderous assault.

He turned to the bots. "Stun weapons only, and *only* if I fire first."

"Affirmative."

The slaves set the sedan chair on the ground and Marajin rose to face him. She wore a sparkling cape of shimmering scales that blended into her fitted cuirass. Silvery vambraces and greaves replaced the jewelry on her wrists and legs just as a helm-like crown had taken the place of the bejeweled tiara she had worn on their first meeting. Clearly the Queen of Un Quan had the idea of presenting a formidable presence.

"Have you come to surrender yourself to my mercy, Warden?" Her voice was loud and calm, reassuring her subjects. But the Warden could see a glint of worry in her eyes. It took a moment to realize that worry was for her missing daughter, and not for the threat posed by the armed robots. "If you have harmed Jynnessa, I can assure you I have no mercy to give. Only pain and destruction."

"The princess is alive and well, Your Majesty. In fact, I have come to take you to her."

"Where is she?" Captain Sappoc blurted, her fists turning pale azure on the shaft of her spear.

The Warden did not look at her. He did not have to, his visor had already target-locked her. "She is in Quan City, what you call The Forbidden City. She is in the company of her intended spouse, Prince Andres, son of King Mascos III."

The Warden saw a snarl ripple across Marajin's beautiful face, her body going taught as if he had struck her.

A feral, anguished roar erupted from Sappoc's throat. She launched her spear at his heart.

The Comet was in his right hand before the shaft left Sappoc's. The blaster bolt caught the spear in flight. The weapon exploded in a shower of flaming sparks and fell to the ground in the midst of the clearing.

Before the other warriors could launch their own spears and arrows, the bots went to work. Stun blasts shimmered and crackled like strobes of lightning. Within moments, the Warden and the two silver men stood facing Marajin alone. The clearing before the castle walls was now filled with cowering slaves and unconscious warriors.

"They are not dead, Your Majesty." The Warden holstered his blaster. "I told you before, I am not a hired killer. I am here on a mission of peace, one which could save the lives of all your subjects. Now I beg you, please come with me to the Forbidden City. Let me reunite you with your daughter."

Marajin's icy gaze scanned the handiwork of the superior technology, flicked to the still forms of the security bots before coming to rest on the Warden's unseen eyes. A quivering sneer turned to a practiced smile on her face. "It would appear that I am now your prisoner, Warden. Do with me as you see fit."

The Warden took a deep breath, relieved. He bowed slightly and beckoned her to the hoverer. "If you please."

He stood in the middle of the glass-and-steel breezeway connecting the top floors of the Administration Center and the Office of Bio-sciences. From this vantage point, the Warden could look out beyond the city's center, past the huge and unused Civic Arena to the Transportation Complex.

"I thought I might find you here."

The Warden turned at Dr. Gamela's approach. "I'm not much use at negotiations. My best efforts usually end up with somebody getting shot, stabbed, or punched in the mouth. Nine times out of ten, that somebody is me."

The scientist joined him at the window. "You do yourself an injustice, Warden. If not for you, the two… rulers would not be speaking."

He knew she had wanted to say "savages," but he let it slide. "You can thank Jynnessa and Andres for that. I may have gotten them to the city, but the kids are the ones who got their parents to share the same room for any amount of time without going for each other's throats."

Gamela followed his gaze to the distant airfields. The glint of sunlight on the damaged hull of the corvette could just be seen. "Well, if there is one thing Thede excels at, it is negotiating. We may be entering the second week of talks, but both Mascos and Marajin have already conceded that there is a minority within their respective populations who seem to prefer the opposite sex. It is our hope that these individuals will prove an adequate sample to begin the repopulation of our world."

The Warden grunted. He understood Gamela's point of view: a scientist only interested in the continuation of her species and civilization. But he thought about the people of whom she spoke, the men and women of Un Quan who had spent their entire lives in societies hostile to their very natures. If this negotiation succeeded and this peace held, it would seem like being released from a life sentence to these individuals.

"And the children?"

Gamela gave him a sly smile. "You are more astute than you let on, Warden. Yes, it only makes sense for the children to begin acclimation and education in an integrated society. We hope that our influence will offset any preconceived prejudices and biases they may have inherited from their parents. We certainly have a much better chance with them than with the adults."

The Warden grunted again. He was confident that she was right. So long as they could keep the adults from wiping each other out, in a generation or two they might just be free from all the hatred and fear. "Just so long as it is 'influence' and not indoctrination."

"What is really on your mind, Warden? You haven't taken your eyes off that ship since I got here."

"I've just been thinking… Now that I'm not fighting for my life or trying to keep others from killing each other, I've had time to think about how I got here in the first place."

"You said there was a hyperspace gate…" Dr. Gamela's eyes widened as the same thought occurred to her. "Someone built it."

The Warden nodded. "Yep. And Einstein-Rosen bridges are not cheap nor easy things to manufacture. Especially seven or eight decades ago, when, by my calculations, that bot would have been dispatched from the Frontier."

He turned to face Gamela. "Whoever built it had a reason. And if they get here…"

The doctor looked at the distant spaceship. "Our technologies will be no match for them."

"Which puts me in a pickle. If I repair the bridge, I open this system up to exploitation and possible invasion… But, I guess you could put a stop to me doing that, couldn't you?"

Gamela narrowed her eyes, her jaw tight. "Yes, we could. But a deal is a deal, Warden. And we cannot hide from the rest of the galaxy forever. Your existence implies that there are probably a few spacefaring civilizations on our side of your Frontier, as well.

"We will get you home, Warden. And when you get there, I hope you will inform your people that we are friends. We will most likely need their help very soon."

The Warden smiled. "It's a deal."

End of Part I

PART II

i.

The Last Star Warden put the rebuilt pirate ship on autopilot and prepared for the spacewalk. The first step of this procedure involved touching the printed image taped to the console for luck. He smiled at the beautiful face in the picture, which he had surreptitiously captured via his visor-cam in an unguarded moment. He had considered commissioning some pinup-style nose art featuring that face for the refurbished ship. But he had decided against it, needing no one to tell him how "impolitic" it would have been.

The Warden had been stranded on the jungle world of Un Quan at the edge of Uncharted Space for almost three months. And though his "hosts" had been more than accommodating since the initial unpleasantness surrounding his arrival, he was glad to finally take the first actual step in securing a return to his own side of the galaxy.

Even if that return would separate him from the smiling face in the snapshot, possibly forever. He tried not to think about that as he entered the ship's airlock.

"This is the Warden," he announced into his GlasSteel helmet's microphone. A notification on his visor told him his spacesuit was secure. He vented the pressure in the small chamber. "Preparing to exit the ship. Coms check."

Over three hundred thousand kilometers away, Dr. Hydrax answered. "We are receiving you loud and clear, Warden. All systems are looking good on our end." The Master of Astro Sciences could not keep the pride out of his deep voice.

The Warden didn't fault that pride. Hydrax and his people had done a heck of a job rebuilding the crashed corvette and adapting their own limited space-probing technology to that of the more advanced Civilized Worlds. The Masters had even successfully rebuilt and refueled the ship's single remaining atomic engine.

At least the Warden *hoped* they had nailed all the pertinent engineering details. He was about to put all the scientific and technological knowhow of the Un Quan Masters to the ultimate test. A test, which if failed, would be his last.

Surprisingly, Dr. Gamela's rather flat voice came over the coms. "Good luck."

The Warden acknowledged the Master of Biology's uncharacteristically sentimental comment with a smile, but did not reply. Checking his Ox levels, he hit the airlock release and drifted into open space.

The DuraSteel tether line slowly unfurled from his belt as he kicked off, separating himself from the stabilized corvette. The Warden turned to witness the splendor of the twin suns silhouetting the ship and three of the binary system's inner planets.

He had travelled from one end of the Civilized Worlds to the other and crossed the width and breadth of the Frontier. He was now the very first Earthman to explore Uncharted Space. But that feeling of physical weightlessness and ultimate spiritual gravity, of being one with the Cosmos, was a thrill that never got old.

"Approaching the bot debris field now." Using the small, shoulder-mounted jets designed by the engineers of Quan City, the Warden maneuvered himself close to the meters-wide scatter of metallic fragments. He pulled the electro super magnet from his belt and powered it up.

The construction and maintenance bot had been sent from somewhere in Frontier Space quite some time ago. The bot's mission had been to build the Einstein-Rosen bridge that would open the Un Quan system to interstellar travel, linking it to the part of the Milky Way now under the influence of the United Planetary Council.

However, the identity of the person or persons responsible for the bot's mission remained a mystery, as the Warden's unplanned arrival had all but destroyed the bot and damaged the bridge. Apparently at the very moment the ERB had come online.

If such coincidences weren't by now commonplace in the Warden's experience, he might have ascribed some self-centered meaning to why he was in this system at this very moment. But he had seen enough to know that the Cosmos simply put people where it wanted, when it wanted. All things happened for a reason.

Holding the powerful magnet with both hands, the Warden scooped up the various parts of the robot. He hoped that once the Un Quan scientists had the pieces, they could rebuild the bot so that it could not only bring the damaged ERB back online, but also give him some clue as to the mission's architect. A glance at the distant, gigantic, metallic rectangle of the darkened ERB told the Warden that it was not standard U.P.C. design.

U.P.C. bridges were much larger, allowing the powerful Star Cav ships-of-the-line access to "troubled" solar systems at a moment's notice. This ERB was big, but not that big. The Warden guessed it would just about accommodate a decent-sized freighter or maybe a luxury cruise-liner. Of course, there were smaller warships out there. Many of these had been acquired by a number of nefarious organizations: pirates and crime syndicates, smugglers and corporate mercenaries, and even a few galactic terrorist organizations. Any of these groups could be responsible for the construction of Un Quan's uninvited Einstein-Rosen bridge.

One thing was certain. Whoever had sent the bot to the Un Quan system had done so with an eye for a future which they might not be around to see. Or with an uncanny certainty that they would. And that unsettling thought made the Warden nervous.

Once the robotic debris was gathered into a sizeable metal ball on the end of the magnet, the Warden turned and used the shoulder jets to propel himself and his prize back to the corvette. Everything had gone smoothly thus far, but if the seals on the airlock weren't perfect, the entire ship could be destroyed in a cataclysmic decompression when he reentered.

The Warden held his breath as he closed the hatch and activated the re-pressurization protocol. There was an unsettling long wait before he heard the conditioned air flowing back into the chamber. The display on his visor told him pressure was normalized, but he still had to wait for the decontamination spray. It would not do to return to the planet's surface with any space-borne bacteria or microbes which might lead to a genocidal pandemic.

Once the bio-scan gave him the all-clear, the Warden doffed his GlasSteel helmet and Ox pack, stowed them, and made use of the zero-g to pull the heavy ball of salvaged metal down the ship's narrow central corridor. In the corvette's snug cargo hold, he secured the robotic parts before returning to the cockpit.

"That was surprisingly easy."

"Congratulations, Warden." Dr. Hydrax had to speak over the sound of applause and cheers in the mission control room to be heard through the coms. "You have made Un Quan's first manned space mission in centuries a complete success!"

The Warden didn't have the courage to tell the good doctor they hadn't yet tested the heat shielding on the ship with reentry. Primarily because that was one worst-case scenario he did not want to think about at the moment. Or for the next few days of his return flight.

"Warden," Dr. Gamela said over the coms. Her voice had assumed the chill with which he had grown familiar. "You will be happy to know that Her Majesty, Queen Marajin XVI will be waiting to see you upon your successful return."

The Warden cringed at Gamela's thinly-veiled sarcasm, his eyes going immediately to the photo of Marajin taped to the console. In the intervening months since his arrival, the acerbic Master of Biology had become the Warden's unlikely sounding board. Probably because she reminded him of Quantum to some degree. As such, the Warden had taken her into his confidence about the unexpected relationship he had embarked upon with the queen of the indigenous female population. Dr. Gamela did not approve of the affair and was not shy about sharing her opinion on the matter.

Deep down, the Warden knew she was right. He and Marajin were like oil and water sometimes, their new courtship peppered with as many heated arguments as endearing smiles. They came from completely different worlds, and not only in a literal sense. She was an imperious ruler responsible for the lives of tens of thousands, possessing a singular point of view forged from a Bronze-Age perspective. He was an itinerant spaceman who had experienced hundreds of cultures and species from across half the galaxy.

But the Warden was just so blasted lonely. And Marajin was, well... just so blasted gorgeous. Despite their mutual attraction and fascination, things could get touchy in a hurry. In fact, Her Majesty had not been happy about his undertaking this mission alone...

The Warden had walked into her suite at the embassy in Quan City the day before the scheduled launch, all smiles and optimistic excitement. He carried a crystal vase filled with red, yellow, and blue exotic flowers grown in Dr. Gamela's private hothouse, and a bottle of purple-colored wine given by Thede the Administrator to celebrate the auspicious flight.

Marajin had been trying on a series of utility suits with a pair of tailors from the Master of Textile's office. The blue-skinned queen did not look pleased with the green-skinned ladies' efforts. Ignoring his gifts, she turned on the Warden as soon as her guards had admitted him. "Good. You are here. Will you tell these *servants* what a real spacesuit should look like?"

One of the tailors frowned and was about to speak, but her companion warned her with a shake of the head.

The Warden set his presents on a side table and moved to intervene before Marajin's royal haughtiness could further harm relations with the citizens of Quan City. "Well, first off, Your Majesty, these ladies are not 'servants.' They are professionals in the employ of the Masters and are helping you out of the kindness of their hearts as much as anything else." He smiled as he spoke in a pleasant tone, hoping to alleviate some of the words' implied criticism.

Marajin had veiled her frosty eyes and sniffed. "You are right, of course. Servants would have gotten it right to begin with."

The Warden's smile had faltered. He cleared his throat and spoke to the tailors. "Can you give us a moment, ladies?"

As soon as they were alone, Marajin's aloof features took on a more playful expression. "And second?"

"Beg pardon?"

"You said, 'first off.' That implies you have at least one more point to make." She began abandoning the sleek, form-fitting silver jumpsuit with slow, practiced moves.

The Warden caught her mischievous smile as he turned his back and sighed. He knew she got a kick out of teasing him, just as she knew how uncomfortable her casual nudity made him. "I could come back in a minute."

"No need. Look, I am already in my robe. Now, tell me what else you have to say."

The Warden turned to see that she had, indeed, donned a silky green robe that clung to her shapely form like a second skin. He ran a hand through his hair and stepped to the sideboard where he had placed the flowers and wine. "I'm not sure that improved things, but okay... Before I get to my second point, I'd like to give you these."

Marajin rewarded the gifts with a royal smile that made him feel like a teenager. She sniffed the flowers. "Beautiful. Though I imagine you got them from that shriveled-up green shrew." She delighted in torturing him about his friendship with Gamela just as much as the Master of Biology seemed to enjoy cajoling him for his romance with Marajin.

"I did, but I've scanned them and they're not poisonous." He opened the bottle of wine with a wink. "Now this is from the Administrator, and he assures me it is the very best from his personal stock. I'm not much of a drinker, so I'll leave it to you to decide."

"Let it breathe. Come join me on the balcony."

He followed her across the elegantly spartan room, allowing himself to admire the muscular sway of her legs and hips as the breeze from the opened window flared the hem of her robe. "As you wish, Your Majesty."

Marajin's suite afforded a splendid view of the gleaming southern edge of Quan City and the untamed jungle beyond. It was a microcosm of the planet itself, a jewel of advanced technology and ancient wisdom hidden in the depths of primordial wilderness and barbaric survival. The Warden always felt a pang of discomfort when he looked out upon the seductive vista, as it offered a promise of home. The temptation to stay here was all but irresistible when in the company of this powerful, challenging woman.

"Do you think we can achieve this?" Marajin said, the wind brushing her long blue-black tresses back from her regal forehead and chiseled cheekbones. Her ice-colored eyes stared out at the towering buildings gleaming in the planet's twin suns. "Can we make Un Quan a 'Civilized World' again?"

The Warden knew what she meant. If the flight was successful, and if they could rebuild the bot, and it could repair the Einstein-Rosen bridge, and if he could contact Quantum or someone else in the Frontier, then the Un Quan system would be accessible by the United Planetary Council, a political organization that, despite its ponderous bureaucracy and endless red tape, was the de facto power in the galaxy. In order to have any part in the U.P.C. or in its authority, petitioning planets had to qualify as 'Civilized Worlds.'

Even Marajin knew that her world fell far short of that mark at the moment. The Warden knew she secretly felt responsible for that, at least in some small measure. As queen of the jungle-dwelling women, she had perpetuated the gender war for the duration of her reign. Even now, he was the only male she deigned to speak with as an equal, and that probably only because he was not a native of Un Quan.

The Warden placed his hand on hers atop the balcony railing and smiled. "Yes. I believe you can do anything you set your heart and mind to. Yes, I believe Un Quan will be a Civilized World." He did not add "someday," but he could tell by the look in her eyes that she heard it nonetheless.

Sliding her hand away, Marajin stood straight. "Good. Then I have my heart and mind set on accompanying you on tomorrow's inaugural spaceflight. It is a singular honor which I will not surrender to a male counterpart."

The Warden grimaced. "Which, I'm afraid, brings us to my original second point."

In the end, Marajin had hurled a potted plant at him, and he had left her suite at the embassy in a very foul mood…

"Thank you, Doctor." Switching off the coms, the Warden briefly wondered if a bad reentry might not be the worst thing that could happen to him on Un Quan.

The shielding held.

The Warden guided the ship into a victory roll as he circled the airfield on the northern outskirts of Quan City. The edges of the tarmac were crowded with blue spectators on the west and yellow on the east. A smaller greenish swarm huddled along the southern edge closest to the heart of the city. This was the group that made him smile.

"Hail the conquering hero." The Warden made the ironic comment with a bit of pride. The two genders had been at war for generations, and yet here they were together to welcome him back from a successful spaceflight. As much as he liked the idea that he had some small hand in the planet's current peace, he knew that the real heroes were his one-time travelling companions, the young Prince Andres and Princess Jynnessa. He could see the newlyweds standing at the heart of the comingled crowd of yellow men, blue women, and green "Ancients"—natives of Quan City—along the airfield's southern edge.

Exiting the landed ship, the Warden trailed an affectionate hand along the spacecraft's fuselage. He had wanted to call the refurbished corvette *Marajin* but settled for the more diplomatic call-sign *M-XVI*, knowing that the male contingent under Andres's father, King Mascos III, would have felt more than a little slighted. As the letters were written in the Warden's own Earth language, no one on Un Quan was the wiser.

Still smiling at the sunlight glinting off the new blue-and-gold paintjob, he was greeted by Dr. Gamela and a team of medical robots. They cut him off before he turned to make for his young friends in the crowd. The elderly, green-skinned Master of Biology did not look happy while the bots performed their scans. But then, happiness was not an expression she wore well.

"I'm fine," the Warden said, doffing his visored cowl. "I ran the ship's checks twice before exiting the craft."

Gamela followed his line of sight to the waving prince and princess. "They can wait, Warden. We have a deal, and you will not be able to honor your end of that deal if you have managed to expose yourself to tumor-inducing radiation or some other hazard during this adventure."

The Warden sighed. She was right, as usual. He had agreed to be Un Quan's representative to the United Planetary Council, when and if they arrived, in order to ensure that the more technologically advanced members did not exploit the system and its populace as soon as the ERB was restored.

"Besides," Gamela added in a lowered voice. "I wanted to speak to you again about... the woman."

The Warden raised an eyebrow. Gamela never referred to Marajin by name or title unless in official company. Most of the Masters, the hierarchy of Quan City, viewed the chromatically and gender delineated inhabitants of the jungle as less-evolved and barbaric subspecies. However, most were better at hiding this social prejudice than Gamela.

"What haven't you said on that topic already? Or has she said something to you?"

Gamela scoffed as they left the shadow of the corvette's wing. The noise was almost drowned out by the gathered crowds' rising cheers. "You know she and I do not speak unless required to do so in the course of the ongoing negotiations. I think her an altogether repulsive person, given to delusions of grandeur and a slave to her unbridled emotions and... biological urges."

The Warden waved at the crowds, smiling while waiting for Gamela to make her point.

"But for all that, I am concerned about her feelings."

This stopped the Warden in stride. He feigned pausing to adjust the strap on his boot to buy a little more time before reaching Andres and Jynnessa. "Her feelings?"

"Yes, Warden. I am not a monster. I understand that the woman has feelings just like anyone else. Feelings which will most likely be hurt when you have had your fill of our backwater little world and its... pleasures—"

"Watch it. I've been nothing but a gentleman with Her Majesty." He stood and walked on. "And I don't intend to hurt anyone's feelings."

"No one ever does. But take care, Warden. The woman is a queen, and injured queens can be dangerous to their own people."

The Warden acted as though he hadn't heard the remark as he accepted the embraces of Andres and Jynnessa and the rigorous handshakes from Dr. Hydrax and his team. Though he smiled and waved, the warning consumed his mind like a supernova consumes a star system.

"Congratulations," Andres said, a broad smile across his golden face. "You have made history on our world."

"I was just the test chimp. The Masters of Un Quan are the true heroes today."

Jynnessa slapped him on the back hard enough to knock the wind out of him. "You're too modest, Warden. If not for you, none of this would be happening."

He smiled at the young princess, her crystal blue eyes glistening. "I should say the same of you. Now, I've been told your mother wants to see me."

This caused Jynnessa's smile to falter. "Good luck."

"That bad, huh?"

Andres cleared his throat and tried his best diplomatic tone. "Her Majesty was in a rare mood this afternoon."

Jynnessa poked her husband in the ribs, still unaware of her formidable strength. "I think she was just worried but didn't want to show it."

The Warden thought that a sweet notion. Though if that potted plant had connected a few days before, the flight would have been scrubbed owing to him having a concussion. "Well, to the embassy I go."

Somewhere deep within the Frontier, about three standard months ago, a long-awaited signal reached its destination.

"*Mission complete. ERB online—correction. Offline. Damaged. Will attempt to—*"

The message's recipient took a long, deep breath and held it. He stared out the bridge's forward viewport, imagining a binary star system very, very far away.

"What are your orders, Commander?"

The Commander released his breath in a long sigh. Turning to leave the bridge, he told the coms officer, "Monitor that channel. Make sure the rest of the fleet is ready to go at a moment's notice. Let me know as soon as another communication is made."

"Yes, sir."

The Warden took a deep breath and forced a smile as he approached the queen's reception hall in the embassy building. He ignored the two armored women wielding spears posted at the door. The imposing warriors returned the favor when he entered the spacious and luxurious room unannounced. The royal guards were familiar with his and Marajin's "arrangement."

His smile faltered when he saw that Marajin was not alone.

Sappoc, the captain of her guard, stood beside the queen on the suns-lit balcony overlooking Quan City. The blue-skinned women were in the midst of a serious discussion. Both turned at his entrance. Marajin's face shifted from frustration to pleasure before sliding into her usual blasé demeanor. The powerful captain's scowl only deepened at the sight of him.

"Ladies." The Warden greeted them with a slight bow. "I hope I am not interrupting…"

"You are." Sappoc's muscular chest heaved beneath her mail vest. Her fists flexed as they dropped to her sides, conveniently close to the silver-chased dagger and sword on her belt. "Go outside and wait to be summoned."

The Warden understood why Sappoc hated him. Though she had tried to kill him on their very first meeting as a matter of course, her feelings were now personal. He had recently learned that Sappoc had been Marajin's paramour. If the warrior captain had once wanted him dead simply because of his gender, that murderous urge had only increased since the queen had chosen to pursue the Warden. The fact that he was a male could only add insult to this injury.

"Nonsense," Marajin said. She wore a silvery diaphanous gown that made her smooth skin appear to shimmer in shades of cobalt, indigo, and azure. Her long dark hair was pulled back and captured in a diamond-studded silver net at the nape of her neck. More diamonds and silver gleamed at her throat, earlobes, wrists, and ankles. "The Warden has travelled a very long way. I'll not make him stand on ceremony. We can continue our discussion at another time, Sappoc. You may leave us now."

The Warden and the warrior captain stared at one another for a moment, he smiling politely while she seethed. Narrowing her sapphire eyes, Sappoc bowed to her queen and former lover before stalking from the room.

The Warden watched Sappoc closely until the doors shut behind her. "She still wants to kill me, you know."

Marajin waved the statement away as she led him back into the stateroom. "As I understand it, she is but one of many. That barbarian, Hurm, wants to string you up and disembowel you, if the gossip around this embassy is to be believed."

The Warden shrugged. Hurm was Sappoc's male counterpart, the commander of King Mascos's army. And while the man did not share similar affections for Andres's father—at least as far as the Warden knew—Hurm's pride had been sorely wounded the last time they'd met.

"Occupational hazard, I suppose... I don't mind so long as your name is not on the list of my would-be assassins."

This earned a coquettish smile from the queen. "Not at the moment, but it has been some time since we last spoke. Come, have some wine and sit with me."

The Warden took the offered goblet and sat on the sofa beside Marajin, thinking this was how he had meant for things to go the last time he was here. He smiled, recalling the first night he had met her, his first night on this planet. The queen had sought to seduce him in a similar setting, though for rather nefarious purposes. Now, he was grateful that she had adopted the Masters' more modest mode of dress for this present occasion. Even fully clad, Marajin's unearthly physical beauty was enough to make him feel stupid and giddy.

He hefted the goblet before taking a sip. "Not as heavy as a flower pot, but at this range it could do the trick."

She laughed. "You know, I was a warrior before I was a queen. If I had wanted to hit you with that plant, you would not have left the room alive."

The Warden smiled, not knowing whether or not she was joking. That uncertainty only heightened the thrill of courting this powerful woman. Yes, he thought, stupid indeed. "Then I guess I should thank you for not killing me."

Marajin glanced over the rim of her goblet. "And how do you propose to thank me for that kindness, *Star Warden?*" The way she said his title made it plain Andres had been right: the queen was in a rare mood. She wanted to play.

The Warden cleared his throat. His spacesuit suddenly felt too tight and too warm. He looked away from those hypnotic, ice-blue eyes. He tried to clear his thoughts as he took in the spartan splendor of the big, ivory-and-silver room with its muted lighting and dark furniture, the black-framed artwork of brightly colored geometric patterns and designs.

"How would you like me to thank you… Your Majesty?"

She took his goblet and set both on the low table, then turned to face him. Resting her head on her hand, she smiled. "I believe you know. You have stirred something within me, Warden. It is an urge that I do not fully understand, but I feel that it is one that only you can satisfy. I have ended my physical relationships with Sappoc and the others—"

The Warden jumped to his feet. "Others?"

Marajin frowned. "Yes. It is customary for a queen to have several paramours. Why does that bother you?"

The Warden paced the room, rubbing his face with both hands. "Maybe Gamela is right—"

Marajin was off the sofa like a loosed arrow. "Gamela? What has that withered, old harpy to do with anything?"

The Warden sighed and checked to make sure there wasn't anything too heavy within the queen's reach. "Nothing. She just gave me some advice that I refused to take."

Marajin crossed the room. Face to face, she stood a few centimeters taller than he. Even on the verge of a rage, the Warden couldn't resist her regal beauty. "What sort of advice?"

He looked away to gather his thoughts. Staring at her, he always found it so hard to concentrate on anything else. "She doesn't want me to hurt your feelings. When I leave—"

Marajin's face rippled, then she broke into an open-throated laugh. At first low and deep, the laughter rose to a mocking cackle. "That is rich. You and the green hag think I am some timid girl to be destroyed by the sudden departure of you, a *male*. The arrogance! The sheer audacity!"

The Warden didn't like that laugh. He could take a lot from a lot of folks. But that laugh bothered him more than the time she had had him tossed into an oubliette, wearing little more than a bathrobe. He grabbed her by the upper arms and pulled her close.

"Look. I'm trying to do the right thing here. I... I care about you, Marajin. I care about Jynnessa. And I don't want to hurt either of you, but you know as well as I do that I can't stay here. Once that ERB is fixed, I've got to go back to my side of the galaxy. To where I belong. And you—Well, I can't be responsible for taking you from your home, from your people. But I can't stay here..."

The laughter ended, replaced by a coy smile. The Warden could feel her body against his as she breathed slow and deep. Her voice husky, she said, "I am no fool, Warden. I know that this... whatever *this* is... it cannot last. But it is something new and exciting, something I find enjoyable. Something that brings happiness to my life. A new kind of happiness I have never known... It is something I want. *You* are what I want. Now."

He kissed her for the first time. It was something he had imagined doing since setting eyes on her, enthroned in her great hall as Queen of Un Quan and he, her prisoner. The reality overwhelmed those imaginings in an instant.

Even as endorphins flooded his body, his mind filled with Gamela's warning and he knew he was a fool. A happy fool for the moment, but a fool nonetheless.

ii.

He rested in his cryogenic stasis chamber. Rather his reconstructed body did. His mind, however, travelled the ether of information that permeated and filled the galaxy. He recalled that somewhere, a long time ago, an Earth scientist had postulated that information was the fifth stage of matter, and it was this information rather than Dark Matter which bound the universe together.

He very much liked the notion, though astrophysics had since moved into other directions. The concept was in keeping with the tenets of so many ancient philosophies: that reality was but the dreams conjured in the mind of God. And when he surfed the galactic data-stream network, it was like being one of God's more lucid dreams.

"Commander."

He was instantly summoned back to the reality and pain of his physical form. It always took a moment to remember that the pain was ever-present and that he had long since become accustomed to it. But that moment was always horrific. He took a deep breath, air filling his artificial lungs and oxygenating the bio-fluids now replacing his blood, powering his few remaining organic components.

"Yes. What is it?"

"We have the signal again."

He opened his eyes, a smile stretching the muscles of his face for the first time in months, if not years. "Very good. Prep the fleet."

As the coms officer signed off, the Commander rose from his stasis chamber like a man reborn. With a thought, he summoned his major-domo: *Prepare my uniform, Saladin. Our day of salvation and blessed rest has finally arrived. We are going to the Promised Land.*

A week after his return from the inaugural spaceflight, the Warden stood beside Dr. Hydrax in the new Interstellar Communications Laboratory. The two men were surrounded by a handful of green-skinned assistants and several silvery bots. These worked at consoles or monitored readouts on the vast array of computers and machinery filling the air-cooled room. The Master of Astro Sciences fidgeted nervously as the data from the ERB bot beamed in.

"I can't believe it," Hydrax murmured. "We haven't done any practical investigation into space exploration in centuries, and now we've had two successful launches and a remote-controlled robotic probe in the same month. What the ancestors would have thought!"

The Warden stood with his arms folded across his chest, watching the meaningless yellow symbols scroll up the wall-sized primary display screen. His wrist chrono had mastered the spoken language of Un Quan, but he still had no idea how to decipher their written words. "So, is the bot making contact with the ERB?"

Hydrax nodded, his jade-colored eyes fixed on the screen. "Yes. It would appear that our repairs on the robot have indeed borne fruit."

The Warden smiled. "You are too modest, Doctor. 'Repair' doesn't begin to cover the scope of what you did with that ball of debris I brought back. I believe you could start building and launching your own ERB bots at this point."

Hydrax grinned at the compliment. "Yes. I believe we could. Though without your U.P.C.'s command codes, our gates would not be connected to the existing ERB network, and would therefore take many, many years before our space program could ever be considered interstellar."

The scientist's grin failed and his brow furrowed. "In any case, I do not think it advisable until we… get our own house in order, as I believe the saying goes. Can you imagine spacecraft carrying those warlike jungle barbarians into the galaxy? Your United Planetary Council would think Un Quan the basest of worlds, and either invade us out of self-defense or quarantine the entire system."

The Warden shrugged. "I don't know. When my people first started exploring space, we were a moment's notice from wiping out our own planet in an atomic war. I guess we were lucky there weren't any more-advanced civilizations keeping an eye on us. Or, if they were, they let us work it out on our own. Besides, in my humble opinion, not every society in the 'Civilized Worlds' is as civilized as they think they are."

A tech turned to Hydrax. "The robot has activated the bridge, Doctor."

The Warden almost laughed in excitement. He raised his chrono to send a message, via the new antennae array, that would travel through the online Einstein-Rosen bridge and find Quantum. The Warden was about to speak to his best friend for the first time in months. He was about to connect with his own side of the galaxy again.

A beeping alarm sounded and a new signal appeared on the screen.

"What is that?" Hydrax demanded.

"Something just came through the gate, sir. Wait, there's another one! Now there's three!"

The Warden activated his chrono, tried to make the connection with Quantum, but got only a spinning icon. The newcomers had jammed the signal. He looked at Hydrax and shook his head. "My message didn't get through. I don't know who they are."

"Try to contact them," Hydrax told the tech. "We need to know what they want."

"Nothing, sir. They are not responding."

The Warden patted Hydrax on the shoulder before heading for the door. "Have the *M-XVI* prepped as soon as possible. I need to get up there and find out what's going on."

Thanks to the efficiency of the Masters' robotic workforce, the rebuilt pirate corvette was refueled and ready to launch by the time the Warden reached the airfield. As he buckled into the command chair, he considered contacting Marajin to let her know what was going on.

He thought better of it, knowing the conversation could quickly turn into an argument. She would demand he take her and a score of her best warriors along to ensure his safety. But the simple truth was, whatever had just come through that gate was bound to be more than a match for twenty-one spear-wielding women, no matter the level of their martial prowess. And he did not want to put any more lives at risk than he already had by reopening the ERB.

This inner debate frustrated the Warden. Just a few months ago he would have been able to blast off to face any possible danger without a second thought or a moment's guilt. But his relationship with Marajin had changed that. He wondered what other scenarios would now have him second-guessing himself. He wondered what the cost of those doubtful hesitations might be.

As soon as the corvette broke the planet's atmosphere, its more advanced sensors picked up the drive signatures of the three newcomer ships. They had fanned out, taking up a defensive position around the repaired ERB. The Warden recognized them, and as the surprise settled in, another ship emerged from the gate. This one an oblong, cigar-shaped transport capable of carrying at least a thousand passengers and crew.

"A Ranger and two Paladins. Star Warden ships… but how?" The lead ship was virtually identical to his beloved *Ranger VII*, the ship he had piloted since the days before the Battle of Draconus Prime. The Paladins were more modern designs—heavier, armored gunships built as much for intimidation as for fire superiority.

The Warden guided his ship toward the formation in an oblique trajectory so as not to be perceived as an attack. The pirate ship had been without munitions when he had liberated it, and the Un Quan had seen no reason to rearm the vessel. Neither had the Warden until now. Though even if it had been fully equipped, he knew the corvette was no match for any one of the three warships now guarding the ERB and the transport.

He hailed the flotilla. "Ahoy Ranger-class vessel. This is the Star Warden. Please state your business in this system."

An automated voice from the Ranger responded. "*Warden, prepare to be boarded.*"

Closing the channel, he muttered, "Well, that doesn't sound very good at all."

Putting the ship on autopilot in a stabilized vector with the engine powered down, the Warden headed for the airlock. He checked his Comet blasters along the way, though he hoped he would not need to use them. Even if he won a skirmish aboard ship, either of the two Paladins could make short work of the *M-XVI* before he could take control of the docked Ranger and get to safety.

He waited as patiently as he could while the metallic sounds of the docking procedure echoed through the hull. After a few moments of the airlock pressurizing, the doors slid open. A broad-shouldered, olive-complected man stepped in. He wore heavy armor resembling a more modern take on the Warden's own spacesuit, a similar visor concealing the upper part of his face. He held a blaster carbine in his hands.

"Do not reach for your weapons," the man said. "I will kill you if you do."

The Warden kept his hands extended away from his sides. His visor scanned the invader, detecting numerous cybernetic enhancements beneath the armor. "You wear the blue."

The man ignored him, communicating with someone else via sub-vocal transmission.

That someone stepped aboard.

The Warden recognized the tall, dark-skinned man in the black and silver Star Warden spacesuit instantly, though he could not believe his eyes. The man did not wear his visored cowl, so his clean-shaven head, piercing eyes, and age-lined features were visible.

"Commander Solomon Jones... but how? You led the attack on Draconus Prime... How can you still be alive? And what are you doing here?"

Jones's grim mouth twitched into a brief smile. His voice was as rich and deep as the Warden remembered. "I could ask you the same thing, Warden. Been a long time since I've seen a Mark II suit. Not since we sent those Mechtechan bastards packing. I'm guessing you're the one they call 'The Last Star Warden' on the Frontier."

The Warden stood to attention. "First Lieutenant—"

"At ease, Lieutenant." Jones's dark eyes scanned the interior of the rebuilt corvette. "The Star Wardens are a thing of the past. I'm all about the future now, and that future starts here, in this system. Now, I'm betting you've got one hell of a story about how you ended up here... But I think we should adjourn to more amenable surroundings if we're going to get each other up to speed."

"Yes, sir. Of course."

Jones's smile broadened. "This is Saladin Karkadan, my major-domo and right-hand man. Give him the command code for this ship, and you can accompany me back to the transport aboard the *Ranger I*. I've got a pretty nice setup over there where we can have a bite to eat, a couple drinks, and a chat."

The Warden nodded, then paused. "I need to contact the people of Un Quan and let them know what I'm doing. Your sudden arrival has them worried that they may be in for an invasion."

"Un Quan? Is that what the locals call this system? I'd thought to call it Nova Sol, myself..." Jones laughed. "But an invasion? Furthest thing from my mind... Go ahead and give them a call. Just tell them that you've met an old friend and will be making introductions very soon. I am looking forward to meeting our new neighbors."

The Warden caught a grin on Saladin Karkadan's face that he didn't like. And he wasn't very comfortable with Jones's "make myself at home" attitude. But he made the call.

Solomon Jones was the greatest Star Warden to ever live, after all.

The trip from the corvette to the transport didn't take long, certainly not long enough to embark on a conversation that the Warden knew would surely span hours. He had so many questions for the Commander. How had he survived over a century since the Battle of Draconus Prime? What had he been doing in that time? Why had he sent the ERB bot to this system? What was his ultimate goal? And why had he brought a small military flotilla to Un Quan?

The Warden didn't fully trust the newcomers, despite his reverence for the legendary man. The man many had once called 'The First Star Warden.' Jones had earned the moniker even though the organization had been around for a few decades before he came to prominence in the First Tuatha War. After his successes against that ancient race, Jones had almost singlehandedly turned the nascent Star Wardens into the elite organization which had defeated the Mechtechan invasion, ultimately saving the galaxy from interdimensional conquest.

The Warden's instinctive misgivings were somewhat assuaged by the Commander's gracious manner and his assurances of peace. Jones wasn't just a hero, he was the Warden's hero. Surely the man could not harbor a villainous objective in coming to Un Quan. Could he?

Once both ships had docked with the enormous transport, the Warden accompanied Jones and Karkadan through the big vessel's corridors to the Commander's private apartments. The Warden noted scores of cybernetically enhanced men and women along the way, going about their duties, eating in the mess hall, exercising in a gymnasium, relaxing in a lounge area, and training on a vast obstacle course. Without exception, every one of these individuals had the mean and bearing of a soldier.

"All of them are veterans," Jones said, noting the Warden's interest. "Most of them, the young ones, are Star Cav castoffs. The officers, the most-senior men and women, however, are what's left of the Star Wardens. Though you won't find any other survivors from our day. I fear we're the last of that generation."

"The cybernetics…"

"Yes. Casualties of war. Heroes. Patriots. All that jargon. The U.P.C gave them all medals, small stipends, and then swept them under the rug. Put them out to pasture in favor of fresher meat. Never mind the services they had rendered. Never mind they are still warriors with more yet to give. Just like you and me."

The Warden raised an eyebrow. "How do you mean?"

The Commander led him and Karkadan into a small apartment, sparsely but elegantly apportioned. The décor was remarkable in its absence. There were no framed images of friends, family, pets, or art on the pale grey walls. Not even framed medals or displayed service trophies. No reminders of a life spent as a peacekeeper or the comrades acquired in that life.

Jones motioned them to a small dinette table set in the back of the front room. "Have a seat and I'll order up some dinner. Arcturan chili okay with everyone?"

The Warden nodded as Karkadan poured three metal tumblers of amber liquor from a carafe at the sideboard. "That's fine. Forgive me, Commander, but what did you mean when you said, 'Just like you and me'?"

Jones typed the order into the wall processor without looking at the Warden. "First, I'd like to know how you got here ahead of me. I went to considerable lengths to keep this gate a secret. And it is very hard to keep any kind of secret for nigh on eight decades. Much less one of this magnitude. To say nothing of the ungodly expense."

The Warden shrugged, allowing the Commander to dodge his question for the moment. "It was an accident. I would say a freak accident on the order of one in a million, but I'm beginning to find that particular variety quite commonplace in my experience."

He elaborated on his adventures since his reemergence into this timeline while they sipped their drinks. His tale culminated with his bizarre arrival in the Un Quan system and the series of events which had led to him sitting at the table with the First Star Warden. Finally, he asked his question again. "What did you mean by calling us *warriors* with more to give? I've never thought of myself as a warrior, Commander. Our job as Star Wardens was always to keep the peace…"

"So, you and a Mechtechan warrior were lost in time for a century. Trapped in that black hole. Is that about right, Lieutenant?"

The Warden cleared his throat, annoyed at the continued sidestepping of the question. "Quantum is more a scientist than a warrior, but that about sums it up."

Jones sat back in his chair, his face hard as flint. "Strange that you'd pal around with one of the worst enemies this galaxy has ever known. But let's set that aside for the moment…"

The Warden frowned. "He is not an en—"

The Commander rose from the table, cutting him off. "If you really were out of the picture for a hundred years, then you don't know what happened to the Star Wardens after we won that war. You don't know the price we paid for that victory. You don't know how dismissively we were treated by the very government we had saved in that battle."

Slowly pacing the room, Jones folded his hands behind his back and spoke in a low, rhythmic tone. "I was seriously injured when the Mechtechan flagship was pushed beyond the event horizon. So were most of the other survivors. We were hailed as heroes, given medals, and great speeches were delivered in our honor. The majority of us witnessed these 'honors' via telecast from our hospital beds. By the time we were back on our feet, the galaxy had moved on to the next news cycle and had forgotten about us.

"I spent years trying to get the U.P.C. to reinstate the veterans of Draconus Prime, to let us rebuild the Star Wardens. But a new regime had come to power and they didn't want to be associated with the previous administration's successes. They took a new bent, more Wardens, not better; meaner ships, not faster. I'm sure you know how that turned out."

The Warden nodded. "I've heard. Scandal and dishonor. Eventual disbandment."

"Yes. Another era, another administration, another shiny new organization. The vaunted Star Cavalry. A military war machine to replace what was once a peacekeeping force. Meanwhile, as more brush wars and more 'actions' were waged, more and more young men and women were fed into the U.P.C. meat grinder."

Jones stopped and faced the Warden. "Well, with my beloved Star Wardens gone forever, I turned to rescuing these new orphans of the galactic industrial military complex. Gathering them up, getting them off the streets and off the drugs, replacing their low-end, government-issue cyberware with top of the line tech. Helping them to find their way back from despair and self-destruction to self-respect and self-actualization."

The Warden rubbed his chin as Karkadan served steaming bowls of chili from the wall processor. "I'm guessing that cost a fortune. And it still doesn't explain how you've managed to live this long."

The Commander laughed but there was little mirth in it. "Several fortunes, in fact. All of them earned the hard way. But no money is ill-gained if it is not ill-spent." The Warden did not like the implications of that statement. "As for my longevity, have you ever heard of cryo-cyber sleep?"

"Afraid I've not come across that one yet. Cryo sleep, sure, but the cyber part?"

Jones touched the base of his skull. "As I said, I was severely injured at Draconus Prime. An injury that required my entire central nervous system to be rewired with cybernetics in order to function. One side-effect of this enhancement—at least once technology had advanced far enough—is the ability to connect my consciousness into the galactic data-stream network. While so connected, my body can be placed within cryogenic hibernation."

Karkadan smiled. "A form of immortality. The Commander can direct his operations from the GDN for decades while his body rests and regenerates."

The Warden swallowed a mouthful of food but tasted only bitterness. He sensed something sinister in all this but wasn't quite sure where it was leading. "Is this a common practice? I'm betting it's an expensive one, which means only the wealthy can… direct their operations in such a manner. It seems like it could cause… problems down the line."

"Problems?" The Commander chuckled as he joined them at the table. "Quite the contrary. Imagine a galaxy where the governing powers are guided by a singular, methodical plan for centuries rather than being tossed this way and that every few years or decades by ideological changes in policy. But, point of fact, Lieutenant, the U.P.C. came to the same conclusion, and recently outlawed the practice."

The Warden set his spoon on the table, a cold chill running down his spine to settle in his gut. His instincts had been right. Jones was up to no good. "Which is why you are here."

The Commander took his first bite with a smile. "One advantage of the hibernation is that, over time, one gains a certain kind of… prescience. About eighty-odd years ago, I could see how things in the U.P.C. were headed, and I concocted this contingency plan. I started probing Uncharted Space, looking for a refuge where I could bring my rescued children. A star system we could make our own, a new utopia free from all the corruption and scandal that run rampant and unchecked in the so-called Civilized Worlds."

"But this system is already inhabited."

The Commander's eyes narrowed. "So it is. But that's a big planet down there and we've already scanned it for life signs. The native population is a fraction of a percentage of what your Un Quan can sustain. I've another transport still in the Frontier. It had a drive malfunction right before we made the jump, but once it gets here, I'll have four thousand able-bodied colonists ready to share our resources and technology with the natives, as they share their world with us. I believe that within the next decade or two, we might even be able to terraform at least one of the inner worlds for future colonization."

The Warden pushed his bowl away. He didn't like the way this was shaking out. It was too much, too fast. "I can talk to the people down there, but I can't guarantee that they'll agree to what you're proposing. The current political situation is… delicate to say the least. They barely trust each other right now. I don't know how they'll cotton to an army of newcomers."

Jones surprised him with another good-natured laugh. "I like you, Lieutenant. You remind me of myself when I was your age. All idealism and diplomacy. I guess I've lost that somewhere along the way. I've become too cynical. Seen too many politicians and warmongers take advantage of those good intentions. I could use you as a member of my command team. Help me keep things in focus."

The Warden blinked. "I'm honored, Commander. But my goal is to get back to the Frontier where I can continue my mission. The mission we undertook when we put on this uniform. The Frontier is still a lawless place, and a lot of good people still need our help. With your resources and followers, we could do exactly what you originally set out to do. We could rebuild the Star Wardens, even acting independently of the United Planetary Council if need be."

Karkadan gave a mocking laugh. "Only if you intend to go to war with Star Cav, Lieutenant. The U.P.C. will not tolerate a challenge to its sovereignty in the Frontier. You've seen how they treat the Undocs and any native populations that get too uppity."

"Karkadan is right, I'm afraid. Else I would be fighting them even now. Star Cav is just too strong at the moment. But here, in the Uncharted systems, I can build an empire that can stand against them in time."

The Warden frowned at the word "empire." He shook his head. "What's to stop

Star Cav from sending forces through that ERB right now? Even with the ships you've got, they won't stand a chance in a pitched battle against a squadron of modern assault scouts."

Jones shrugged and took another bite of chili. "As soon as my other transport gets here, which should be within the next thirty-six standard hours, we're blowing the bridge and sealing this system off for good. It'll take them another seventy or eighty years to get here the old-fashioned way. By then, we'll be ready for them."

The Warden went cold all over. The bridge was his only hope of ever getting back to what he now thought of as home. Though the prospect of living out his days with Marajin in the service to the legendary First Star Warden was appealing, he could not fathom abandoning Quantum on the other side of the galaxy. More than that, he knew in his bones he wasn't meant to stay here in this constructed fantasy. His place was on the Frontier, just as it had always been.

Even more pressing, the Warden now understood that Jones and his cybernetically enhanced troops would invade Un Quan, despite the Commander's protestations to the contrary. He would give the people of the planet the opportunity to say "yes" to his proposal, but he had come too far to allow them to decline his magnanimous offer of friendship.

"Hernan Cortez," the Warden said as he rose from the table. "A conqueror of Earth's antiquity. He brought a handful of mercenaries to the Americas, plundering and laying waste to an entire civilization. That's who you are, Commander Jones. And I can't be a party to that. If you'll excuse me—"

Jones moved faster than the Warden could have imagined. And he hit a whole lot harder. Ninety-odd years of advances in cybernetic technology struck the Warden with such ferocity that he lay sprawled on the carpeted floor before he knew he was hurt.

"I was afraid you'd say that, Lieutenant." Jones stood over him as Karkadan fitted the Warden with gravity shackles and removed his gun belt. "Sorry we had to do this the hard way, but as you'll soon discover, I am a man who always gets his way in the end. You don't accomplish the things I have if you're willing to take *no* for an answer."

The Warden felt like he'd been hit by a meteorite as Karkadan hauled him to his feet. "Come along, Lieutenant. We've already got a berth set up for you in sickbay. Don't want to be late for your surgery."

The Warden tried to question the remark, but his jaw was broken.

iii.

The Commander stared at the three bowls of chili on the table. He thought about resuming the meal, but his appetite was gone. He stepped to the room's porthole and stared out at this new, virgin region of space. He wanted to drink in the view, revel in the untold possibilities it offered. But he could not summon the enthusiasm. The unpleasant encounter with the Lieutenant had soured the moment.

"Why?" he asked the empty room. "Why does he not see what I see? He, of all people..."

Jones closed his eyes, letting his mind reach out to touch those of every man and woman under his command. Of course, he could not sense those aboard the other transport, still trapped in the Frontier by mechanical problems. He felt their absence as acutely as if he had lost a limb. An unpleasant experience with which he was more than familiar.

Still, he took strength and inspiration from the courage and faith of the rest of his troops, his children. In his way, he loved them as any father would. And like a loving, protective father, he would move heaven and earth to make a home for them. He had already sacrificed so much to get them this far; he would let nothing stand in his way now.

He opened his eyes, ocular implants magnifying the image of the distant planet until he saw the cloudy green orb of Un Quan as if he were but a hundred kilometers above its surface. "You are our new home, our safe haven. Once the young Lieutenant has become one of my children, he will see you in the same light."

The Warden must have blacked out somewhere along the way. When he came to his senses, Karkadan was nowhere to be seen. The Warden lay stretched on a bunk in an elaborate medical bay, soft light gleaming on white walls, polished chrome, and flat-screen monitors. A middle-aged man in a white tunic stood beside one of these monitors, observing a series of readouts.

"Yes, the analgesic is taking effect. He's ready for prep." The medic turned and nodded at someone outside the Warden's field of vision. "Restrain him."

A pair of men in black jumpsuits stepped forward and took hold of the Warden's arms. The man to his left had a PlaSteel cranium and multi-faceted bionic eye replacing the left side of his head. The man to the right had a chrome robotic left hand.

The Warden's skull felt like it was coming apart, but he didn't give the orderlies a chance to get a firm grip. He came off the gurney like a shot, both fists connecting with the undersides of the two men's jaws. Though he packed nowhere near the punch Commander Jones had, the Warden's strikes benefited from the same element of surprise.

The two cybernetic medics fell back, stunned if not staggered.

The Warden grabbed the man to his right and slammed him head-first into the metallic cranium of his counterpart. Feeling the orderly go limp, the Warden lashed out with a mule kick, sending the other attendant across the room to crash into a tray of surgical equipment.

Leaping from the bed, the Warden turned his attention to the surprised doctor.

The man reached for a com panel on the wall. He found his hand pinned to that wall by an expertly-hurled laser scalpel. Arching his back in surprised agony, the medic tried to scream but was rendered unconscious by a ferocious right cross.

The Warden swooned against the bunk, lightheaded and in excruciating pain as the wave of adrenaline subsided. His face had become so swollen he couldn't move his mouth to speak. He felt like his eyes might soon swell shut. He needed to get off this ship and back to Quan City before more of Jones's cybernetic troopers found him. But first, he needed to know what kind of surgery the Commander had planned for him. His gut told him it was somehow related to Jones's ultimate scheme.

Rifling the medical supplies for a health booster hypo, the Warden then connected his wrist chrono to the sickbay computer and initiated a download. He'd have to wait until he was somewhere safe and secure before he could check the data.

Not discovering his Comets or any other weapons in sickbay, the Warden set out to find a way off the transport. Fortunately, his spacesuit had not yet been removed, and since coming aboard, he had seen several men and women wearing the updated versions similar to Karkadan's. By keeping his distance and walking with a casual purpose, he was able to move about the ship without drawing attention to himself. Luckily, he didn't run into the Commander or his major-domo before finding his way to the docking bays.

Still unable to speak, and fighting to keep his eyes open, the Warden approached the deck officer as if on official business. He stood a polite distance away until the man dismissed a couple of techs after accepting their maintenance report.

"Yes?" The deck officer said, his cybernetic eyes scanning the data pad in his hands. "What do you need?"

The Warden punched him in the throat, dropping the man like a block of lead in supergravity.

Glancing around to make sure none of the other techs or mechanics had seen the incident, the Warden dragged the unconscious officer behind a stack of blaster-cannon ammo crates and checked the data pad.

The *Ranger I* was currently being refueled and all six landers aboard the transport were under DNA lock, but the *M-XVI* remained unattended. It seemed it was considered such a useless hulk that once Karkadan had disembarked, no one had given it any further thought.

That sparked an idea.

Using the unconscious deck officer's thumbprint, the Warden entered a disengage-and-discard order for the pirate ship into the logs. As soon as the transport's bridge crew saw the ship leave the bay on their sensors, the order would come up, and they would let it drift away without any undue attention. The order would also be relayed to the rest of the flotilla.

He hoped.

The Warden considered the possibility of a bored gunner on one of the Paladins using the abandoned corvette for target practice before he could fire up the engine. With that happy thought in the back of his mind, the Warden made to steal the ship for the second time.

Again acting as if he belonged, the Warden boarded the *M-XVI*. Hurrying to the cockpit, he strapped into the command chair, took a deep breath, and issued the order to disengage from the massive transport.

A long pause stretched into eternity while the ship's refitted computer made the necessary communication with that of the transport. By the time the access was granted, the Warden realized he hadn't taken a breath in over a minute. When the loud clunking of magnetic clamps releasing the corvette echoed through the hull, he would have whistled with relief if his mouth still worked.

His left eye had swollen shut. Swallowing was painful by the time the corvette drifted far enough away from the transport to breathe easy. As it turned out, the transport had been taking a less-than-leisurely approach to Un Quan during his meal with the Commander. The two Paladins had remained to guard the ERB at the edge of the system. Even though the gunships were now out of firing range, the transport still possessed half a dozen batteries along each flank, more than capable of making short work of the unarmed *M-XVI*.

Once he had reached a position and vector that would make his approach to the planet look like the ship had fallen into Un Quan's gravitational pull, the Warden engaged the *M-XVI*'s rebuilt engine and made good his escape. When blaster and rocket fire didn't immediately follow, he sat back and accessed the data he had taken from the medical computer.

Despite the swelling, both his eyes went wide when he read the information. If he could have spoken, he would have said, "Sam Hill."

"Why did you let him escape?" Saladin Karkadan demanded as he strode into the Commander's office.

Solomon Jones had known the question was coming before the officer entered the room. Jones stood at the porthole, watching the dim light that was the pirate corvette disappear into the planetary shadow of Un Quan. Tilting his head, he briefly wondered what his answer would be. Several reasons came to mind, and he was not entirely comfortable with all of them.

"The Lieutenant is doing what I would have ordered him to do in any case." Jones turned and smiled at his subordinate. "Only somewhat sooner. He may not technically be on our side at the moment, but I am confident the end result will be the same."

Karkadan frowned. "Sir?"

The Commander sat behind his desk and steepled his fingers. "I had intended to send the Lieutenant down to inform the locals of our coming as soon as he had recovered from the procedure. He has seen the superiority of our forces and the scope of my plan. He understands that like Caesar, I have crossed the Rubicon of Uncharted Space. Just as he understands that the primitives on that planet stand no chance against us in an all-out armed conflict. He has no choice but to advise them to accept a peaceable occupation."

"We could have simply opened communications with them, destroyed one of their abandoned cities as a show of force if need be. There is still the chance that the Lieutenant will advise them to resist. His manner at dinner would indicate that option, at least in my opinion."

Jones shrugged. "True, but if the natives are inclined to resist, it is better to flush out their firebrands in open conflict rather than once we are down there and among them. They still hold a considerable numeric superiority. If they feigned capitulation, then rebelled after we had committed ourselves to colonization, we could easily find ourselves in a protracted guerilla-war of attrition. One which we might never win. As the 18th Century's War for American Independence has shown us, my friend, home-field advantage counts for a lot in these sorts of affairs."

Karkadan narrowed his eyes but remained silent.

Jones smiled. "You think me sentimental? You think I let him get away because of some misplaced sense of nostalgia? Perhaps there is some truth to that, even if I choose to deny it… You are young and do not remember the Halcion days when our silver ships flashed across the forever night of Frontier Space. You do not know the fire and glory of that epic battle with the Mechtechan devils, our great and pyrrhic victory."

Swiveling his chair to stare out the window again, the Commander said, "But that man, the Lieutenant does. He and I are perhaps the last in this galaxy who do. We were made of stronger stuff in those days, men and women of steel who forged a galactic civilization and kept it safe… Maybe you are right, and I do not want to have a gunner destroy such a man with the squeeze of a trigger from hundreds of kilometers away. No, if I must kill him, I'll have the decency to look into his eyes when I do it."

"Cybernetic master program." Doctor Gamela frowned as she scanned the data scrolling on the wall-sized display screen in her lab. "Implanted into every single soldier, you say? Ingenious work."

The Warden scowled at the medical bots ministering to him. "I'm glad you admire it. I think that technology might just be what will conquer your world."

The Master of Biology turned and raised an eyebrow. "You think so? You have said that this man, this Solomon Jones, currently only has some two or three thousand troops at his command. The jungle savages alone number almost a hundred times that. And, I'm sure I needn't remind you, this city has remained independent for nigh a millennia, in spite of a world-wide war with advanced technology. Our ray shielding protected us from aerial bombardments centuries ago. I doubt even this Commander's space-borne gunships can penetrate it."

The Warden sat up and stretched his repaired jaw. "This is something completely different. I know Jones, and he is a force to be reckoned with. I've never seen the kind of iron will, the single-minded determination that man has. That, coupled with his mastery of strategy and tactics alone should give you cause for concern."

The Warden waved at the monitor. "But now this... If he can guide his cybernetically enhanced veteran troops with pinpoint accuracy, almost as if he were there in person, then his margin of error goes from very slim to almost nil. Even if Mascos's and Marajin's warriors could match his troops' firepower and modern training, they could never hope to match this level of combat coordination."

Gamela looked again at the data, seeing something he did not. The Master of Biology narrowed her eyes and stroked her narrow chin. "I wonder if there might not be a way to..."

Thede the Administrator, entered the lab accompanied by Dr. Hydrax and a half dozen armed robot sentinels. Thede was a pale shade of green when he announced, "The off-worlders have landed near one of the abandoned citadels to the north. It appears they are preparing to march on Quan City."

The Warden noticed Thede did not make eye contact. The de facto head of the Masters may as well have accused him of bringing this calamity upon them and their world.

Hydrax cleared his throat. "We have been able to monitor their communications to some extent. It seems they intend to land three-fourths of their troops while holding the rest in reserve. They are keeping a warship in orbit directly above this city to provide cover for the march... We have nothing that can challenge that type of three-dimensional superiority."

The Warden shook his head in frustration, then made for the door. He did the mental calculations. With six landers, it would take maybe ten or twelve hours to land the proposed assault force on the planet's surface. They had only that much time to come up with a plan. And a handful of hours after that, Jones's other transport with the balance of his forces would come through the ERB, and the system would be sealed off forever.

Like Hernan Cortez, Jones would "burn his ships," and he would conquer or die.

"We need to set a war council. Mascos and Marajin are about to have to learn how to work together for real. And they're going to have to do it fast."

iv.

Solomon Jones stepped from the landing craft into the hot, humid air of his new world. He smiled as he took his first breath of fresh, unfiltered air in over a year. He marveled at the sudden overwhelming sensation of total freedom, the thrill of knowing that he was light years beyond the reach of the corrupt U.P.C. and the warmongering Star Cavalry.

Shielding his eyes as he stepped from the lander's shadow—more out of habit than necessity—he gazed up at the orange glow of the sky edged by the jungle's dense blue-green canopy. Wisps of pinkish clouds drifted past the twin suns as they approached their zenith. He mentally adjusted the focus of his aural receptors, listening beyond the methodic sounds of his troops and equipment establishing their operational base, to the untamed cacophony of the millions of living things out in that jungle.

One of those living things attacked him. Or attempted to.

Jones plucked the insect from the air a moment before it could alight on his exposed cheek. Gently grasping its elongated golden body between his bionic fingers, he studied the nervous twitch of its six scintillating wings and the frantic spasms of its like-numbered legs. He stared into the multifaceted greenish blue eyes above the needle-like parasitic proboscis.

Crushing the alien bug between his fingers and discarding the pulped remains, he hoped the creature would be the only casualty of his colonization of Un Quan. He did not put much stock in that hope, however. His extraordinarily long life had given him far too many reasons not to. Turning to Saladin Karkadan at the head of his guard detail, he said, "We made it, my friend. We are home."

Karkadan nodded, returning the smile. "Yes, sir."

The Commander's spirits were so buoyed by the moment that not even his major-domo's unspoken doubts could detract from the experience. He was finally home, after so many years and so many campaigns...

"Yes, Saladin, we are home. And if we must, we will fight for it."

The war council was an unpleasant necessity for all concerned. The Masters, having grown old in a society long past the need for physical violence, were not at ease taking a backseat to their bellicose cousins, the monarchs and captains of the jungle tribes. King Mascos III and Queen Marajin XVI and their subordinates, Captains Hurm and Sappoc, respectively, had yet to fully overcome their generational gender-based hatred for one another. And the Warden was uncomfortable taking the lead in defending the planet's native inhabitants from his own kind, led by the man he had once idolized.

Especially when he knew it was his own personal desires which had given Jones access to Un Quan.

All would have preferred to hold the proceedings via digital teleconference rather than sharing a room with the other parties. However, due to the technological superiority of the invaders, they could not risk such signals being intercepted by the orbiting ships' sensors. Surprise and uncertainty were among Un Quan's few advantages in the coming conflict, and the defenders could ill afford to relinquish these assets. If Jones was overconfident enough to allow his own communications to be monitored, it was not a mistake the Warden and his confederates were willing to make. The council was held in a fortified chamber in the lowest level of the Administration Building.

Thede and the other Masters sat at one end of the room's long conference table. The Administrator still found it hard to make eye contact with the Warden, though his tone held no overt sense of judgement or remorse. "I suppose capitulation is out of the question?"

"I can't tell you that." The Warden stood at his place at the opposite end of the table, flanked by Mascos and Hurm on his right and Marajin and Sappoc on his left.

"But my gut tells me you surrender only if you're willing to sacrifice your own culture and way of life, your independence and personal freedoms. I've spoken with Jones and seen what he has become. Whatever happened to him after his heroics at Draconus Prime, it has convinced him that the only way for a society to ever truly be at peace is total, unwavering, lock-step conformity."

Dr. Gamela nodded. "My initial assessment of the cybernetic implants described in the data retrieved by the Warden confirms this. Once a subject is so equipped, his or her free will can be overridden by the master program at any time. This Commander Jones would eventually become, in effect, an all-knowing and all-powerful deity if allowed to implant these devices in the inhabitants of Un Quan."

Marajin raised her chin, looking on the Masters with disdain. "We would rather die first."

Mascos slammed his brawny golden fist on the polished tabletop. "As would we. By the moons, these off-worlders will know they've been blooded when we're done with them. And if they do conquer Un Quan, they damn well will have earned it!"

The Warden sighed. "Look, I'm here to tell you we can't win this fight. But I'm also telling you, you can't afford not to try. Once Jones blows that ERB, there will be no help from anyone, and you'll be trapped in this system with his spaceships and cybernetic soldiers. We have to fight, and we have to do it now because time is running out."

Thede shook his head and clasped his hands on the table in front of him. "Then we will fight. The resources of Quan City are at your disposal, Warden. Tell us what you need and we will get to it while you and the King and Queen discuss specific strategies..."

An hour later, once the plans were made, the Warden and the representatives of the jungle tribes rose from the table to put those plans in motion.

Mascos placed his hand on the Warden's as he turned to leave. "Have you thought about my proposal, Warden? I must confess, I have thought of you often since the night you came to my bedchamber."

The Warden reddened as he saw Marajin's eyes go wide. Clearing his throat, he stammered, "I—I'm quite flattered, Your Majesty." Extricating his hand with as much grace as he could muster, he took an unconscious step closer to the queen. "But I must reiterate that my... my affections lie elsewhere."

Mascos frowned and narrowed his eyes at his lifelong rival, then flashed a smile at the Warden. "Then the... *object* of those affections has my grudging admiration and envy... Look for us on the field of battle, Warden. If we cannot be lovers, then at least we will be brothers-in-arms. In any case, I hope you enjoy the josco fruit."

The Warden nodded and tried to ignore Hurm's hateful scowl as the two men left the room. He turned to explain the situation to Marajin but was stopped by her throaty laugh.

"You should see the look on your face, Warden." The queen touched the edges of her brilliant blue eyes. "I did not know I had such a *royal* rival for your attentions. I must redouble my efforts if I am to keep you in my thrall!"

Sappoc cleared her throat and glared at the Warden, but he ignored her just as he had Hurm. "If you're finished having fun at my expense, I'd like to arrange your escort back to Castle Sarquis before we gather the troops."

This ended Marajin's mirth. "What? You would allow Mascos to win glory for his people by leading them in battle while robbing me of such an honor? How dare you?"

The Warden felt the formidable woman's rage boiling the air out of the conference room. "Look. We don't have time for this, so I'll lay it out loud and clear as I can. Mascos, for all his royal position, is a goon. If he doesn't come back from this fight, then his son, Andres, will make a much better king. But you—"

There his reasons ended. Marajin's daughter, Jynnessa, was just as capable a leader as Andres, and Marajin was just as obstinate and resistant to the new peace as was Mascos. But the Warden did not have strong feelings for the king.

"But what?" Marajin's frosty eyes narrowed, her jaw set. "Am I no warrior?"

The Warden glanced at Sappoc. "Please wait outside."

"No."

Marajin waved a dismissal to her captain without taking her eyes from the Warden's. The two lovers stared hard at one another until Sappoc left them alone in the conference room.

The Warden stepped close and took her in his arms. He kissed her with all the passion and confusion he had wrestled with over the past three months. When they finally separated, he looked deep into her eyes. "I've lost too much in my life to risk losing you now. Not when I know that this fight is my fault. If something happened to you… I could never forgive myself."

Marajin stroked his jaw more gently than she'd ever touched him. She smiled her coquettish smile and stepped away. "Very well, Warden. I shall retire to Castle Sarquis to await word of your victory. Perhaps then you will tell me by what name you are called among your own kind."

The Warden rubbed his chin and was about to tell her his name, but she left the room before he could make up his mind.

"Mud," he said to the ceiling tiles. "My name is mud."

The Commander stood on the ramparts of the captured fortress, watching as Karkadan led the assault force into the jungle. A thousand armed and armored cybernetic veterans of the U.P.C.'s wars of conquest and policy marched in perfect military precision behind a squadron of six hover tanks. Equipped with threshers, these armored behemoths cleared a path through the undergrowth as they advanced. A score of jet bikes flitted along the small army's flanks, weaving in and out of the towering tree trunks and zipping above the canopy.

Solomon Jones smiled, sensing the confidence and the resolve of every trooper under his direct command. He felt the clammy heat clinging to the infantrymen's armored uniforms, smelled the pungent floral aromas filling their nostrils, and heard the cries and calls of birds and animals fleeing before the army's march.

With a thought, he adjusted the course of the scouting jet bikes, widening their scope of reconnaissance. The tanker gun crews broadened their fields of fire accordingly. The unerring efficiency of his war machine still delighted Jones. Since acquiring his master program, he had spent over three decades fighting in Frontier brush wars and corporate campaigns as a mercenary. Thirty-odd years of bloodshed in service to corruption and greed so he could build this tight-knit community of brothers-and-sisters-in-arms. But now that they were here, in Uncharted Space, it would all be worth it. They were finally free.

"Yes," he murmured to the jungle wind, admiring the fighting force he had built. "When a warrior masters his weapon to such a degree that it is an extension of his own body, his own will, he has become all but undefeatable. When a general can claim such mastery over his army, he is invincible... A lesson I would spare the poor, primitive natives of this world. A lesson I would spare the young Lieutenant, though I fear he will force my hand in the matter."

The Commander's fear was soon justified. Only a few hours had passed since Karkadan began his march when a wedge of sensor-camouflaged robots and hover cars burst from the jungle on the column's left flank, blaster and ballistic weapons ablaze in fire, smoke, and thunder.

A dozen troopers went down under this surprise attack, but the men and women of Jones's command immediately responded with a devastating counterattack. The bots and hoverers that weren't instantly destroyed turned and fled into the jungle.

Karkadan sent his jet bikes in pursuit.

Before Jones could countermand this order, he was alerted to a mass of gigantic life-signs charging the tanks at the head of the column from the south. The gun crews opened fire, blaster cannon bolts turning the green jungle ahead into a crimson inferno. Even so, a score of maddened monstrosities stormed through the flames, debris, and carnage. The abominations—resembling a cross between gargantuan serpents and equally large crustaceans or arachnids—hit the hover tanks like rabid battering rams. The troops behind the armored vehicles scattered as the monsters continued their frenzied stampede through the lines.

Jones shifted his focus to this threat and his troops immediately enacted his unspoken orders. The heavy-weapons teams deployed armor-piercing rockets at close range and the spider-saurs were brought down in thunderous, meat-hurling explosions before they reached the second brigade of infantry.

The column had come to a complete halt. Troops crouched in firing stances, their weapons sweeping the jungle on all sides. The tank crews scrambled to disengage their vehicles from the mammoth corpses atop them. At least one armored vehicle had suffered such damage that it would be inoperable for quite some time. A score of dead and wounded troopers lay sprawled in the wake of the monsters' rampage.

The Commander called back his jet bikes to secure the column's flanks from another attack. As the lightly-armored vehicles circled round to the battle site, a hail of arrows riddled the lead bikes. The arrowheads were equipped with explosive tips. Three jet bikes and their riders turned into roaring clouds of flame and black smoke, streaking through the canopy like burning meteors.

Jones shook his head, seeing the battle dozens of kilometers away as if he were in its midst. "Why must you vex me, Lieutenant?"

The remaining bikes strafed the jungle with blaster fire as they sped back to the column, laying waste to great swaths of vegetation and the Un Quan warriors hiding within.

The small aircraft arrived just as a massive wave of golden-skinned men in primitive armor and helmets came screaming and howling out of the southern jungle. Karkadan focused his troops' fire on the charge, decimating the assault as the jet bikes swooped in to rake the attackers with blasters and rockets.

Jones ordered the troops in the rear to advance to the head of the column on the double. Even though his people were better armed and armored, they were sorely outnumbered by the yellow men. The natives made use of armor-piercing vibro-spears and explosive arrows, which proved more than adequate at close range.

The Commander heard a gust of wind from his troops in the field before realizing it wasn't wind at all. A thousand explosive-tipped javelins and arrows streaked from the undergrowth to fell dozens of advancing soldiers like grain before a scythe. As his forces took up firing positions to face this new threat, Jones understood that he was now engaged along three fronts.

Focusing on the crew aboard the orbiting *Ranger I*, Jones gave the command: "Orbital bombardment at close quarters." He gave the exact coordinates of the enemy, knowing not a single one of his troopers would suffer from friendly fire. "Bring the rain."

The Warden stood among the front line of male warriors of Un Quan, an automatic carbine from the Masters' armory in one hand and a blaster pistol in the other. Mascos's men fell to his left and right, but they did not break their swarming, howling charge. The humid air—thick with hurled javelins, spears, and loosed arrows—smelled of scorched metal, smoke, and blood. But each archaic missile was answered by a half dozen blaster bolts. Deafening explosions erupted all along the jagged battle lines as the invaders' grenades answered the explosive tipped weapons of the natives.

The sky boomed with unnatural thunder. White-hot bolts of energy crashed through the jungle's canopy to vaporize handfuls of Un Quan men at a time. The resulting shockwave hurled dozens more through the air like broken toys.

The native assault faltered in the face of this godlike onslaught.

"Orbital bombardment," the Warden murmured, his ears ringing.

The first Un Quan soldier turned and ran. Others followed and the rout began.

"For Un Quan and for glory!" King Mascos III shouted to his men, a flashing scimitar held high above his helmed head. "Death to the invaders! No retreat! No surrender!"

A blaster bolt sheared the king's arm off just below the elbow.

The Warden dropped his rifle and grabbed Mascos as he fell. "Your Majesty! We can't keep this up. We must pull back!" He shouted above the devastating explosions.

The king gnashed his teeth against his pain. "Never! I've still one good arm. Give me a blade!"

The Warden turned to the bloodstained Hurm as he knelt beside them. "He's in shock. Get him back to Quan City along with everyone else. Save as many as you can."

The captain frowned as blaster bolts and wounded men fell around them like rain and leaves in a storm. "What of you?"

The Warden grabbed up the discarded carbine and turned to the enemy center. "I'm going to try and end this slaughter."

Sprinting and weaving through the hellish firefight, the Warden knew the safest place to be was among Jones's troopers. The Commander would not use an orbital strike unless he was absolutely certain that his own men were safe. A certainty given him by his cybernetic master program.

Behind a wall of blaster bolts and auto-fire, the Warden charged headlong into the front rank of cybernetic invaders. That's where he came face-to-face with Saladin Karkadan.

Jones's major-domo waved his troops off as the fighting began to flag. Hurm had sounded the retreat and the invaders were not pursuing. "I'll handle the Lieutenant. Regroup and prepare to resume the march."

The Warden discarded his empty weapons. He saw that the female assault on the enemy's rear had also failed under the fury of the orbital bombardment. Huge sections of blasted and burnt forest stretched to either side of the column. Medics moved among the wounded cybernetic soldiers, but no such succor was offered to the broken and twisted blue and yellow bodies scattered upon the smoking ground or dangling from shattered trees.

Karkadan smiled. "Did you really think you and these... primitives could stand against us, against the Commander?" He waved his armored hand at the carnage and desolation. "This didn't have to happen, Lieutenant. We only wanted to share this world with the Un Quan, but you have made us fight for it. You are responsible for this."

The Warden swallowed hard against the truth of the statement. "I know about the cybernetic master program, Karkadan. You know as well as I do that Jones would have insisted the natives get the implant in order to secure his 'peace.' In my book that amounts to slavery. Masters don't 'share' with their slaves, do they?"

Karkadan's smile turned into a scowl. "You imply that I am a slave?"

"No. I'm *telling* you that you are a slave. That technology gives you all your information, your direction, your purpose... your very opinions. Don't you ever question what the person on the other end of that technology wants you to think, to believe, to accept as the truth? Do you ever question why?"

Karkadan's hands curled into fists. "I'll kill you."

The Warden ignored the threat, his attention drawn to the sound of high-altitude engines passing overhead.

Karkadan laughed, his anger banished. "That? Oh, that is the sound of two landers carrying the balance of our forces to capture the strongholds outside the city. Did you really think the Commander would let you listen in on our communications without a reason?"

The Warden's heart stopped. He turned in the direction of Castle Sarquis, far to the southeast. His plan had relied on the two monarchs throwing the vast majority of their forces into this fight, leaving but a skeleton crew to defend their home fortresses. "Marajin..."

Karkadan signaled a jet bike to land beside them. "Believe me, Lieutenant, if it were up to me, I would indeed kill you right now. But the Commander wishes you to return to your Quan City and deliver these terms of surrender." He transmitted a signal to the Warden's wrist chrono before directing him to the parked jet bike. "When we arrive at the city gates in a few hours, the inhabitants must lay down their arms and allow us full occupation. If not... what is the old saying? We will put everyone in the castles to the sword."

The Warden shook his head as he mounted the bike and started the engine. "Karkadan, think about what you just said. If you truly wanted to kill me and it was really up to you, do you think you'd let me go? Do you retain any actual free will at all?"

Karkadan's face rippled with uncertain emotion, but that was the Warden's only satisfaction before rising into the air. Opening the throttle on the jet bike's engine, he sped back to Quan City in utter defeat and despair.

V.

Jones slumped against the ancient stone parapet, placing his face in his hands. The victory had been complete, the enemy routed, his superiority demonstrated. And yet, sixty-three men and twenty-one women would not rejoice in that victory; would not see the rewards of their sacrifices. Seventy-nine others would awaken in the medical bay tomorrow, having given up yet more of their own organic tissue to secure the freedom this planet promised.

Closing his eyes, Jones let the tears glide down his weathered cheeks as he recited every name, remembering every face. Recalling every moment when he had found them, in the soup kitchens, the rehab centers, the shelters, and the ghettos of over two dozen worlds. He allowed himself this private moment to weep for the loss of these, his children.

He did not question if this profound sadness, this personal sense of loss was a byproduct of the cybernetic master program. If the notion had ever crossed his mind, he would have dismissed it as a price well worth paying. In fact, he would have deemed it the greatest achievement in military technology. Leaders should feel at least some shadow of the pain and suffering of the men and women under their command. If every general, admiral, monarch, and politician in history had carried such a burden then perhaps mankind would have been a far less warlike species.

Clearing his throat and brushing the moisture from his eyes, the Commander stared into the jungle, seeing his army preparing to resume the march. The casualties were loaded onto support vehicles for return to the base. Come nightfall, the dead would be ceremonially interred in this new soil, thereby hallowing the conquest of Un Quan.

"And then," Jones said aloud. "The young Lieutenant will be called to account for every single grave."

The Warden leapt from the jet cycle as soon as it touched down on the landing pad atop the Administration Building. Thede and a quartet of silvery robotic guards were there to meet him.

"I'm sorry, Thede. My plan failed… The battle's lost… Here're Jones's demands." He held out his wrist chrono, sending the dictated terms of Un Quan's surrender to the Administrator's computer. "I hate to leave like this, especially now, but I've got to get to Castle Sarquis as fast as possible. I've got to—"

Thede put his hand on the Warden's shoulder, still splashed with King Mascos's blood. "Warden, you need to come with me."

The Warden felt cold all over. There was something in the Administrator's soft, yet commanding tone that told him all he needed to know. He shook his head, refusing to believe it. "No. I've got to get to Marajin. There may still be enough time to help her escape."

Thede gently guided the Warden to the elevator. "The Queen is not in her castle, my friend. I am sorry."

The world, the Cosmos itself, lost all meaning. One moment, the Warden stood on the windswept rooftop ruing his failure to save this planet, desperate to rescue Marajin. The next, he moved through space and time as an empty husk, numb to all sensation. Before he knew it, he stood outside a hospital room guarded by two battle-weary blue women. Tears carved lines through the soot and grime on the stoic warriors' faces. Their crystalline eyes gave him no notice as he removed his visored cowl and stepped into the room.

Dr. Gamela, Captain Sappoc, Princess Jynnessa, and Prince Andres stood at the bedside. The Warden looked at their downcast faces, seeing sadness, anger, anguish, and sympathy. He could not look at the body covered by the bloodstained sheets. His chest constricted, his throat tightened, and a stinging pain filled his eyes. The silent room smelled of antiseptics and death.

A sigh, a repressed sob slid past the Warden's lips.

Jynnessa turned her contorted features to him. He saw hatred in her tear-filled eyes, so much like her mother's. "This is your fault!" In a moment, she crossed the room and struck his face. It paled in comparison to the punch Jones had given him, but in many ways it hurt so much more. He almost welcomed the blow, silently hoping more would follow.

"Jynnessa," Andres said, taking her by the shoulders and pulling her away before she could strike again. "Come. There is much we must do." The golden prince gave the Warden an inscrutable look as he led the weeping princess from the room. That look conveyed either disappointment or pity. Both possibilities were equally bitter.

Sappoc stepped to face the Warden. Her low-spoken words were as surprising as Jynnessa's rage was to be expected. "Her Majesty cared for you, spaceman. I… am almost convinced you cared for her, and that is why you wanted her to avoid battle. But you are a foolish male, filled with pride and a false sense of superiority. She was our queen, and as such, she chose to lead her people against this threat rather than cower behind castle walls. Marajin was among the first to fall in the battle, but she was also one of the first to strike at her enemies.

"You underestimated her and were never worthy of her affections, spaceman… But I, for one, do not hold you responsible for her death. In time, the princess will come to the same conclusion."

The Warden stood in silence as Sappoc left the room. Closing his stinging eyes, he took a deep, shuddering breath and stepped to the bedside. He finally looked upon the pale blue face of Marajin XVI, Queen of Un Quan, the woman he had come to love. Even in death she was beautiful, but the fire, the passion, and the power that had made her the person of Marajin had fled the fractured mortal shell.

He shook his head, fighting back tears and the pain that forced the air from his lungs. His chest shuddered as he struggled against that sudden, crushing pain. Gasping for breath, the Warden muttered, "But I *am* responsible… for all of it…"

Dr. Gamela's cool voice cut through his agony like a scalpel. "The barbarian woman is right about one thing. You are a foolish male, filled with pride and a false sense of superiority."

The Warden rubbed his eyes and looked at the green-skinned Master of Biology, unsure of what he'd just heard.

Gamela glared back, then her face softened as she looked upon the peaceful countenance of the dead queen. "If you would but think, Warden, you would come to the conclusion that you are not responsible for this disaster. We know that this Commander Jones has had his eye set upon our system for a very long time. He was moments away from launching his conquest when accident, coincidence, or fate intervened by causing your arrival to damage the bridge. If that hadn't happened, we would already be his slaves and you would have never been the wiser."

She looked him in the eye. "But your arrival helped to forge a peace between the two warring factions, thereby offering us a future as the genders might someday again be reunited into one people. That peace also gave us a chance to fight back, to resist Jones and the impending slavery he intends to impose upon us. Yes, a considerable number of Un Quan have died today, including this woman. But what little I knew of her and what I know of these proud, fierce warriors, I believe they would much prefer facing death in battle than being doomed to a life of collective thralldom. Your tears may serve your grief, but your guilt does a disservice to Marajin's valor and sacrifice."

The Warden gave a begrudging chuckle, as much to alleviate his anguish as to acknowledge her words. "You may have missed your calling by going into the sciences, Doc. You'd have made one heck of a general with speeches like that."

"I shall leave you with her for a short time."

The Warden touched Gamela's wrist as she turned to leave. "Thank you. But I've got one last card to play. Here's the data I gathered from Karkadan a little while ago." He touched his chrono, sending the information to the Office of Biology's central computer. "See if you can do what we talked about earlier."

The doctor nodded and departed.

Alone, the Warden turned to the pallid face of Marajin. Tears rolled down his cheeks as he stroked her lustrous blue-black hair. One great sob shook his entire frame before he mastered himself. He knelt and kissed her cold lips. Rising he cleared his throat and said, "I am sorry... But I promise you this: I'll join you in the Cosmos before I let your world become enslaved. Your daughter will sit on your throne, and she will rule over a free and united people."

He composed himself and headed back to the fight.

vi.

Three hours after saying goodbye to Marajin, the Warden stood outside the northern walls of Quan City, along with Thede, Captains Hurm and Sappoc, and most of the uninjured survivors of the battle. Andres and Jynnessa had taken over six hundred volunteers from both gender factions into the jungle to prepare a guerilla resistance should this last-ditch effort fail.

The Warden, wanting the bloodshed to end as soon as possible, had not approved of this plan. But he knew he had no foot to stand on in the matter. Jynnessa refused to speak to him and Andres intended to support his wife's quest for vengeance to the bitter end. In his heart, the Warden knew he would do the same in their shoes.

Thede and some of the other Masters had proposed waiting until the invaders were inside Quan City, then using high-pressure pumps to unleash the radioactive river water on the unsuspecting occupiers. Fortunately, Dr. Gamela had sided with the Warden's plan, pointing out that even should the tactic eventually destroy the enemy, the city's dwindling populace would certainly count it a Pyrrhic victory.

The ground shook at the approach of the cybernetic army, and the humid jungle air hummed with the sound of jet and anti-g engines. Brightly colored birds scattered from the canopy, crying out and taking wing against the gold-orange sky as they fled the horde's approach.

Thede shook his bald head, glancing sadly over his shoulder at the silvery ramparts and towers of his beloved city. "We stood against a war that all but destroyed our civilization and survived the ensuing millennium of decay around us. And yet, Quan City falls in a single day."

The Warden took a deep breath. He looked at his chrono, noting the empty circle on the tiny screen. "Maybe not. Just do as they say and hopefully everything will turn out in the end."

Sappoc scoffed. "*Hopefully!* It seems that too many of your strategies rely on hope, spaceman. We can still fight."

The Warden watched as the tanks broke the tree line, the jet bikes speeding ahead. "I'll not argue that. And before it's all said and done, you may still have to fight for your freedom. But for right now, trust me. Kneel today so you can stand tomorrow. Better yet, if all goes well, you may not have to fight at all."

Hurm growled. "I should have gone with Prince Andres. If King Mascos weren't recuperating in this city, I would have."

The tanks drew up several hundred meters away from the walls and stopped. A line of jet bikes hovered above them. The Warden watched as Karkadan's armored form emerged from the lead tank's hatch to sit atop the turret, waiting.

"I guess we go to greet our new overlords." Thede was unable to keep the bitterness from his voice. With a regal stride, he led the Warden and the two captains across the grassy clearing.

When they got within ten meters of the tanks, Karkadan spoke. The vehicle's loudspeakers amplified his translated voice so the conquered army could hear the conversation. "I am Saladin Karkadan, representative of Commander Solomon Jones. We have come a very long way to seek shelter on your world, but we did not receive the greeting we had hoped for. I fear you have been deceived by this man." He stood and pointed at the Warden. "He has filled your heads with lies about us. We did not come as conquerors, but as refugees, as colonists, as friends seeking succor from a galaxy that has abandoned us. We mean you no harm, but we will defend ourselves to the utmost should hostilities again arise between us."

Thede stepped forward and bowed. "I am the Administrator of Quan City, and on behalf of my people, I welcome you to our world. Please forgive our initial opposition. As you say, we were misguided in this. Having now seen the strength of your arms and the merit of your intent, we humbly seek an end to further hostilities and do hereby acquiesce to your submitted demands. The city… and the world are yours."

The Warden's jaw flexed as he witnessed the formal surrender of the planet to these invaders. Invaders his personal desires had given access to this world. The grief he felt for Marajin's death was tightly bottled up somewhere deep inside, but he felt it burning like a ball of solar flame in his heart. He tried to remain calm but Karkadan's mocking sneer caused his blood to boil. He was thankful he wasn't wearing his Comets or else, plan or no, he would have been sorely tempted to blast the man to pieces.

"Well then," Karkadan said. "Have your troops come forward to stack arms before us. Once this is done, we will move to occupy the city. But first, I will take custody of the criminal responsible for today's violence."

Thede tilted his head. "Criminal?"

Karkadan pointed at the Warden. "This man is an officer in the Star Wardens, a branch of service under the authority of Commander Jones. He is formally charged with treason against his brothers-and-sisters-in-arms. I will take him to the Commander's headquarters, where he will face trial and summary execution for this crime."

"But surely this tribunal should be held here." Thede gestured to the city. "This man did what he did, perhaps misguidedly, in the defense of the planet's inhabitants. I know there are many here, myself included, who would stand in his defense."

The Warden touched the Administrator's shoulder. "Thank you, but that won't be necessary." He met Karkadan's gloating gaze. "He's right. I have always lived by the code of Star Law, and Solomon Jones is the arbiter of that code on this world. I'll go peacefully."

No visible signal summoned the jet bike the Warden had taken from the battlefield. As it landed in the clearing, Karkadan leapt from the hover tank to trade places with another jet cycle's pilot. "Come along, Lieutenant. I can trust you not to try anything as you know that any rash act on your part will result in swift and draconian punishment for our new neighbors." The armored soldier leered at the natives of Un Quan as he said this.

The Warden climbed onto the bike. He cast a surreptitious look at the quarter-filled circle on his chrono's screen. "Let's go."

With that, he and Karkadan rose into the darkening sky and headed north to face the Commander. The Warden spared one backward glance. The blue and yellow troops formed up to surrender their primitive weapons beneath the tanks' blaster cannons and the hovering jet cycles. The ranks of cybernetic soldiers watched in grim silence. He knew that directly overhead, unseen beyond the clouds, Jones's *Ranger I* orbited, its weapons zeroed in on Quan City.

"You gave up rather easily." It was Karkadan's voice coming through the Warden's earpieces, but he recognized the observation to be the Commander's. "I expected at least one more heroic fight from you. Perhaps a last stand behind the walls of your adopted city, like James Bowie and David Crockett at the Alamo."

"I've brought enough bloodshed to these people."

"Earlier… you said the name, Marajin…"

The Warden turned a glare on Karkadan as they sped above the canopy, his teeth bared.

"Ah! Now I see. You went native. You went soft. That's what took the fight out of you."

The Warden lowered his head, opened the throttle and redlined the jet cycle's engine. Even though he knew he should play for more time. As he broke away from Karkadan, he heard the major-domo's laughter over the coms. He could have closed the channel, but the Warden chose to let the man's mocking cruelty fuel his determination. There was only one chance left to pluck victory from complete and utter defeat.

The Warden would not fail to take that chance.

The abandoned fortress Jones had taken as his HQ was nowhere near as impressive as either the female-held Castle Sarquis or the males' Castle Vear, but it was a formidable structure nonetheless. Not least because of the automated blaster cannon newly installed at strategic points along the aging, crenelated bastions. The Warden's visor noted these targeting him as he descended into the clearing surrounding the five-story structure, but he paid this danger little mind. He knew Jones wanted the satisfaction of killing him face-to-face.

To the north of the stronghold, on a low hill, a company of men used heavy equipment to dig and fill graves. Dozens of them. The Warden closed his eyes and tried not to wonder how many of those dead troopers were the grandsons and granddaughters of the men and women with whom he had served a century before. He tried, but failed.

He leapt from the jet cycle before it skidded to a complete stop on the turf outside the fortress's gatehouse. The Warden shouted: "I'm here, Jones. You wanted me and now you've got me. Time to quit playing games with your little toady as your proxy. Time to do your own dirty work like a man."

A squad of armored troops carrying blaster carbines emerged from the gatehouse as Karkadan landed behind the Warden. "You will accompany us to see the Commander," one of the soldiers said.

The Warden shrugged, falling in behind Karkadan as the troopers surrounded him. The tiny circle on his chrono was now almost half full.

They entered the castle, which must have been an industrial plant before what the native Un Quan called "The Dark Times." The building was a maze of ancient and crumbling machinery, conveyer belts, and rusty catwalks, stairs, and ladders. Ensuing generations had since turned these into easily-defended breastworks, workshops, and living quarters before eventually abandoning the location.

Jones's people had added their off-world technology to this inner space: Generators powered light panels affixed to the walls and ceilings, and soft-sounding ventilation fans diminished the jungle's heat and humidity throughout the structure. At least a full company of armed cybernetic men and women moved about the fortress with unnatural military efficiency.

The Warden thought of a giant ant farm, each worker and drone mindlessly guided by the will of the queen. Only in this case, that "queen" was a megalomaniacal military genius with superhuman speed and strength. A man who had already flattened the Warden without breaking a sweat. And he was about to face that man again, surrounded and unarmed.

There were worse ways to die, the Warden was certain, but none came to mind offhand.

They climbed a rusty staircase that wrapped around the main chamber's walls and led to the uppermost story. An automated door opened at their approach, admitting them into a completely refurbished office space. This occupied the entire top floor of the fortress, its weather-stained walls lined with great windows providing a panoramic view of the surrounding jungle. An array of new computers, monitors, and communications equipment filled the center of this space. These were manned by six technicians in grey jumpsuits who did not acknowledge the arrival of Karkadan, the Warden, and their armed escort.

Jones stood at the opposite end of the room, his hands folded behind his back, chin resting on his chest as if in thought. He wore his black and silver Star Warden uniform as before, but now his cowl and visor were in place.

"Thank you, troops." Jones's deep voice was quiet but powerful in the big room. "That will be all."

The techs rose from their consoles without a word and made for the door with the armed troopers. Karkadan turned to go, as well, but paused, a pained expression on his face. Slowly he turned to face the Commander. His voice was raspy, as if he were in pain. "Begging your pardon, sir, but I request permission to attend the tribunal."

Jones raised his chin. "That won't be necessary, Saladin. Please return to the city to oversee the surrender."

Karkadan took another step toward the door but paused again. The Warden could see perspiration on the exposed portion of his face, rolling down from beneath his eye-concealing visor. Karkadan was challenging the cybernetic master program.

"Go ahead, Karkadan," the Warden said. "Tell him how much you want to see me beg. How much you want to see me suffer for challenging him. You deserve that, don't you? You've never questioned him in all the time you've served him, and yet he has shown me so much more respect than he ever did you. Isn't that right?"

Karkadan turned, his teeth gnashed in a rictus. His entire body shook and his voice rose in a throaty growl. "Yes, dammit! I deserve this, Commander. I deserve to see you make him crawl before you crush the life from him. After all I've done for you, without question. I... I demand it."

"Enough!" Jones stepped forward, a movement the Warden thought betrayed some lack of control. "You demand nothing of me, Karkadan. You are a soldier, and a soldier who does not follow orders is less than useless. Now go, do as I say."

The Warden smiled cruelly at Karkadan, but the cruelty was not genuine. He understood the heroic effort the man made, attempting to override the circuitry commandeering his mind. But he knew the smile would enflame Karkadan's emotions, just as his remarks had at the battle's end. When the Warden had seen the weak spot in Jones's cybernetic mastery before passing it on to Dr. Gamela. "You heard the man, Karkadan. Go about your business like a good little soldier while the grownups have a chat."

The Commander crossed the spacious room with preternatural speed, backhanding the Warden to the floor in a blur. "Silence!"

"How much?" Karkadan shuddered like a man in the grip of a deadly fever, blood trickling from his nostrils. "How much of who I am... have you taken from me?" His hand slowly moved to the holstered blaster on his hip. "How much of me... is actually you?"

The Warden shook the starbursts from his aching head and tried to rise from the floor. Blood spilled from his broken nose and split lips. "No, Karkadan. Don't do it."

Jones grabbed the man's wrist as he drew the weapon. Karkadan's horrific scream and the sound of rending metal filled the room. In a blur of motion, the Commander tore the man's cybernetic arm from his organic shoulder.

"You will be fine." Jones's voice returned to a calmer tone. He stood over Karkadan, who lay convulsing on the blood-splattered floor, slipping into shock. "We'll get you fixed up and back on your feet, just like we did when we found you in that flophouse on Vega Prime. You remember that, don't you, Saladin? A decorated Star Cav Black

Ops captain with over seventy-five confirmed kills in twenty-one successful missions, you were passed out in a pool of your own waste and vomit."

Tossing the severed, blaster-wielding arm across the room with diminished rage, the Commander sighed. "Yes, my son, how much of you is me, indeed?"

The Warden regained his feet, noting the nearly-full circle flashing on his wrist chrono's screen. "I cannot believe you are the same man who led us into the teeth of that alien armada and black hole all those years ago. What could have possibly happened to turn you into… this? You used to lead by example and inspiration. Now you rule by brainwashing your followers and physically assaulting them if they question your authority. You used to be a hero, but you've become a monster."

Jones turned, his mouth a flat line. "As I told you, Lieutenant, you were not there to see what the United Planetary Council did in the wake of Draconus Prime. I was. For every bit of it. And I do not need to justify myself to you or to anyone else. Not ever."

"Maybe not." The Warden pressed a button on his chrono, signaling Dr. Gamela and Dr. Hydrax now that the circle was full. "But you should think long and hard about justifying yourself to the man you once were."

A distant rumble echoed through the jungle from the direction of Quan City.

Jones turned as a flash against the darkening sky heralded something launching from the captured city. He swayed for a moment in uncertainty. He touched the back of his skull with a trembling hand. "What have you done?"

"I've done nothing… but provide a distraction." The Warden took a deep breath, trying hard to master the overwhelming surge of grief, rage, and exultation that swept over him. "But while you've been focused on me, the scientists of this 'primitive' planet have just released a global pulse that stimulates the amygdala of human brains. Apparently, the sudden flood of chemicals and hormones temporarily disrupts the signal of your cybernetic master program… How does it feel to be alone, Commander?"

The Warden didn't tell him that the flash they had seen was the *M-XVI* launching with a robotic pilot and a deep-space communications booster aboard.

Jones's face contorted behind his visor, a furious howl erupting from his throat. He flew across the room to strike the Warden like a ghostly thunderbolt.

This time the Warden was expecting the attack and rolled with the impact. Skidding across the floor with no more than a few bruised ribs, the Warden found Karkadan's severed arm and retrieved the blaster pistol still clutched in the metallic hand.

"Even without the master program, I can still signal the Paladins," the Commander growled as he moved to one of the control panels. "I can still destroy the ERB. With the troops I already have here, we can still take this world."

The Warden fired. Not at Jones, but at a specific piece of equipment he had noted upon entering: the master communications console.

The device exploded in a shower of sparks and smoke. "You have relied on your master program and connection to the GDS for so long that you don't even wear a simple wrist chrono, Commander. Now you can't stop Un Quan calling Star Cav for help."

Jones turned, his hands knotted into powerful fists. His mouth was a hard white line in his dark face. Before he could retaliate, a series of signals came over the Warden's wrist chrono:

"*Commander, please come in! We've lost connection! We have destroyed a ship launched from the planet… but not before it sent a deep-space communication! Please advise!—Wait! Something's coming through the ERB—*"

"*Attention, Paladin class ships, this is the* U.P.C.S. Silverheels. *Stand down and prepare to be boarded, or we will open fire. This system is now under the provisional protection of the Star Cavalry. This is your only warning.*"

The Commander, Solomon Jones, the man once called The First Star Warden turned. All the fight had gone out of him like the light from a dying bulb, and he looked like a very tired old man in a powerful young man's body. He peeled the cowl off his shaved head, his coal-black eyes accusing the Warden. "You've let the wolves in the door. I wanted to seal this part of space off from the corruption, greed, and exploitation that are the hallmarks of the 'Civilized Worlds.' I might have been an emperor, but I would have been a benevolent and just one."

"I'm sure every tyrant in history has said the exact same thing." The Warden shook his head. The moment, the victory felt as hollow as his soul. The pulse had turned his emotions inside out, filling him with remorse, grief, and guilt over the loss of Marajin and the hundreds of others who had died today. He wondered if he could ever get over those feelings. He wondered if he would ever want to.

He knew he could never forget Marajin. As brief as their time together had been, it had been one of the most exciting periods of his life. And now it was over.

"I should not be surprised that you are the first human to explore the region of your galaxy dubbed Uncharted Space." The familiar voice coming over his chrono was the only thing in the entire Cosmos that could possibly have lifted the Warden's spirits at that moment. "However, I must admit a certain amount of disappointment that you decided to do so without me."

The Warden blinked back tears, cleared his throat, and spoke into the chrono. "My apologies, my friend. I promise to make sure that you are with me the next time things go completely and unpredictably sideways."

"Of that I have very little doubt," Quantum said.

"I'm just glad you got here as quickly as you did." The Warden and Quantum walked the corridors of Quan City's Administration Building. "If you hadn't, I'm not certain I could have kept Jones from blowing the ERB and rallying his troops."

Quantum paused in a bar of sunlight falling through one of the broad hallway's floor-to-ceiling windows. "When you disappeared, I immediately set about trying to find you. I spent twenty-eight standard days reconstructing the rather ridiculous set of variables which resulted in your random discharge from the Einstein-Rosen bridge network. Accessing the network and determining that you had not exited from any of the seventeen-thousand, nine-hundred, seventy-three registered bridges took far less time.

"Given these data, I could only conclude that you had been destroyed in the accident or had emerged from an unknown bridge. If you were dead, there was nothing to be done, so I assumed you were not. From this assumption, it was a simple matter of looking for ERB energy signatures in non-network star systems. Again, this took considerable time and resources. Fortunately, Commander Morris of the *Silverheels* was willing to help."

"So, when we got the bridge back online, you located us. Why didn't you and the *Silverheels* come through then?"

Quantum almost seemed to smile. "Human bureaucracy. Commander Morris could not get authorization from Star Cav. However, when we received your prerecorded call for help sent by the Un Quan, the commander made an executive decision to 'render assistance.' We were already on standby near the ERB in Pegasus Five, the closest network star system to the Un Quan gate."

The Warden smiled, grasping his friend's shoulder. "What would I ever do without you, Quantum?"

"You appear to have done moderately well here in my absence."

"Moderately." The Warden's smile failed as he turned to look at the guarded room at the end of the corridor. "Will you come with me?"

Quantum shook his head. "I do not comprehend the inhabitants of this dimension's need to mourn their dead. We Mechtechan understand that matter and energy are fluid and universal. The ending of biological life is merely a transference of that universal energy. I fear my... indifference would not serve you on this occasion."

The Warden nodded. Quantum's confession was as true a display of sympathy as a human embrace. Taking a deep breath, the Warden strode alone to the room where Queen Marajin XVI lay in state.

Sappoc and Hurm stood guard, both in highly-polished ceremonial armor, both stoic as statues. Neither challenged him as he passed through the tall sliding black doors. The room was a high rotunda, with an open iris in the domed ceiling. Golden sunlight slanted through this iris to fill the ivory-paneled space. An elevated, black-draped catafalque, upon which rested a polished ebony casket with silver furniture occupied the center of the room.

A tall figure, all in white, stood beside the shining black coffin.

"Jynnessa," the Warden whispered. "I... I am sorry. I'll come back—"

The uncrowned queen turned, reached out a strong blue hand. "No. Warden, please."

Looking into her red-rimmed eyes, he saw none of the hatred he had the last time they'd met. He gave her a sad smile and took the offered hand. She pulled him into a tight embrace.

"I'm so sorry, Jynnessa..." It took everything in him not to break into sobs.

"As am I." She eased out of his arms and brushed at her eyes. "I know it was not your fault."

The Warden was not so sure about that, so said nothing. He turned and looked at the peaceful face of his lover, who appeared to be but sleeping in the coffin.

Jynnessa squeezed his hand. "It was not your fault, Warden."

He nodded, his eyes fixed on Marajin.

Clearing her throat, Jynnessa stood beside him. "Un Quan was destined to change sooner or later. I've known this my whole life, ever since I discovered the prophecy. And change is rarely easy, or even peaceful."

The Warden sighed and shook his head. "The prophecy. The words of a long-dead scientist. Those ancient words led you and Andres to search for and ultimately find Quan City... That seems like a children's bedtime story told a long, long time ago."

Jynnessa smiled, reached up and brushed the tear from his cheek. "Yes. I remember seeing you fall from the sky in your burning ship. I thought you were the harbinger of that change, our new age of enlightenment. And it was you, Warden, who made our search possible and even successful."

The Warden returned the smile as best he could. "I wasn't the harbinger, just a rocket-jockey who got caught up in the plot. Jones was the architect of your change, Jynnessa. He'd planned for Un Quan's 'new age of enlightenment' long before you were born. When I came here, I remember thinking this place could have been a new Eden. But all that is about to change. And I'm not certain that it will be for the better."

Jynnessa's eyes filled with a fleeting shadow of that familiar rage. She looked again on the face of her dead mother and her expression softened. "But Jones is now in the custody of your Star Cav and his soldiers are disarmed and under guard. Dr. Gamela has begun removing the cybernetic master chips from their brains. I am confident that justice will ultimately prevail and these so-called Civilized Worlds will treat us fairly in the days to come."

The Warden put his arm around Jynnessa's shoulders and thought about the political delegation being prepared by the United Planetary Council. He thought about Jones's warnings of corruption and warmongering. He thought about how Star Cav might exploit Un Quan as a stepping stone in the conquest of Uncharted Space. And he thought of his responsibility not only for the past few days' bloody events on Un Quan, but also for the planet's foreseeable future.

"Justice will prevail and Un Quan will be treated fairly. I'll make sure of it." A sad smile worked its way across the Warden's face as he recalled the fiery passion and indomitable will that had so attracted him to Marajin XVI, Queen of Un Quan and the warrior woman he had loved. "I owe it to her."

End of Part II

PART III

i.

"**S**ir. There has been unauthorized interstellar activity in System UQX."

The watch commander moved to the intelligence officer's station. The flickering light from observational command's countless holographic displays shimmered on his bronze scales like tiny rainbows. "UQX? The quarantined system at the edge of the Imperial Frontier?"

"Yes, sir." The intelligence officer tilted her uncrested head, her silver eyes shining.

Accessing the pertinent data via the collective consciousness, the watch commander narrowed his eyes. "Is it a Malcontent operation?"

The female officer shook her head. "This is a completely new energy reading, not analogous with anything we have seen the rebels use before."

This answer did not reassure the watch commander. The Malcontents were constantly developing new and dangerous technologies to further their goals. "What is the nearest vessel?"

"Admiral Thargrimm's *Bellicose*, sir."

The watch commander hesitated a moment. Thargrimm had the reputation of being the most ruthless commander in the Imperial Fleet. If it was Malcontent activity, he was indeed the best man for the job. However, if someone else, perhaps a new culture or civilization, were behind the strange readings… "No scientific craft closer to UQX?"

"No, sir. Besides, as this activity occurs in the Frontier—"

"Yes, yes, I know." The watch commander frowned. "The Frontier is the purview of the military. Too many Malcontents have fled into the region… Very well, dispatch the *Bellicose*."

"What orders, sir?"

Before the watch commander could reply, the Hierophant's voice filled the thoughts of everyone in the observational command, via the collective consciousness. "Threat assessment. Admiral Thargrimm is at his discretion on how best to deal with any perceived threat to the Hrothshaar Empire. Any Malcontent presence is to be utterly eradicated. In any case, if the natives of the quarantined planet have availed themselves of interstellar technology, the entire system is to be purged for reclamation."

The intelligence officer blinked, looked to the watch commander for confirmation.

"You heard the Supreme One. Relay the order."

"Yes, sir. Hailing the *Bellicose* now…"

The Last Star Warden stood outside Quan City's Civic Arena and stared at an overcast sky the color of a sucking chest wound. The jungle planet's firmament was normally a golden orange on sunny days, but some element in the atmosphere combined with the light of the system's twin suns to turn bad weather into horror shows. Given the recent bloodletting the world had seen, the bloodletting for which he had been largely responsible, the Warden thought the grisly, gloomy day quite appropriate.

Though he had been reunited with Quantum, the Warden had made this trip alone… Alone… He had come to feel more alone with each passing day of his life. First, he had been lost in time, returning to the galaxy decades after everyone he had ever known had passed away. Then, another freakish accident had stranded him here, on Un Quan, in Uncharted Space, cut off from the Frontier, the reach of the United Planetary Council, and the entire human race. But all of that isolation paled in comparison with this new form of loneliness, the sudden, violent loss of someone he had come to love.

Marajin…

The Warden shook the grief and guilt from his thoughts as he approached the security checkpoint. This was manned by armed Star Cav marines and the Masters' silvery security bots. He had a reason for coming to the facility, one which might have serious galactic repercussions. That is *if* the information he sought had any bearing on the current negotiations between the Un Quan and the U.P.C. delegates.

The Civic Arena had long been vacant. The sterile citizens of Quan City had grown old and small in number since the "Dark Times" of the ancient Agenda Wars. However, in the wake of the illegal invasion from the Frontier, the vast colosseum had been put to use as an improvised internment camp for the POWs of the brief but bloody conflict.

The Warden presented his wrist chrono for scan at the checkpoint. "The Warden to see Saladin Karkadan."

The marine sergeant checked the Warden's ident code against the information on his datapad, pushed his blue beret back from his chrome visor and nodded. "You're clear, sir. I wouldn't hold out much hope for any good conversation though. That one hasn't said a word since he cleared med-hold."

The Warden grunted at this friendly warning, expecting no less. He would have preferred to speak with Commander Solomon Jones, the architect of the unsanctioned invasion of Un Quan and Uncharted Space. But the legendary man was being held in a maximum security cell aboard the Star Cav destroyer, *Silverheels*, orbiting high above the planet.

The ship's commander, under direct orders from the U.P.C. diplomatic delegation, had strictly forbidden any contact with Jones, so the Warden would have to get his information elsewhere. He hoped that Saladin Karkadan, Jones's major-domo might supply some answers before things at the summit got out of hand.

When he thought of what the battle had cost him and the people of Un Quan, all they had lost, he decided it was probably for the best that he didn't speak to Jones face-to-face. Just thinking about that possibility caused him to gnash his teeth and flex his fists. It was so much easier to let the pain of Marajin's loss turn to vengeful rage.

But the Warden knew that would do nobody any good.

A Star Cav corporal and a silver security bot escorted the Warden through the outer walls of the massive arena, past locker rooms and concession areas which had been converted into holding cells and cafeterias. These were occupied by Jones's cybernetic army, now under the watchful eye of marines in heavy power armor and reinforced battle-bots bristling with stun cannons and EMP generators. He was led down onto the field where a huge prefab city had been erected to hold more of the captive veterans, men and women Jones had gathered from Star Cav's own wounded castoffs.

As the Warden passed these hardened warriors, he sensed bitterness and anger mixed with confusion and despair. Thanks to Jones's cybernetic master program, they had labored under the belief that their every thought and action in invading Un Quan had been justified. They had expected total success, having been electronically infected by Jones's own fanaticism.

Now, as prisoners, they could not fathom how their years of planning, superior training, and unmatched firepower had been undone. They could not understand how their Commander, who must have seemed a god to them in their cybernetic enslavement, had so utterly failed.

Thunder rolled in the blood-colored sky and a few moments later, red rain began to fall.

A prefabricated PlaSteel building guarded by two more marines and another heavy-duty battle-bot stood at the south end of the pitch. Even though Karkadan had shown no signs of aggression and possessed only a single arm, his military record as well as his high position in Jones's army obliged such precautions. The Warden's credentials were scanned again and his Comet blasters taken before he was admitted into the cell.

Saladin Karkadan lay on a small bunk in the spartan room. His muscular frame was sheathed in a grey jumpsuit rather than the heavy blue armor he had worn in the Warden's previous encounters with him. The right sleeve of the jumpsuit was conspicuously empty, Karkadan having lost the cybernetic appendage for daring to resist Jones's electronic mastery.

The black-ops officer turned at the Warden's entrance, looked at him with deadpan eyes, then rolled back over on the cot to face the wall.

"Saladin, I'd like to talk."

No reply.

The Warden took a deep breath. "You know, the Masters of Quan City have remarkable medical technology. Maybe even better than the Civilized Worlds. If you cooperate with me, we can look into the possibility of replacing your arm with a biological one. Maybe good as new, maybe even better."

Karkadan didn't move.

The Warden paced the small space, which was devoid of any sense of occupancy save for the obstinate man on the cot. "Okay, cooperate with me and maybe we can get that level of help for all the troops under your command."

After a very long silence, Saladin Karkadan turned over and sat up, his broad back to the corner of the cell. "What do you want, Warden?"

The Warden almost sighed with relief. "We need to know how Jones was able to pull this entire operation off. I know he left some very important names and places out of the summary he gave me when he brought me aboard the transport. Who did he work for to make the money required to finance everything? What unsanctioned and unlawful operations did he take part in before coming here? What kinds of deals did he cut to fly under the radar, and with whom? In short, I need you to tell me all your boss's dirty little secrets."

Karkadan laughed, rubbed his face with his only hand. "Why? Even if I could tell you every sin the Commander committed in the past hundred years, what good would that do now? You stopped him from achieving his ultimate goal. You, Mr. Big-Bad Phantom Lawman, Avenging Angel of the Frontier, kept the greatest military leader of the modern age from finding a refuge, a new home for all us freaks chewed up and spit out by the U.P.C.'s ever-hungry war machine. Good on you. Isn't that enough heroic derring-do for one month?"

The Warden inhaled sharply. There was some truth to Karkadan's retort. The details of Jones's criminal past might be useful in an ongoing investigation into corrupt politicians and corporations in the Civilized Worlds. Someday. But what bearing would they really have on the current negotiations with Un Quan?

Even if Saladin did divulge a smoking gun that showed government cooperation—or at least tacit consent—in Jones's invasion of the planet, that information would have little to no impact on the U.P.C.'s political and technological criteria for admission to the Civilized Worlds. Most of Un Quan still existed in a Bronze-Age society, and there was no unified world government to promote global stability. The fact that Jones's invasion had forced the planet into contact with the U.P.C. and its advanced technology was merely academic. At least as far as the politicians were concerned.

"What are you really doing here, Warden?" Karkadan smiled, pleased by the Warden's consternation. "Do you honestly think anyone in power in the U.P.C., the corporations, or even Star Cav is going to step up and admit to wrongdoings? Wrongdoings that will allow your pet planet into the exclusive club that is the Civilized Worlds? Especially when those very people in power are the ones who stand to gain the most by exploiting Un Quan to the fullest... Come on, old man. Grow up."

Jones had told the Warden as much at the moment of his defeat. "*You've let the wolves in the door...*"

The Warden nodded as he left the prisoner. Karkadan hadn't admitted anything, hadn't given him anything useful. But he had confirmed the Warden's suspicions that someone, if not an entire conspiracy, was in fact behind Jones's operation. Karkadan was biding his time, waiting for this mysterious faction to offer a better deal than the Warden ever could. Of course, if Karkadan was holding too much information, that deal might earn him nothing more than a flag-draped coffin.

Leaving the Civic Arena, the Warden walked through a crimson deluge on his way back to the Administration Building. The visit with Karkadan had been a waste of time, as he had expected it to be. It had, in fact, been a distraction, another way to avoid dealing with the loss of Marajin, a way to avoid dealing with the guilt he felt for her death and everyone else who had died in Jones's invasion.

Perhaps he had thought if Karkadan had rolled on the mysterious powers-that-be, the Warden could have vindicated himself, at least in his own mind, for the tragedy. He shook his head at the foolishness, the selfishness. Marajin's beautiful face would forever haunt his thoughts. Just like the wild, staring eyes of Maximo Ryan, the crazed constable of Cibola Seven he had shot while under the telepathic influence of a mad Tuatha. Both would still be alive today if they had never met him.

"Warden." Quantum's voice came through his wrist chrono. "The negotiations are about to resume. Shall I tell the delegates to begin without you? I can have the *Ranger VII* ready to go in ten minutes. You can leave these negotiations to the professionals, and we can get back to our work in the Frontier."

The Warden shook his head in silent frustration. As happy as he was to be reunited with his friend, Quantum's tendency to exclude all else in the face of logic added another stressor to the situation. In Quantum's mind, there was no good reason for the Warden to remain on Un Quan, participating in a diplomatic situation for which he was clearly unqualified.

Added to this unwanted advice, Dr. Gamela—having become the Warden's confidante in Quantum's absence—urged the Warden to seek comfort in his grief before investing himself in the negotiations. She suggested he do this by sharing time with the other two people who had been closest to Marajin: her daughter and heir, Jynnessa, and her bodyguard and former lover, Captain Sappoc. The problem with this was that Jynnessa filled the Warden with more sadness and guilt whenever he looked at her, and Sappoc had hated him from the first moment she'd set eyes upon him.

"No. I'm on my way. I'll be there shortly."

The Warden signaled for a hover car to pick him up. Slipping into the small vehicle's cabin, he wiped rain from his face and let the interior fans dry his spacesuit. He stared out the window at the shining city, now the color of blood in the storm, dreading the return to the conference room.

The Un Quan delegation consisted of Thede, the Administrator, representing the

Masters, King Mascos III representing the male jungle tribes, and the newly crowned Queen Jynnessa I, representing the indigenous females. The Warden was supposed to be their collective advocate, but the three factions could not completely agree on any one item of debate. Added to this, arrayed against him was a formidable delegation from the U.P.C.

The diplomatic team was helmed by Ambassador Kayla Castille, an ambitious Earth politician trying to make history on her first lead assignment. The fact that the U.P.C. had not sent a senior diplomat was not a good sign. Backing Castille were General Leonidas Bohr, a highly decorated Star Cav senior-command officer riding out his last days until retirement, and a junior member of the United Planetary Council, Ch'Koh Pah from Silesia—possibly chosen because of his green skin, as a show of solidarity with the Masters of Quan City. Both of these gentlemen seemed content to sit and listen while the firebrand Castille dictated the course of negotiation.

"I'd rather fly into the teeth of a pirate armada…"

Solomon Jones sat alone in his cell. Alone for the first time in seeming ages. He could not feel his troops, his children, not a single one of them. The sensation was devastating. Each of his hand-picked warriors had become a living extension of himself in the decades since he had accepted the cybernetic master program. He had lost the greater part of his identity.

Or had he?

In that profound solitude, Solomon Jones, the man once hailed as "The First Star Warden," rediscovered a part of himself he had thought lost quite some time ago. A part of himself almost remembered when he had met the young Lieutenant, the infamous "Last Star Warden." Jones had lived long enough to appreciate symmetry in the Cosmos when he saw it. And there was most definitely the mark of Intelligent Design in the unlikely circumstances which had caused the two men's paths to cross at the very moment of his long-laid plan's fruition.

Solomon Jones began to think of himself as an individual again, something he had

not done for a very, very long time. He began to think of his own wants and desires, specifically his continued survival, and his legacy. He thought about the consequences of his recent failure, and what those consequences could mean to those who had enabled him on his path of conquest, and what they would mean for those who had served him.

He understood that, though he was currently secure in a detention cell aboard a Star Cav warship, surrounded by guards and armored plating and blaster batteries, he was in fact at his most vulnerable.

Not only had the cybernetic master program been stripped from his cerebral implants by the Un Quan scientists, but the internal energy cell that powered his augmented cybernetic body had also been downgraded, effectively reducing him to the physical ability of an invalid. His armored carapace had been removed, baring the skeletal superstructure of his rebuilt body. He was naked and exposed.

Someone would come for him, and soon. He simply knew too much and posed too great a threat to galactic security to ever be allowed back into Frontier Space, much less the Civilized Worlds. That was the problem.

Now, alone in his cell aboard the *Silverheels*, high above the planet of Un Quan, Solomon Jones turned his prodigious mind and experience to solving this problem.

ii.

"The United Planetary Council has very specific criteria for worlds petitioning membership. Specifically, at bare minimum, the planet must boast a Level 1 society on the cusp of attaining Level 2." Kayla Castille's rich, lilting voice filled the conference room as if she addressed the U.P.C. and its 1900+ representatives rather than the half dozen people in attendance. She stood tall at one end of the long polished darkwood table, her athletic physique sheathed in an expensively tailored grey suit. It was clear to the Warden that the young, green-eyed brunette intended this negotiation to be hers and hers alone. "I am afraid that Un Quan is, by definition, a Level 0."

Flanked by the imposing bull-necked, silver-haired General Bohr in his medal-festooned blue dress uniform and the impassive yellow-eyed, green-skinned Councilman Pah, Kayla Castille would have been the center of most shows. However, at the moment, she faced off against the Last Star Warden in his hallmark blue-and-silver spacesuit as he represented the interests of two monarchs and a city of super scientists.

Thede, the Administrator of Quan City wore golden hoop earrings and his heavy chain of office over a scintillating, multicolored robe. The gold-skinned King Mascos, the stump of his brawny right arm encased in a portable bio-tank, wore crimson robes and bronze jewelry. Queen Jynnessa was resplendent in her mother's silver crown and regalia, her muscular blue frame draped in shining silk.

The Warden felt tension rise at his end of the table, King Mascos bridling at the woman's patronizing smile while Thede clucked his tongue in consternation. Queen Jynnessa took a long, deep breath. The Warden imagined the young warrior queen would prefer to solve this matter with a feat of physical action rather than endure these ponderous proceedings.

He felt the same way.

Rising before anyone could voice a rebuttal—particularly Mascos, re-growing an arm making him crankier than usual—the Warden cleared his throat. "Of this we are all aware, Ms. Castille. However, you and your colleagues must concede the unprecedented circumstances which have brought us to these negotiations. Un Quan did not 'petition' the U.P.C. so much as they were invaded by it."

Castille frowned. The general and councilman to her sides both raised affronted eyebrows but said nothing. "That is an unfounded allegation, Warden. And an insult, if I am to be frank. In fact, I believe the U.P.C. is being more than fair in even conducting these negotiations, all things considered."

The Warden smiled. "Meaning?"

Castille folded her arms and stared at him. "For one, we are allowing not only your presence, but also your participation, Warden. This is done strictly out of respect for the natives of Un Quan in naming you their advocate. You do not exist on any database we can find, and therefore, according to Star Law, should not be afforded the rights and privileges of any citizen of the U.P.C."

"Clearly you haven't dug deep enough into your databases. And if I hadn't providentially been forced to intervene in this incident, Jones and his troops—all trained by Star Cav and equipped with U.P.C. military hardware, I will point out— may very well have succeeded in conquering this system. And despite what he has claimed, there is no proof that Jones was not acting under someone else's orders...

"But all that is beside the point, ambassador. What matters here is that this planet has been exposed to technology and influences from our side of the galaxy. You and I both know that, now that the cat is out of the bag, every corporation and freebooting adventurer with a spaceship is going to come looking to see what the Un Quan system has to offer. And that is to say nothing of the fact that the door to Uncharted Space is now wide open. We've seen what Jones and his crew almost accomplished in a single day. We can't allow a larger operation to exploit this planet and its people. Admission into the U.P.C. is the only way to guarantee that sort of protection."

General Bohr cleared his throat. "We could always pull back to the Frontier and blow Jones's bridge. Call it no harm, no foul."

Thede interjected with a practiced smile. "That would indeed be a simple solution, General. However, we now possess much of the technology necessary to build our own Einstein-Rosen bridges and deep-space vehicles. Our studies have even begun accessing your network codes, eventually enabling us to connect any bridge we might construct with yours. I realize this is not in strict accordance with your U.P.C.'s laws of technological advancement, but there you have it. As the Warden put it, 'The cat is out of the bag.'"

Castille placed her hands on the table and glared at the Warden. "This, thanks to you. According to the gathered statements, you are the one who provided this level of technology to the scientists of Quan City. And by doing so, it was you who ultimately gave Jones access to this system."

The Warden folded his arms and bared his teeth. The accusation had scored a direct hit. "I did. But Jones worked under the U.P.C. and Star Cav's noses for eight decades while putting his plan together. If I hadn't come here by accident, he would have been here months ago on purpose. So, don't go trying to lay this all at my doorstep."

Jynnessa stood. "The Warden's arrival has helped us move toward a unified civilization. Is that not one of the requirements for admission to the United Planetary Council, Miss Castille?"

The human woman relaxed her expression as she faced the blue-skinned queen. "It is, Your Majesty. However, moving toward a unified civilization is a far cry from actually having an established, stable global socio-economic infrastructure. Un Quan is at least three or four centuries away from that level of civilization."

Thede shook his bald head. "Not so, ambassador. Un Quan had just such a civilization a millennium ago, and we still have the building blocks here in Quan City to recreate that global society. Now that the Warden has helped the age-old gender war come to an end, I believe that we may achieve what you are talking about in a few generations."

Castille sighed and shook her head. "A few generations—"

A holographic projection of Commander Morris, the captain of the *Silverheels* appeared above the conference table. "Please forgive the intrusion, ladies and gentlemen, but I'm afraid we have a potential crisis on our hands."

For the first time Councilman Pah looked interested as he rose from his chair. "What's going on, Commander?"

"Long range sensors have picked up a rather large signal approaching this system at a speed we've never seen before."

The Warden used his chrono to link Quantum into the conversation. "Is it a comet?"

Morris shook his head. "If it is, it's the fastest comet in recorded history. And if it is, I fear it could be a system-killer."

The commander's words hung heavier in the air than did his holographic image.

General Bohr slowly stood. "Well, until we have more information, I recommend we adjourn these proceedings as they may be all but academic in the near future. Ms. Castille, Mr. Pah, you will accompany me back to the *Silverheels.*"

The Warden scowled at the old soldier. "You can't mean to abandon these people, General."

"Until we know how much time we've got, there's no sense making promises we can't keep, Warden. If space and time allow, we will put in place a plan of action to evacuate as many people as possible. But, ultimately, my responsibility, Star Cav's responsibility, is to the citizens of the U.P.C."

Jynnessa gave a throaty, sarcastic laugh, sounding very much like her mother. "Which means your evacuation plans will begin with the soldiers who came to conquer our planet, I presume."

Bohr did not answer. He gave a curt bow and led the U.P.C. delegation from the room.

The Warden glared at them as they left. "Don't worry just yet. We'll think of something." He raised his chrono and said, "Quantum, meet me at the airfield. We're going to see if we can intercept that thing in the *Ranger* before it gets too close."

"I am running the pre-flight diagnostics as we speak, having anticipated your preferred course of action."

The Warden spared Jynnessa a hopeful smile as he headed for his ship.

"Admiral Thargrimm, we will arrive in the target system within the hour. What are your orders?"

"So soon? Someone must have noted our approach..." Thargrimm took a deep breath, slowly dragged his attention from the incredible vista of hyperspace unfolding outside the *Bellicose's* bridge. He turned to his newly assigned second in command, a slender, uncrested female named K'Luk. "Slow to maximum temporal space velocity and approach UQX from the far side of the system. Extend scans to maximum range and see what is waiting for us. This may be the finest combat ship in the Imperial Fleet, but if interstellar activity has occurred in that barbaric system, it is highly probable that it did not originate there. We could be approaching a Malcontent trap."

Commander K'Luk bowed slightly to her superior. "Yes, sir."

Thargrimm folded his hands in the small of his back as he returned his attention to the collective consciousness. "In order to make a plan, K'Luk, one must first have actionable information. Remember that. Information is the foundation of every good strategy, and thus every worthy military victory."

The admiral did not sense his subordinate's mind as he returned to the vast sea of species-wide knowledge, assuming that the young officer was too preoccupied with fulfilling her orders and making a good impression. Thargrimm was well aware of his reputation and elevated status in the Hrothshaar Imperial hierarchy, just as he was aware how that reputation placed many an underling in such consciousness-depriving awe. He did not hold this against these lesser minds as he had worked long and hard to acquire that reputation, and harder still to maintain it.

Peace had prevailed for far too long in the Empire, and he was a man bred for war. The ongoing skirmishes with Malcontent flotillas and terrorist cells did not constitute warfare in Thargrimm's mind. The actions felt more like the base work of an exterminator rather than the valorous efforts of a warrior.

Shielding these secret thoughts from the collective consciousness, Thargrimm rejoiced in the hope that this mission would result in the unleashing of his flagship's considerable arsenal. Against a *real* opponent. He hoped, too, that whatever they found in the quarantined system would prove worthy of elevating his status even higher in the eyes of the Radiant Council. Perhaps even an appointment to that august body. Such an appointment was the first step on the long road to being named the Hierophant, the Supreme One, ruler of the Hrothshaar Empire and most of the known galaxy.

Every plan requires solid intel and recon. That was one truth Solomon Jones had come to rely upon in his very long existence of conflict. So, in order to come up with a solution to his particular problem, he needed to know what was going on in the wider world outside his cell. To that end, he still had a trick or two up his sleeve.

The Un Quan scientists may have scrubbed his neural pathways of the master program, but they had not deprived him of the hardware he had used to explore the galactic data-stream for decades. Hardware that would allow him to interface with the *Silverheels*'s central computer system.

Having been a lawman and a prisoner aboard Star Cav ships in the past, he knew his way around a brig. He understood that behind the PlaSteel panels of his cell, there were pipes and conduits, cables, and wires—the ship's respiratory, circulatory, and nervous systems. He merely had to find the right set of wires and splice his neural net hardware into the system, and the ship's sensors would become his eyes and ears. If he played his cards right, he might take control of even more systems. The ship's coms would become his voice, and its weapons his fists.

The trick was doing this without getting caught. Jones glanced at the black orb in the ceiling of his cell, the *Silverheels*'s ever-watching eye. He knew the camera was linked into a network of other security cameras and fed to the brig's central control panel. There, a bored or tired Star Cav marine sat staring at a bank of monitors switching from feed to feed. Jones needed to know how many feeds there were per monitor, and how often those feeds switched. Once he had that information, the rest would be child's play.

He had seen the control panel and the guard when he'd been brought aboard and placed in his cell. But he'd still been groggy following the medical procedures he'd endured in Quan City. He needed another look now that his faculties were again sharp and his resolve fixed.

"Guard!" he shouted. "Guard! I need help!"

The Warden guided the *Ranger VII* up into Un Quan's crimson atmosphere, the silvery ship rising on a thunderous cloud of white flame. He sat at the controls of his beloved craft, feeling more at home than he had in months. If the cause for this reunion hadn't been so ominously dire, he might have indulged in a smile. He spared a glance at the photograph of Marajin he had attached to the console and took a deep breath.

"So, what do we know about this thing?"

Quantum sat in the copilot seat, monitoring the readouts. His three-fingered hands brought up a holographic display. This showed a hexagonal map of the star systems of the unexplored arm of the galaxy. A bright point of light, marked by time stamps and measured speeds, glowed in several of these systems. An almost straight line connected these points to the Un Quan system.

"Dr. Hydrax was giving me a tour of his Astro Sciences lab when I noted a strange signal at the extreme edge of his deep-space astronomical observations. With his permission, I made some modifications to the search algorithms and realized this signal was in fact a large body moving at phenomenal speeds. I sent this data to Commander Morris, who was able to use the *Silverheels*'s more advanced equipment to isolate and assess the object."

The Warden glanced at the holographic readout as the ship broke the atmosphere and entered the forever night of space. "There's something… *off* about its movements. What am I missing?"

Quantum turned, his antennae doing slow twirls above his big black eyes. "I am surprised you noticed. The object does not seem to be moving between the systems so much as… appearing in them, then disappearing to reappear in the next."

"Is it using ERBs? Could it be a ship of some kind?"

Quantum shook his head. "We have detected no energy signatures indicating any kind of wormhole, artificial or natural. This object, whatever it is, simply teleports—for lack of a better word—from system to system, apparently picking up speed in the process."

The Warden rubbed his chin. "Well, that sounds like an intelligent act to me. It's either a ship or a… a creature of some kind. I've heard the old spacers' tales of giant wandering monsters. Born and bred in the heart of deep space, they roam from planet to planet in search of food. I always thought they were just stories told to spook the rookies, an extension of the old maritime sailors' traditions." He looked again at the display. "But…"

Quantum made a clucking noise. "There is nothing in our present data to suggest a biological entity. The variables required for such an organism to evolve in outer space are so extreme as to be virtually impossible."

The Warden shrugged, somewhat relieved. But he knew as well as Quantum that space was infinite, and infinity meant infinite sets of variables. Anything was possible somewhere out there in the Cosmos.

"Well, I'm sticking to the belief that whatever it is, it's intelligent. That means we are more than likely about to make First Contact with another spacefaring species."

Quantum turned back to his controls. "According to your own histories, those rarely go very well."

The Warden grunted at the accuracy of the statement.

iii.

"Admiral, a craft has left the planet and appears to be on an intercept course."

Thargrimm stroked the bone ridges of his chin and glanced at his first officer. "From the planet? Not one of the vessels in orbit?"

K'Luk shook her uncrested head. "No, sir. This one seems quite small in comparison to the others detected by long-range scans."

Thargrimm scoffed. "The largest of which is miniscule in comparison to the *Bellicose*. I had hoped for more of a challenge if things come to blows, but I fear these interlopers will simply turn tail and run as soon as we enter the system. Especially if they are nothing more than a ragamuffin flotilla of Malcontents."

K'Luk nodded. "We have initial scan results coming in now." With a wave of her hand, the commander summoned a three-dimensional image to hover in the air of the spacious bridge. The image depicted a slender, dart-like craft powered by three wing-mounted atomic engines.

Thargrimm touched the glowing display, shifting the perspective to get a complete look at the ship. "No design with which I am familiar... I cannot find it in the collective consciousness... That insignia, the silver planet orbiting the golden sun. I wonder if that is the symbol of UQX's nascent military... Odd choice if so, considering it is a binary system... Can we get an image of the crew?"

K'Luk closed her eyes, concentrated, and projected two humanoid characters onto the holographic display. For reference, she also summoned the images of the green, blue, and yellow natives of UQX from the archives.

"Definitely alien," Thargrimm said, appraising the two figures revealed as the interceptor's crew. "This pinkish one is similar in form to the indigenous peoples of UQX, save for pigmentation, while the blue one resembles a subspecies only in skin color."

K'Luk smiled. "Then we will be making First Contact, Captain, something that has not happened in over a thousand years."

Thargrimm raised a hoary eyebrow. "If you would but recall your history, Commander, you would understand that this is not a cause for excitement, but rather one for special concern."

Six feeds per monitor. Thirteen seconds per feed. Continuous, non-randomized loop.

Solomon Jones had gathered this information when the guard led him past the brig's control station to sickbay, where a Star Cav medic had been nice enough to replace his bio-fluid cables. Jones had complained of dizziness and weakness, blaming the sub-par medical attention he had received from the scientists of Un Quan. In truth, the green-skinned Masters had done a remarkable job in "putting him back together" after stripping him of his power.

However, the lower quality, industrial cables that were standard issue aboard Star Cav dispensaries made for a much better means of splicing his neural pathways into the ship's command network. And now that he was safely tucked away in his cell again, he could get to the work of solving his particular problem.

Six feeds per monitor. Thirteen seconds per feed. Continuous, non-randomized loop.

That meant he had sixty-five seconds in which to work between his cell's feed displaying on the guard's monitor. Sixty-five whole seconds.

He recited Whitman as he got to work.

"*A noiseless patient spider,*

I mark'd where on a little promontory it stood isolated..."

"Sam Hill..."

The Warden stared at the enormous alien spaceship as it emerged from the shadow of one of the system's smaller inner planets. He honestly thought he'd never live to see a craft larger than the SuperCorp Sun Smasher, but this speeding, cigar-shaped behemoth dwarfed that experimental monstrosity. The fuselage was a contorted, almost writhing twist of bulges and orbs spiraling around a central elongated axis. Each of these dull, metallic protuberances appeared to be alive with moving gun turrets and rocket batteries. There were no visible engines to be seen anywhere on the thing.

Quantum scanned the craft. "There is something particularly strange about the vehicle's structure. It does not appear to be complete, or rather it is in a state of constant reconstruction."

"Bio-signs?"

"In excess of five thousand. Some strange chromosomal configuration, sharing similarities with mammalian, reptilian, and amphibian DNA."

"Here be dragons..."

Quantum tilted his head.

"We're in what we call 'Uncharted Space.' At the edge of our maps. On Earth, way back in olden times when men sailed the seas in wooden ships, fearing they might sail too far and tumble off the rim of the world, the mapmakers would draw fantastical beasts on the edge of the known with the warning, *Here be dragons.*"

Quantum returned his impassive gaze to the leviathan now overtaking them. "Your obscure reference appears to be appropriate."

The Warden opened a hailing frequency and hoped his ship's translators were up to the task. "Attention approaching vessel, this is the *Ranger VII* of Earth, a planet located on the opposite side of this galaxy. Please identify yourself and state your business in the Un Quan system."

There was a moment's pause before every piece of equipment capable of making sound erupted in a high-pitched squeal. Quantum slapped his hands to the sides of his head, protecting his pointed ears. The Warden pulled his cowl from his head as the inner speakers nearly blew his eardrums.

Quantum touched the console with a shaking hand. "They scanned our audio files, apparently in an attempt to learn our language."

The Warden winced, running a finger inside his right ear and stretching his jaw. "Heck of a way to say howdy."

"*Ranger VII, this is the* Bellicose, *flagship of the Hrothshaar Imperial Fleet. Please power down your engines and prepare to come aboard.*"

The Warden and Quantum exchanged glances. The *Bellicose* was now a few thousand meters from the *Ranger VII*'s nose, and the metallic monster obscured all of space. The constantly shifting gun turrets rolled around the alien ship's hull like hungry and deadly insects. With a shrug, the Warden deactivated the engines. "He did say, 'Please.'"

As soon as the *Ranger VII*'s engines were dormant, the Warden and Quantum found themselves—and their ship—inside a cavernous docking bay filled with menacing-looking assault craft. Phalanxes of hulking armored troops marched between the orderly rows of parked fighters, the alien soldiers each standing almost three meters tall.

The Warden blinked. "Did I black out? What just happened?"

Quantum shook his head. "I would surmise that the alien ship moved *around* us in a similar manner as it moved through space. I have insufficient data to formulate a hypothesis as to how this is done."

"*Crew of the* Ranger VII, *you will please exit your craft.*"

The Warden strapped on his gun belt as he headed for the hatch.

"Do you think that is a good idea?" Quantum asked.

"They've made a point of showing us their guns. They can see mine. Let 'em know we're not entirely cowed."

Quantum shrugged and attached his own sidearms to the thighs of his spacesuit.

The Warden checked the readout beside the hatch before exiting. "Looks like they breathe the same kind of air we do, so we won't need helmets and Ox."

"That is comforting."

The Warden smiled, finding Quantum's comment amusingly sarcastic even if it wasn't intended to be. Taking a deep breath, he donned his visored cowl and led his friend out of the *Ranger VII* and into the belly of the alien behemoth.

They were met by a score of soldiers. Their heavy armor reminded the Warden of something from a storybook or a historical documentary, something akin to what knights would have worn in Earth's Middle Ages. Matte black with gilded, gothic edges and high-crowned, face concealing helms, the eight-foot-tall warriors were intimidating to say the least, even if they hadn't been wielding multi-barreled carbines in their clawed hands.

"You will follow us."

"After you."

The Warden and Quantum fell in step with the armed escort, proceeding from the massive, oval-shaped hangar. The soldiers did not demand they surrender their weapons, which the Warden found interesting. The gesture was a clear signal of the aliens' martial superiority, as was the route they took through the landing bay.

The Warden catalogued at least fifty smaller craft being prepped under hovering globes of white light, ranging from single-pilot, bat-winged fighters to heavier, wasp-like assault ships and bulky orbital weapons platforms. He guessed there was an equal number of vehicles on the unseen side of the hangar. The *Bellicose* was aptly named. The flagship was a self-contained operational theater of war just waiting for a venue.

"You get the feeling they're showing us all this stuff for a reason?"

Quantum glanced around the busy hangar. "Clearly they are not overly impressed by us or the *Ranger VII*. Otherwise, they would not be so confident as to openly display their military assets."

"Something tells me this is just the appetizer. I've a sinking feeling there'll be a bigger demonstration of their perceived superiority served up as a main course before our tour is finished."

At the far end of the hangar, they stepped onto an elevated, bronze-colored platform. The leader of the detachment made a gesture with his hand. Walls of dull metallic hexagonal panels sprang up from the platform's edge to encapsulate the group. A moment later, the enclosed platform began to move.

Quantum looked at the walls appraisingly. "Preprogrammed nanobot construction and anti-gravity technology. However, I see no electronic interface, no wireless network." He addressed the officer, "Excuse me, but what is the basis of your operating system?"

The Warden was not surprised when the soldier did not respond. Grunts were grunts no matter which side of the galaxy they came from.

Presently, the anti-g platform came to a stop and the walls disintegrated, revealing a spacious, bronze-floored room with rows of gilt-arched viewports curving up to the high-vaulted ceiling. Balls of golden light hovered at intervals between these windows, giving the chamber a warm and pleasant glow. The far end of the room was dominated by a three-dimensional holographic display of the Un Quan system. Two tall figures in crisp black, leathery uniforms stood before this display, their backs to the new arrivals.

The twenty armored troopers stepped off the platform and took positions along the chamber's walls. The two figures at the opposite end of the room turned and approached. The Warden and Quantum moved to meet them.

"Salutations. I am Admiral Thargrimm, and this is my first officer, Commander K'Luk." The speaker was as tall and imposing as the armored soldiers. Thargrimm's voice was deep and raspy, as might be expected based upon his appearance. The Hrothshaar admiral looked like one of those fabled dragons of yore in human form, with bony crests framing his jawline, brow, and crown. His skin was a beautiful network of tiny golden scales touched with blue. The musculature of his face seemed surprisingly human for all that, his platinum-colored eyes possessing a not unfamiliar cunning and intelligence.

"Well met, Admiral Thargrimm. I am the Warden from Earth, a member of the United Planetary Council, and this is my friend, Quantum, a Mechtechan scientist." The Warden smiled politely as he made the introductions, noting the demure pose of K'Luk as she stood slightly behind her superior officer. The female Hrothshaar was almost as tall as Thargrimm, but less bulky with a sleek, serpentine build. Her face was scaled in a dull copper tinged with pale green, and devoid of the male's prominent bone ridges.

"I cannot agree that we are well met, Warden." Thargrimm inhaled deeply. The Warden got the sense that the admiral was smelling them, taking in their scents. "You and your kind are invaders of the Hrothshaar Empire, and I have been sent here to resolve the problem."

The Warden took a deep breath of his own. He hated these sorts of negotiations, knowing better than most that he was not the right person to handle them. "I can honestly say that we did not come here as invaders, Captain. In fact, it was a remarkable set of bizarre circumstances which brought us here." The less said about

Jones's incursion, the better. "But don't take my word for it, sir. Presently, a delegation of ambassadors from the U.P.C. are in orbit above Un Quan. I am certain they would be more than happy to speak with you on this topic, as well as begin the process of opening communication with your empire."

A cruel smile crossed Thargrimm's lips, revealing a neat row of fangs. "I am certain they would, Warden. However, I am not a politician nor an ambassador. I am a warrior. I follow orders, and those orders are to remove the interlopers from the Empire's frontier and to purge this system for reclamation."

"Purge… for reclamation? That doesn't sound very good."

"On the contrary." Thargrimm continued to smile as he beckoned them to one of the windows overlooking the inner desert world below. "It is a unique innovation in terraforming technology."

With a wave of his hand, Thargrimm launched a torpedo from his enormous ship's arsenal. The Warden watched the missile strike the planet's atmosphere and explode, sending out a brilliant blue shockwave that soon enveloped the entire world. Even from high orbit, the cataclysmic volcanic eruptions and tectonic upheavals could be seen on the planet's surface.

"In a dozen or so years, that planet will be habitable. I will do the same to all the planets in this system. So, please go tell your *delegation* that they are to take their people and withdraw from Hrothshaar space immediately. Else I will unleash considerably far more force in dealing with the small flotilla you now have in orbit around UQX… I believe you called it Un Quan."

The Warden gnashed his teeth. "Un Quan is already a habitable planet with a sentient population. You can't do that to them."

Thargrimm scowled, the bone ridges on his forehead extending slightly. "Yes, a *barbaric* sentient population. When we explored this system long ago, the race was locked in a genocidal war of self-destruction. Owing to their comparative level of technology, the species was labeled a possible threat and the system was quarantined. Standing orders declare that if the inhabitants of UQX ever gain interstellar space travel, they are to be exterminated."

The Warden flexed his fists, frustrated by the knowledge of *how* the Un Quan had gained access to interstellar travel. "You can't do this."

Thargrimm stepped close and scowled. "You can't stop me. Now go, tell your people to leave. I will temporarily hold position here. You have until UQX's orbit brings it in view of this planet, about seventy-two of your standard hours by my reckoning. That is the only *diplomatic* concession you will get from me, Warden."

"...Mark'd how to explore the vacant vast surrounding,
It launch'd forth filament, filament, filament, out of itself..."

"I really must insist that you and your... companion come aboard the *Silverheels* to continue this discussion, Warden." Kayla Castille tried very hard to maintain the appearance of authority over these proceedings, but the Warden doubted she was fooling anyone. She had been dispatched by the bureaucratic higher-ups to cobble together a simple appeasement policy for a primitive world in a backwater system, not to embroil the United Planetary Council in a First Contact situation with a galactic empire possessing inexplicable technology.

Queen Jynnessa raised her voice to the array of monitors displaying the U.P.C. delegation, "And I must insist, Ambassador Castille, that these proceedings now bear far more importance to the people of Un Quan than they do your so-called *Civilized* Worlds. So, if turning tail when things get hard is the U.P.C.'s preferred manner of handling things, by all means, gather your toys and go."

"This is an interstellar incident, Your Highness," General Bohr said from his monitor screen. "You'll forgive me if I point out that you do not have any experience with such matters."

"You mean other than an army of ex-U.P.C. soldiers invading our planet, General?" Jynnessa shot back.

The Warden stood and raised his hands to silence the frustrated and heated retorts from his constituents. He and Quantum occupied the embassy's conference room in Quan City, along with all nine of the gathered Masters, King Mascos, his captain Hurm, his son and heir, Prince Andres, Queen Jynnessa, and her captain, Sappoc. The U.P.C. delegates were present via digital transmission from the relative safety of the Star Cav destroyer, *Silverheels*.

"And you'll forgive me, General, if I point out that this has not yet become a military situation." The Warden waited for everyone to settle down before continuing. "Though I'd bet the farm on the fact that Admiral Thargrimm would be more than happy if it did. Which tells me we *all* need to make sure it doesn't."

Castille cleared her throat. "I demand to speak to this Thargrimm. As the duly appointed representative of the United Planetary Council, that is my right."

The Warden sighed. "I feel comfortable in speaking for the admiral on this matter, Ms. Castille. He doesn't care about your rights. Or anyone else's for that matter. He cares that he has a job to do, and the bloodier that job, the better as far as he's concerned. It is *our* job to make sure it doesn't pan out that way. All of us, the people of Un Quan and the delegation from the U.P.C."

General Bohr stroked his chin. "Perhaps this seventy-two hour stay is a sign of weakness. Perhaps he has to recharge his batteries or something after that hell-bent-for-leather trip to get here. Perhaps we should go ahead and strike now. I can have a dozen assault scout squadrons and six or seven destroyers and light cruisers through Jones's half-ass gate within sixty hours."

The Warden shook his head. "I think that would only result in getting all those crews killed and escalating this into a full-fledged war between the U.P.C. and this Hrothshaar Empire, sir."

"Then why does Thargrimm wait if he is so strong?" Castille asked.

Prince Andres offered an explanation. "Perhaps he doesn't want to start a war, either."

The Warden nodded. "That's part of it, I think. He doesn't want to start a war that he's not certain he can win. And at the moment, the U.P.C. is just as much an unknown variable to him as the Hrothshaar are to us. I think he's using this time to watch us. He's gathering intel, cataloging how we react to the situation."

Bohr exhaled. "All the more reason to show strength. If we tuck tail and run, it'll only invite these bastards to invade *our* Frontier."

King Mascos banged the glass globe of his arm's bio-tank on the table with a scowl. "I agree with the red-faced Bohr! If we are to die, then let us do it fighting. Like *men!*"

"Stupidly, you mean," Sappoc said, causing Hurm to rise from his seat at the table. Sappoc stood to meet him.

The slender Andres rose and scowled at the muscular warriors. His voice was low and hard. "That's right, you two. Act like savages. Make it easy for the U.P.C. to abandon us so this Thargrimm can destroy our planet. Now sit down and be silent."

The Warden nodded at the young prince, noting the approving smile Jynnessa gave her husband. The Warden said, "Now, if we can get back to brass tacks… Thargrimm said something about this world being visited a long time ago, during the Agenda Wars by his description. That is why Un Quan was isolated from the Hrothshaar Empire's expansion."

Dr. Hydrax said, "That was over a thousand years ago. Perhaps their technology was not advanced enough to invade and conquer us, or to destroy us outright back then."

"No."

Everyone looked to Quantum. He had spoken but not with his own voice. He sat very rigid, his big, black eyes fixed on a spot on the opposite wall. His antennae, normally slightly drooped or slowly twirling, now stood perpendicular from his elongated, blue cranium.

"No. It was not our technology that stayed us from destroying or annexing your world. It was our government. A millennium ago, the Hrothshaar Republic governed much of what has since become the Empire. However, as time passed, the Rule of Law was replaced by Majority Rule, which led to anarchy and the near collapse of our civilization. This crisis, in turn, gave rise to the Supreme Hierophant and the Empire. During these epochs of upheaval, your little system was all but forgotten as wars were fought against threat after threat, both foreign and domestic."

"What is going on?" King Mascos whispered, edging away from the apparently possessed alien.

Dr. Gamela stepped close and examined Quantum. "He appears to be in good health, but in a trance of some kind." She turned to the Warden. "You said the Hrothshaar technology seemed to work as if by 'magic.' Psychic or telepathic connection, perhaps?"

Quantum spoke again in that strange, almost effeminate voice. "Yes. Our spiritual bodies have evolved alongside our physical forms, allowing us to interact with reality on different planes of perception. This one is sensitive to these planes, allowing me to make contact with you in this manner."

The Warden knelt beside his friend. "Who are you? What do you want?"

"An ally... To help..." The voice sounded weaker and Quantum's head drooped. "Will contact you again, soon…"

Quantum's big eyes fluttered with uncharacteristic blinks as he sat up. "What… happened? I have the strangest sensation that I have acted foolishly."

The Warden smiled and clapped him on the shoulder. "I'll explain later."

"In the meantime," Castille said, "we still haven't got a plan of action."

The Warden faced the monitors. "If it's action you want, I know the perfect man for the job."

Councilman Pah scoffed. "What do you plan to do this time, Warden? Challenge this Admiral Thargrimm to a fistfight?"

"No. I want to talk to Commander Solomon Jones."

"…And you O my soul where you stand,
Surrounded, detached, in measureless oceans of space…"

iv.

"They are either heroically brave or immeasurably foolish. These interlopers have not begun evacuation procedures in the past six hours." Admiral Thargrimm stood on the bridge, watching the data come in from the advanced probes and long-range scans. He turned his attention to the three-dimensional holographic display of the system. "Perhaps they believe reinforcements will come through that prefabricated wormhole."

He knew that was a doomed hope, if indeed that was where the enemy's strategy lay. Once scans had revealed the nature of the structure, he had dispatched a squadron of stealth fighters on a roundabout route through the system. They had since taken up ambush positions near the outer gas giant, within easy striking distance of the bridge. On his word, they would destroy it, or, alternately destroy any spacecraft emerging from it.

"Commander," Thargrimm said. "Are the bombers loaded and ready?"

K'Luk stepped to his side. "Yes, sir."

"Then perhaps our unwanted guests need another demonstration of our sincerity."

"Are you ordering a preemptive strike on the alien flotilla, sir?"

Thargrimm turned on his subordinate with a low, rumbling hiss, surprised at the shock in her voice. "No. Though I would hope that you would not find such an order... questionable were I to give it, Commander."

"No, sir. Not at all. My reaction was merely based on the timetable you—"

Thargrimm ignored her and touched the holographic image of the planet closest to UQX, the one covered in an ocean of mercury. The gesture signified a command sent through the collective consciousness, a command immediately answered by thirty bomber crews. The crews boarded their ships and winged through space en route to the designated target.

"...Till the bridge you will need be form'd, till the ductile anchor hold,
Till the gossamer thread you fling catch somewhere, O my soul..."

The Warden and Quantum guided the *Ranger VII* toward the *Silverheels*'s docking bay, having received reluctant permission to meet with Solomon Jones. Surprisingly, most of the opposition to the meeting came from Councilman Pah, the Silesian showing far more interest in the matter than anything since his arrival on Un Quan. However, the Warden pointed out that not only had Jones once defeated an alien armada equipped with superior technology—the Mechtechan at the Battle of Draconus Prime—but also possessed the unique perspective of a general capable of commanding his forces with the precision of thought. This argument convinced Castille and Bohr to overrule Pah.

For his part, the Warden had second thoughts on confronting the Commander. Since the arrival of Star Cav had ended hostilities between Jones's cybernetic forces and the natives of Un Quan, the Warden had ruminated on the death of Marajin. And though he still felt a great deal of guilt for her loss, he had come to shift a significant portion of that blame to Jones. He was afraid of what he might do to the man when next he saw him.

Quantum adjusted the guidance rockets as the Warden powered down the main engines for docking. "What do you hope to learn from Jones that might resolve this situation?"

The Warden shrugged. "I don't know, maybe nothing at all. I've just got a hunch, a gut feeling that Jones still has a part to play in all this. I mean, none of us would even be here right now if not for him. It was his plan and singular drive which has brought us to this impasse."

Quantum made a clucking noise that reminded the Warden of Dr. Gamela. "I fear your sojourn on this planet has unduly fostered your poetic nature. I shall have to redouble my efforts in cultivating your logical thought processes in the future."

"Nice."

The sensors picked up a vast array of ships swinging around the system's twin suns at attack speed.

"*Attention* Ranger VII, *disengage docking protocol. I repeat, disengage docking protocol. We are now under general quarters and going to battle stations.*"

Quantum maneuvered the ship away from the destroyer. The small Star Cav flotilla and Jones's captured ships fired their main engines, moving into a defensive screen above the planet. "It would appear that Admiral Thargrimm is not a man of his word."

The Warden frowned, unable to reignite the *Ranger VII*'s engines for another three minutes while they went through their cooling routine. Charging the ship's cannons, he prayed they wouldn't need to use them. "You ever heard of a guy named Musashi? He was a legendary warrior from Earth's ancient past. He won a lot of duels to the death, many of them by showing up early or way late to a scheduled fight and taking his opponent by surprise."

"Not very sporting."

"War is never a sport. Like Musashi, Thargrimm understands that."

The speeding bomber formations veered off before approaching an attack vector on the Un Quan blockade. Instead, the thirty ships descended upon the small, nearby world of liquid mercury. The Warden watched in awe as the ships unloaded their payloads with amazing precision, turning the planet into an atomic holocaust with the intensity of a tiny sun.

The global inferno still burning white hot in their wake, the ships returned to the far side of the system in perfect order. Without so much as a communication to the Star Cav vessels. The entire operation had been conducted with the workaday efficiency of a routine drill. And yet a world had been utterly destroyed.

Quantum turned to the Warden. "I believe Admiral Thargrimm is growing impatient with our dearth of alacrity in leaving this system."

The Warden said nothing, trying hard not to imagine that kind of fury being unleashed on the people of Un Quan.

Solomon Jones sat alone in his cell aboard the *Silverheels*. And yet, now he had become the *Silverheels* and so was anything but alone. Of course, with the red-alert situation at hand, none of the two-hundred officers and crew were aware of this fact. Not yet at any rate, but that was soon to change.

"I'm surprised they sent someone of your elevated status, Councilman." He had to speak up to be heard above the clarion of alarms. He could have spoken through the intercom system, but that would have spoiled the surprise.

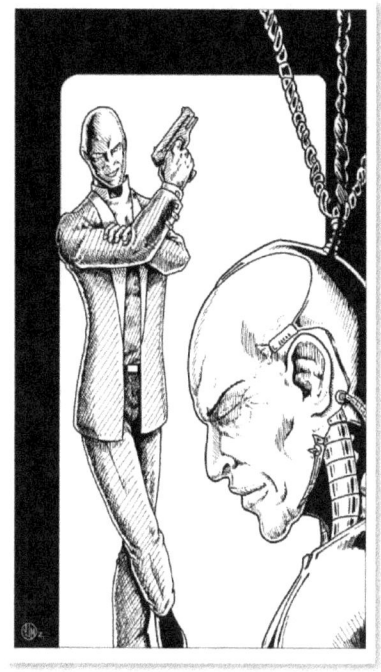

Jones did not open his eyes to see Ch'Koh Pah standing on the other side of the force barrier of his cell. He did not need to open them to see the small, untraceable blaster pistol in the politician's hand. The ship's internal security cameras were now his eyes. The same security cameras Pah believed he had successfully disabled before embarking on his mission of assassination.

"Before being appointed to the council, I worked the intelligence game for quite some time, Jones. I thought you'd have known that." Pah smiled as he activated the blaster's power cell.

"Oh, I do, Councilman. I also know that you are straining at gnats by coming here to make sure I keep your bosses' secrets. It seems to me that something much bigger is going on out there."

The Silesian laughed and glanced at the red lights flickering in the hallway. "It has been said, 'Never let a good crisis go to waste.'" He deactivated the cell's force barrier and raised the pistol.

An automated turret dropped from the ceiling at the end of the brig's hallway and fired a single blaster bolt. Councilman Ch'Koh Pah's headless corpse collapsed to the blood-spattered deck a moment before the sirens and alarms faded.

Jones smiled and turned his attention to the goings on outside the *Silverheels*, his new body. He witnessed the burning of the mercury world and the victorious departure of the bomber group through the *Silverheels*'s sensors, his new eyes and ears. He felt the ship's docking bays prepare for the arrival of the man he had once hoped to make his protégé. The man who had ultimately been his undoing.

Taking a deep breath, Jones waited to speak to the Last Star Warden. Quite possibly for the final time.

Admiral Thargrimm smiled, observing the bombers' return to the *Bellicose*. There would be no debriefing as he had witnessed the mission's success via the collective consciousness. While the crews had performed admirably, he had focused on the enemy ships surrounding UQX, studying their response to the perceived attack. He was more than satisfied that the pathetic flotilla could not stand against an assault from his support craft. There would be no need to commit the *Bellicose*, itself.

Thargrimm's musings were interrupted by a summons within the collective consciousness. The Radiant Council required a status report.

Hurrying from the bridge, Thargrimm made his way to his personal quarters. He darkened the lights and stood in the room's center, his hands folded at his back and chin resting on his breast. He took a deep breath and sent his mind across space and time to join with his superiors in the Council Chamber of the Imperial Palace in the city of Xaxnir on the planet of Hrothsha. With his undivided focus on the chamber and its important occupants and theirs on him, the connection created was far more real than any synthesized hologram. Thargrimm believed he was actually breathing the air of his home-world, over a hundred lightyears away.

"Admiral Thargrimm," the Hierophant said in a raspy voice, her silver and black robes of office enveloping her withered frame. At her advanced age, the Hierophant's silver-scaled crown and face were adorned with the bony crests and ridges like those possessed by males. "What is the status of the UQX situation?" The question, like this communion, was a courtesy given out of respect for Thargrimm's rank and reputation. The information was readily available via the collective consciousness.

Thargrimm bowed to the Supreme One and the six members of the Council flanking her. These occupied an elevated and curved podium, the black, gold, and red banners of the Empire draped behind them. Bright yellow sunlight bathed the crystal-domed rotunda. "The situation is well in hand, Your Excellency. The interlopers in the UQX system are aliens from beyond the Frontier and not Malcontent refugees as first suspected. Though they appear to have a large power structure and are an organized collective of various worlds and species, their comparative level of technology poses very little threat to the Empire."

A hulking, red-scaled male in gilded black robes at the end of the table leaned forward. "This assessment is based on what, exactly, Admiral? They do have interstellar capability do they not?"

Thargrimm nodded. "Yes, Lord Fingaar. But this technology relies on the artificial manipulation of wormholes rather than accessing the higher dimensions to fold space and time as we do. This requires vast amounts of energy and resources to achieve, not to mention the considerable time to manufacture and deliver such devices to distant systems. We have nothing to fear from this United Planetary Council."

The Hierophant hissed. "That remains to be seen…"

"Yes," Lady Sinthaire said from beside the Supreme One, her black scales glinting in the golden light. "For all we know, this United Planetary Council could be delivering these artificial wormholes to every system along our borders as we speak. And we have yet to determine the size of their military. You may be facing a mere scouting expedition, not a battle group."

Thargrimm nodded in acknowledgement of the critique. "This is true, my lady. "However, I have gathered valuable information concerning their military structure and capabilities from this small sample. I am confident that ours is the superior force in every conceivable way."

Lord Fingaar glanced at his colleagues. "What about the system itself? Have you begun the reclamation project?"

"I have initiated terraforming on one of the eight planets and have destroyed another, both as object lessons to the intruders in an effort to hasten their departure from Imperial Space. Although I am confident that I could easily win a military engagement with the aliens, I did not think it wise to attack them without cause."

The Hierophant nodded. "Yes. Wise. We control a vast Empire spanning the width and breadth of this part of the galaxy, but our resources are not without limit. And with the Malcontents pricking us like so many thorns, we would not wish to become embroiled in a war with an unknown agency. However, if these aliens persist in defiance, the security and the honor of the Empire must be upheld. You cannot, under any circumstance, withdraw from the UQX system without the complete success of your mission, Admiral Thargrimm."

"I understand and obey, Supreme One."

"Something's wrong." The Warden sensed danger as soon as he boarded the *Silverheels*. Admittedly, that wasn't a great leap after witnessing the Hrothshaar bombers destroy an entire planet as a simple show of force. "Commander Morris should have sent someone to meet us."

In fact, the docking deck was empty.

"Perhaps the crew is still under general quarters?"

The Warden glanced at a nearby inert light panel. "No, the red alert has been rescinded. Things should be back to normal." He raised his wrist chrono and opened a channel to the bridge. "Commander Morris, this is the Warden. Is everything all right?"

The answer came from the ship's intercom system, and the voice was not that of the *Silverheels*'s commanding officer. "I would not say that, Lieutenant. Everything is not all right, but it is under control. *My* control to be precise."

The Warden looked at Quantum, a sinking feeling in his gut. "Jones."

"Correct. Now, if you'd be so kind as to meet me in the brig, I'd like to have a chat with you."

The Warden and Quantum moved in that direction. "Where is everyone, Jones? What have you done with the crew? Where are the diplomats?"

Jones laughed from the speakers overhead. "Everyone is fine, Lieutenant. Well, not everyone... but for the most part, everyone aboard this ship is sleeping soundly at their post or in their quarters. Once I gained control of operations, changing the atmospheric mixture for a short time was a simple task. Do let me know if you feel yourself getting drowsy on your walk."

The Warden sniffed the air and detected a stale quality. "You said not everyone was fine. What have you done, Jones? Don't you think you're in enough trouble without adding murder and sabotage to your list of crimes?"

Again Jones laughed. "Murder? No, this was self-defense, pure and simple, as footage from the security cameras will prove. As for sabotage, well... if everything goes the way I want, I may just be able to help you with your Hrothshaar problem far more than Morris and his staff could. That is why you wanted to see me in the first place, isn't it?"

Quantum glanced at the Warden. "I wonder how long he has been in control of the *Silverheels*'s systems. If he has accessed all the communication and sensor logs and officers' journals, he may have a more complete picture of what exactly is going on right now than any single one of us."

"Listen to your blue friend, Lieutenant. Give me what I want and you, the U.P.C. crews and representatives, and the natives of Un Quan have a good chance of living happily ever after. But do hurry. If I have to administer another dose of bad air to the crew, I'm not entirely certain there won't be long-term adversities."

The Warden knelt beside a crewmember slumped against a bulkhead. The young woman was unconscious and would probably suffer from a severe headache when revived, but otherwise seemed to be in good health.

"Warden..."

He turned at the odd tone in Quantum's voice to see his friend standing rigid in the hallway, his antennae erect and his eyes vacant. "Oh no. Not now."

"Warden," the voice said again. "Listen to me. My name is K'Luk and I am the first officer aboard the *Bellicose*, but I am also an agent of resistance fighters the Empire has dubbed Malcontents. I am here to help you foil Thargrimm's plans..."

The Warden stepped close to his possessed friend. "That's great, K'Luk, but right now we're kind of in the middle of something. Can you come back later, maybe in a half hour or so?"

"No! I don't have that much time. You need to know that the Radiant Council has ordered Thargrimm to succeed in this operation at all costs. Either you defeat the *Bellicose* or Un Quan dies."

"But how? Even if your warship was a conventional vessel, we haven't the firepower in this system to match it. How can we hope to overpower something that can move with the speed of thought?"

"I have imprinted information on this one that will help. It is my hope that your U.P.C. will join us in our fight against the tyrannical Imperial government—Wait!—"

Quantum's back arched, a horrific cry escaping his throat like nothing the Warden had ever heard, and then the Mechtechan collapsed to the floor, spasming in unconsciousness.

"Quantum!" The Warden gathered his friend into his arms.

"Damned traitor." Thargrimm hissed as he dropped the two parts of K'Luk's carcass to the blood-splattered floor of her quarters. After his communion with the Radiant Council, Thargrimm had noticed his first officer conspicuously absent from the bridge. Not sensing K'Luk within the collective consciousness, he had searched the ship. "Damned Malcontent."

Battling the primordial rage and bloodlust threatening to steal his reason, Thargrimm took deep, long breaths to calm himself. He focused on his elite spiritual training, the training that allowed one to keep secrets and thus climb the social hierarchy. Retreating to his private psychic construct, he kept his thoughts from slipping into the collective consciousness.

He could not let it be known that a Malcontent had not only become a member of his crew but in fact his first officer. He would have to discover how the terrorists had accomplished this travesty and rectify the situation with more bloodletting. Much more bloodletting.

But for now, he had to focus on the mission at hand. There would be ample opportunity to cover up K'Luk's death in the coming confrontation. Of that he was certain.

Regaining complete control, Thargrimm closed his eyes and accessed the communications network. Speaking in a calm, clear voice, he addressed the alien flotilla orbiting the doomed planet. "Attention, invaders from the United Planetary Council. As you have shown no respect for the rather generous timetable I have given you to withdraw, I hereby rescind the offer. You will commence evacuation procedures immediately or you will be destroyed. That is all."

Sending another thought to the command bridge, he gave the order, "Launch all fighters."

V.

"Oh dear," Jones said. "The rest of the ships in the flotilla are asking for orders. It seems everyone with any authority is currently asleep aboard this vessel. What should I tell them to do, Lieutenant?"

The Warden gently shook Quantum until his friend regained consciousness. Turning his attention to the overhead speakers, he said, "You heard Thargrimm. If that transport doesn't descend and begin taking aboard refugees right now, he's going to do to us what he just did to that planet. So, if you want to talk, then I highly recommend you tell the other ships to start the evacuation immediately."

"Very well, Lieutenant. But I am still waiting for my *quid pro quo*."

Quantum rubbed his head as he got to his feet. He looked at the Warden. "I think I might know how to stop them. I will need to work with the scientists of Un Quan to do it. But time is of the essence." He gave a brief summary of his idea, based on the information K'Luk had imparted to him.

The Warden addressed Jones. "Let Quantum go back to Quan City as part of your... magnanimity and we'll talk."

"Fine. Now hurry."

After making sure Quantum had regained all his faculties, the Warden sent his friend back to the docking bay while he hurried to the brig. Things were happening fast now, and they were running out of time. Jones's complete control over the ship's operations alleviated this shortage to some degree by opening every hatch, even the secured ones, ahead of the Warden's approach. Meanwhile, the Commander maintained a running play-by-play over the speakers.

"Sensors are picking up over a hundred small ships on the far side of the twin suns. They are approaching Un Quan at attack speed."

The Warden frowned as he entered the brig. "A hundred? The *Bellicose* must have had at least one more hangar bay..." This rumination was lost when he approached the holding cells and saw the bloody remains of Ch'Koh Pah. "You killed a councilman...?"

"Self-defense, as I said." The audio speakers then replayed the bantering exchange between Pah and Jones before the fatal shot was fired. "Remember those questions you asked when I surrendered? Well, it seems Pah's superiors were afraid I might decide to answer them."

The Warden stepped into Jones's cell and came to an abrupt halt. The thing sitting on the bunk was a grisly remnant of the legendary man. The Commander's powerful cybernetics had been stripped down to the bare essentials, and his organic head and face had shriveled and flaked as if in the earliest stages of desiccation. He appeared little more than a human skull on a metallic skeleton.

Any residual hatred the Warden might have had for the man was instantly replaced by loathing and pity.

That is, until he looked into Jones's piercing black eyes. They were still alive with a cruel, cunning intellect. "Not much to look at, am I? Not this body at any rate. But spare me your pity, Lieutenant. I wear a new skin of PermaSteel armor plating. Atomic engines are my legs, torpedoes and blaster cannon my fists. And that is nothing compared to this ship's supercomputer which now serves as my intellectual playground."

The Warden stepped closer. "Well, I'm here to talk. Tell me what you want."

"You first. What did you want from me before I took control of the *Silverheels?*"

In truth, the Warden had a list of things he wanted from Jones: contrition, remorse, atonement, even a genuine apology. Any sign at all that the man who had once led him into Draconus Prime was still inside this metallic monstrosity. Any sign that he felt at least a little of the Warden's own guilt for the bloodshed the two of them had wrought on Un Quan. "I want your military expertise. How do we beat Thargrimm and that war machine out there?"

"That is the wrong question, Lieutenant. You can't beat him. Not with the pieces you have on the board."

The Warden tried hard not to look at the time ticking away on his chrono. He tried hard not to grab the cybernetic corpse in front of him and shake it until it begged for mercy. "Fine. Then what is the right question?"

"First, answer me this, Lieutenant: What do you have more of in this system than Thargrimm does right now?"

The Warden shook his head in irritation.

"Diplomats, Lieutenant, diplomats. He has the warriors, but you have the negotiators." Jones's ashen face flicked into a brief smile. "*How do we bring Thargrimm to the negotiating table?* That is the right question."

"I'll bite. How?" He hadn't come to play Twenty Questions with Jones.

"First, I want your assurance that you will do all within your power to force Un Quan, Star Cav, and the U.P.C. to agree to my demands. Give me your word of honor and I will tell you."

The Warden flexed his fists, feeling utterly helpless as an apocalypse amassed on metal wings somewhere just outside Un Quan's orbit. And it didn't help that he was forced to treat with the man—or whatever Jones had become—responsible for the death of the woman he had loved. "What are the demands?"

"First, I want an unconditional pardon granted to all my troops. They should not be held accountable for my crimes. Second, I want the inhabitants of Un Quan to bestow citizenship on those troops wishing to remain on their planet as peaceful colonists. Third, the U.P.C. will allow safe passage back to the Frontier for those who do not, as well as reinstating their military pensions. And I want a full and impartial investigation of every single name on this list."

The Warden's chrono chirped as data beamed to it. He glanced and saw a long, undulating list of names. Names of very important, very powerful people in the Civilized Worlds. He took a deep breath. "Is that all?"

"And I want a full-honors Star Warden funeral."

The Warden nodded. Jones understood he would not survive returning his consciousness to the frail thing sitting in the holding cell. This was the Commander's endgame. But the Warden couldn't let him off the hook that easily. "First, I want to hear you apologize for all the damage you've done to the people of Un Quan. You realize that if you'd never sent that ERB here, none of this would be happening. The Hrothshaar would still be ignoring this system."

Jones's dark eyes narrowed in his emaciated face. "And you would never have gone native, Lieutenant. You would never have found this world and its people. And, according to the records aboard this ship, you would never have helped unite them."

The Warden clenched his jaw. He never would have known Marajin.

Jones sighed in a very human way. "I have my regrets, Lieutenant, as all men do. In fact, I am certain I have more than any man alive, considering how long I've lingered on in this existence. Do I wish things had gone differently here? Absolutely. Did I allow the cybernetic master program to unduly influence my personality? Probably. But I know that what I did, I did for the right reasons. I am sorry for the violence and for the woes I have wrought not only here but all across the Frontier.

"But if you are completely honest with yourself, Lieutenant, you know as well as I do that the Hrothshaar would remember this system eventually, and one day they would still come for Un Quan."

The Warden stood silent for a moment. "Very well, I give you my word of honor as a Star Warden that I will do all within my power to see these, your final wishes, carried out, Commander Jones. Now, how do I get Thargrimm to negotiate instead of annihilating us?"

"You give him what he most desperately wants."

"Meaning?"

"From what I've gathered, this Thargrimm is a warrior, taking orders from higher-ups, just like every other soldier in history. Soldiers are ultimately pawns, and every pawn secretly dreams of becoming a queen. I'm guessing that Thargrimm—who made a point of declaring his ship as the flagship of his empire's fleet—is both dedicated and ambitious. This tells me that he sees himself only one or two squares away from the edge of the board, and thus gaining his crown."

"We don't have time for games, Commander. Just tell me straight out what I need to do."

"I am telling you, Lieutenant. You give Thargrimm whatever he needs to add another ribbon to his chest, another oak-leaf cluster to his collar, another star to his epaulet, another silver ring to his arm, or whatever it is that his people do to reward and honor military achievement. You give him another square on the board. You give him a victory. A *military* victory."

The Warden nodded. "We don't just withdraw. We surrender?"

"It's how you beat me, remember? You buy the time you need to spring your trap. We take the *Silverheels* and give it to him as a trophy."

"And over two-hundred prisoners?" The Warden stalked around the cell and shook his head. "He already holds all the cards, and you want to give him our one ace? Well, not our only one..." He thought of the plan Quantum had briefly outlined in the corridor.

Jones chided him with weak laughter. "For all your bravery and dumb luck, you really aren't the brightest star in the sky are you, Lieutenant? I was listening when the alien spy contacted your Mechtechan friend. And as the blue boy pointed out, I've got a better picture of all the variables in this situation. Including a very big, *clear-as-day* pair of variables right at the heart of the system."

The Warden raised his head. "The twin stars."

"Yes. I don't care how fast the *Bellicose* is, you get it trapped in the barycenter between those suns and one of three things will happen before it can escape."

"The three body problem."

"So, you did pay attention in your astrophysics class. Depending on the mass of the ship and the gravitational pull of the two stars, the *Bellicose* will either be crushed, torn apart, or ejected from the system by force."

"The only catch is getting that monster into the barycenter."

Jones chuckled. "After seeing what you have accomplished up to now, that shouldn't be a problem for you, Lieutenant."

The Warden did not share the Commander's confidence in his abilities on this particular occasion. He did, however, have complete faith in Quantum, Dr. Gamela, and the people of Un Quan.

Thargrimm sat alone in his darkened cabin. His eyes glowed in the dim light reflected through the window from the planet below. Explosions of green, red, and violet lightning rent the frothing firmament of the terraforming world, remaking the planet in the Hrothshaar Empire's image.

As impressive as the spectacle was, Thargrimm paid it no heed. He focused on other places and times, and other planes of reality. He wandered the collective consciousness in search of his deceased first officer's memories. He needed to know how K'Luk had passed the fleet screenings, how she had infiltrated his crew—the most prestigious assignment in the Imperial Fleet—who her contacts were, what her mission had been, and, most pressing at the moment, what information had she passed to these U.P.C. aliens.

Ordinarily, this would not have been a difficult exercise for one so well trained in accessing the higher dimensions as Thargrimm. However, it appeared that the Malcontent spy had been equally well-trained. No matter where he went among the thoughts and memories of the crew, there was a grey space around the mental image of K'Luk. It was as if she had been forgotten the moment each crewmember left her presence and not thought of again until she reappeared in the normal course of duties. He could not find a place to start his investigation, he could not find a thread to pull to unravel her conspiracy.

This level of anonymity hinted at some preternatural ability far surpassing any training or esoteric study Thargrimm had yet encountered. If the Malcontents were capable of such prowess in moving undetected through the collective consciousness, there may be no limit to what they might achieve if left unchecked. This realization frightened Thargrimm, but it frustrated him more. As he had told K'Luk upon embarking on this mission, information was the foundation of every good strategy, and now he found himself with a gaping hole where that essential information should be.

The communications officer's consciousness addressed him: "The aliens have begun evacuation of UQX, sir."

Thargrimm returned to the material plane of consciousness. "Order the battle craft to hold their position within striking distance. Reinforce the stealth craft at the wormhole." He did not trust his enemy. The man calling himself The Warden gave the impression of one inclined to reckless and daring misadventure. These aliens could not win a fight here, but they might still be capable of hurting his force, and thus his reputation.

"Yes, sir."

"I am on my way to the bridge." Thargrimm stood and activated the lights of his cabin, made a quick appraisal of his clean uniform and hurried into the corridor. If the alien evacuation was genuine and not some ploy disguising an attack, then this encounter would be a success. However, if the Warden and his allies did try something, a decisive victory would go a long way in gaining Thargrimm access to the Radiant Council. After all, no other military commander had bested a rival power's forces in combat in several decades.

As his hopes rose, however, Thargrimm's keen instincts warned him that there may be some danger yet lurking in this system. If not to his ship and crew, then certainly to his ambitions. K'Luk's treason still remained an unknown variable.

"I vehemently protest this *negotiation*." Ambassador Castille's nostrils flared as she faced the three men in the small room. She was the only civilian present, and it was clear that she was fighting tooth and nail to maintain her authority over this diplomatic mission. "Jones has hijacked this vessel *and* killed a member of this delegation—a sitting councilman, no less!"

The Warden stood with his back against the ship's ready room wall, arms folded across his chest. "An act of self-defense which has been borne out by audio and video evidence."

Castille glared at him. "Systems over which Jones has complete control. He probably doctored them!"

The Warden shrugged. "He didn't doctor that unregistered blaster in Pah's hand, and there's no way Jones could have physically placed it there, wired to his spot in his cell as he is."

"I still refuse to treat with him. He is a criminal."

Jones's voice came over the intercom speakers. "I have not been formally tried, much less convicted, ambassador. And, under Star Law, I am innocent until proven guilty. Besides, I am not asking for anything for myself save a decent funeral. I think I've earned at least that much, considering you would never have been conceived, much less born if not for my actions at Draconus Prime."

General Bohr sighed heavily. He sat at the small conference table with Commander Morris, rubbing at the residual pain in his brow. "I can... petition Star Cav and the Joint Chiefs on behalf of Jones's troops' benefits. However, the issue of the pardon will ultimately be decided by the United Planetary Council."

The Warden said, "Ms. Castille, if you can convince one of your superiors to bring forward the motion, I will testify on the troops' behalf. We have sufficient scientific and medical data from Dr. Gamela's research into the cybernetic master program to make a solid case."

"I will take it under consideration. However, as long as Jones retains control of this ship and its systems, he is essentially holding a gun to our heads during these negotiations. It is very hard to come to a compromise when one is not being treated as an equal."

Jones laughed. "Equality is a myth, Ambassador. In every encounter and every interaction, one party always holds more influence and power than the other. Now, the fact that you think I am the one holding the gun is rich. I have nothing save the hope that my legacy will be to save the men and women who bravely and honorably served under me. As soon as I turn over control of this ship, I am one with the Cosmos, free of all worries and concerns. You, on the other hand, still have that big damn Hrothshaar battle group out there to deal with. So, what is it going to be?"

Castille frowned, chewing her lower lip in silent consternation.

The Warden guessed she wanted to consult her superiors back in the Civilized Worlds, or at least play for more time to think. But there was no time. He helped her along with her decision. "But, putting all that aside for now, Jones's plan is the best we've got to deal with Thargrimm and his ultimatum."

Commander Morris rubbed at his temple in frustration. "As long as he refuses to give us control over this ship, it is the *only* plan we've got. Essentially, he will only give me my boat back if I agree to give it to that monster out there."

General Bohr cleared his throat. "Jones is technically a terrorist, Warden, and standard procedure is to never negotiate with terrorists."

Jones's voice filled the room. "Perhaps, but Star Cav Black Ops certainly had no qualms about hiring this 'terrorist,' General. I can display the particulars of several missions on the room's screens, if you'd like."

Bohr huffed. "That won't be necessary!"

The Warden stepped to the window and stared out at the rows of over a hundred gleaming black assault craft silhouetted against the system's twin suns. "Besides, General, I would hardly call any of this 'standard procedure.'"

Castille pointed at the Warden. "You still haven't told us how this plan is going to work. We give up to these aliens, become their prisoners, and then what? Why are you not telling us everything? Are you in cahoots with Jones? Have you been his errand boy all along?"

The Warden kept his eyes focused on the menacing fighter craft just a few thousand kilometers away. "I'm keeping some cards close to the vest, Ambassador, because our opponents in this situation show a remarkable knack for psychic communication. The fewer people who know what we've got planned, the less likely the Hrothshaar will find out before we're ready to put that plan into action."

Bohr ran a hand through his silvery hair. "I still say we should call Star Cav for reinforcements. Even if Jones controls this ship, we could get a couple of dozen that he doesn't here within a few hours."

The Warden shook his head. "And what do you think Thargrimm will do as soon as another warship enters this system, General? Besides, if I were him, I'd already have the ERB under guard. If they decide to destroy it, we're all done for and the U.P.C. may never know exactly what happened here."

Commander Morris leaned back in his chair. "I believe it was General George S. Patton of the 20th Century who once said, 'A good plan today is better than a perfect plan tomorrow.' And right now, I don't see another plan on the table. I certainly can't think of one."

Castille sniffed. "Actually, he said, 'A good plan *violently executed* today is better...' But that's all military intelligence can fathom: violence and executions. There has to be another way. There has to be a diplomatic solution."

The Warden nodded. "I agree. We just have to find it, and I think Jones's plan is the best way to buy the time to do so. But in order to put that plan into action, we have to give him what he wants."

Castille rolled her eyes and crossed her arms. "Fine. If we survive this nightmare, I will petition every councilperson I know to propose general pardons for Jones's troops."

Morris sighed. "Well, this is still a warship, Warden, and Star Cav, though in service to one, is not a democracy. We can't simply have a vote with majority rule. We must follow the chain of command."

Castille scoffed. "Even under these circumstances?"

Morris stared at her evenly. "Especially under these circumstances, Ms. Castille. Now, I am captain of this boat, but am outranked by General Bohr. I defer to your seniority, sir. What are your orders?"

Bohr stood and slowly moved his massive frame around the small space, his chin on his chest. The Warden could tell the aging soldier was none too happy to have this, possibly the most important decision of his lengthy military career, being foisted upon him at its conclusion.

And yet, the man rose to the occasion. Bohr halted, stood straight and said, "Signal the *Bellicose* and request terms for our surrender."

Jones's voice came over the intercom. "Excellent. Now, as soon as the people on Un Quan agree to give amnesty to my troops, I will return control of this ship to you and I shall shuffle off this mortal coil."

The Warden sighed, fearing the negotiations taking place in Quan City were far more heated than the debate which had just concluded in the ready room.

vi.

"Surrender?" Thargrimm raised his brow ridge in surprise.

"Yes, sir," the communications officer said. "The largest of the alien warships, designated *Silverheels*, has requested terms for their surrender. They claim they cannot remove their personnel from the planet in a safe and timely manner. As an acknowledgement of our tactical superiority in this situation, they are suing for mercy."

Thargrimm narrowed his eyes, sensing a trap. He mentally prodded the helmsman for a sensor report.

"We have detected strange energy readings aboard the craft, as well as some slight fluctuations in the crew's life-signs. However, the ship has not powered up its energy weapons, nor armed its projectile warheads."

Thargrimm pored over the details of the sensor report, noting that the fluctuations seemed to coincide with the time of K'Luk's treachery. "What are they playing at…?"

"What shall I tell them, sir?"

Thargrimm nodded to the communications officer. "Tell this… *Silverheels* to confine crew to quarters, to approach at one-quarter speed, and prepare to be brought aboard. We will then send an armed detachment aboard their ship to retrieve the command crew and the one called Warden." He hoped that by questioning the officers and the Warden, he might learn more about K'Luk's mission and the overall goals and abilities of the Malcontents.

As the message was relayed, Thargrimm sent a mental command to the assault force, ordering two fighter wings to escort the alien craft back to the *Bellicose*, while the remainder of the attack ships targeted the rest of the flotilla in preparation for battle. Once the alien ships were destroyed, the flight leaders were to target the population centers on the surface of UQX.

If this is a trick, it will cost them dearly.

"Clemency? You cannot be serious!"

The Warden stared through the monitor on the *Silverheels*'s bridge at the flustered face of King Mascos. "I understand your feelings, Your Majesty. Believe me. I do. But we've got bigger fish to fry here than these soldiers. Most of whom genuinely came here looking for a new and peaceful life. You have the power to give them that, and by doing so, give your planet and your own people a chance at a future."

Queen Jynnessa showed far less emotion than her father-in-law as she said, "You ask a great deal, Warden. These men and women came here to our world as combatants and invaders. They killed so many and almost enslaved the rest of us. And now you want us to embrace them with open arms?"

The Warden did not look at the other people on the bridge, knowing Castille, Bohr, and even Morris were silently appraising him, second-guessing his every word. They knew the success of their desperate ploy depended on convincing the natives of Un Quan to cooperate. The *Silverheels* moved inexorably toward captivity as the conversation unfolded.

"I want you to take a chance on them. Just like you took a chance on me once upon a time. I, too, was a captive spaceman from the other side of the galaxy, if you recall. And if you hadn't set me free, well…"

He watched as Jynnessa raised her chin. "If I hadn't freed you, then we would still be at war with the males, and we would never have discovered the wonders of the Ancients. We would not be moving toward the rebirth of our civilization."

The Warden didn't say anything for a moment. "You give me far too much credit, Your Majesty. But just the same, I honestly believe that the men and women you now have under arms can offer you an even greater chance at that rebirth. If you don't agree to this, the Hrothshaar may very well destroy this entire system."

As this exchange took place, the Warden noticed Dr. Gamela and Thede conferring quietly at their side of the table. After a moment, the Administrator cleared his throat. "We of Quan City are not necessarily opposed to adding these individuals to our population. Dr. Gamela has reason to think that their genetic makeup is similar enough to our own that it will only strengthen our depleted genepool. However, it is our concern that this large a migration will seriously damage our culture. We need assurances that this will not happen."

The Warden raised both eyebrows behind his visor. At first, he had no answer to this unexpected concern. But, looking at the blue, yellow, and green people at the table and remembering his experiences on the planet of Un Quan, he said, "Well, Thede, just look at yourselves, those of you gathered in that room. Tell me what you see."

He watched the natives glance at one-another, then study the members of the other factions. No one spoke for fear of saying the wrong thing.

"I'll tell you what I see," the Warden said. "I see a proud race of warriors and enlightened scientists. The people you are holding prisoner are nothing if not warriors and scientists. As Dr. Gamela can tell you, and as you have seen all too well for yourselves, their blood is just as red as your own. We are all the same color on the inside. If you can get past the differences that are only skin deep, then you should have no problem with assimilating the troops who wish to join you."

"Very well, Warden. We will confer."

"Holy Cosmos!"

The Warden looked up from the monitor at Commander Morris's exclamation. The *Silverheels* had just cleared the twin suns and hove into view of the *Bellicose*. The massive warship still orbited the violently terraforming world like some gigantic demon perched above a portal to hell.

Bohr stood at the forward window, his hands folded at his back. Shaking his head, the big man said, "What we could have done with a ship like that in my day..." Then, quietly, "What can we hope to do against it now?"

Castille moved close to the Warden and spoke in a low voice. "You say these... people look like dragons? Do you... think they'll eat us?"

The Warden placed a hand on her shoulder and gave her a comforting smile. In his experience, every militaristic spacefaring race had evolved from predators. Still, he said, "For all I know, Ambassador, they could be vegetarians. Besides, I don't plan on giving them the chance to try."

"Warden," Thede said, drawing his attention back to the monitor. "We have come to a decision. We agree to Commander Jones's *request.* The troopers who choose to remain on Un Quan will be afforded the full rights and privileges of its native population, including responsibility to its laws and customs."

"Thank you." The Warden glanced at the speaker above his head. "Does that work for you, Commander?"

After a lengthy silence, Jones's voice replied. "Yes. Thank you. But, before I go, may I have a private word, Warden?"

The Warden paused. His resentment for the death of Marajin resurfaced, but he fought it down. "Absolutely."

Taking his leave of the bridge, the Warden hurried to the brig and Jones's cell. Though countless thoughts flew through his mind like blaster bolts in a firefight, the Warden kept coming back to the notion that Solomon Jones, his one-time hero and later enemy, was the only other member of his generation left in the entire galaxy. Now he was about to die.

And I truly will be the Last Star Warden...

"So glad you came." Jones did not speak through the ship's intercom system. His voice was weak and raspy, like a man dying of thirst. The Warden turned to the water dispenser in the cell's wall, but Jones stayed his hand. "Don't bother. It will only come back up and keep me from saying what I need to say."

The Warden stepped close to the metallic skeleton that had once been the First Star Warden. He knelt and looked up into the man's dark eyes, still alive and human though so much else of him was not. "All right. I'm here."

Jones's claw-like cybernetic right hand moved slowly to rest on the Warden's left shoulder. "I want you to know that I truly am sorry..."

The Warden nodded but said nothing.

Jones's eyes looked away, as if spying something in the distance. "And… at long last, I am afraid… I have lived so long that I have forgotten how to die. I have become something so… unnatural, I don't think that part of the accepted cycle of things is still in me…"

The Warden swallowed. "What are you saying?"

Jones looked at him again. "I'm saying, Lieutenant, that I need you to kill me. I can't keep my word and give this ship back, as it is the only thing tethering me to this existence… And I don't want to go…"

"If you don't, you'll die anyway. This ship is the only thing signifying any hint of a threat or opposition to Thargrimm in this system. If you don't surrender, we're all dead."

Again Jones's eyes went distant, tears forming along the lower lids. "It is a hell of a thing… After all these years, all the fights, the battles, and the victories… my final act will be one of defeat…"

"No." The Warden put his hand on Jones's shoulder. "This is your plan, and I think it will work. And when it does, this will be your victory. Possibly even more significant than Draconus Prime."

Jones's desiccated lips curled back in a death's head grin. "That… was just luck. I had no idea it would work."

"It was an act of faith, then. Well, have faith in this, Commander, and let go.

You've earned your rest, your freedom to join the Cosmos. Your watch is done, Star Warden."

A long, shuddering breath rattled the cybernetic frame. Jones's dark eyes narrowed, as if trying to impart one last thing to the Warden.

"Thank... you..." The light went out of those eyes and the cybernetic body went completely still. The lights in the cell flickered and a squeal of static erupted over the intercom.

A few seconds later, another voice came over the speakers. "*This is Commander Morris. All systems are back under our control. All nonessential crew are ordered to remain in their quarters. That is all.*"

The Warden slowly got to his feet. He stood to attention and snapped off a crisp salute to Solomon Jones. Then backing away, he raised his chrono and requested a medical team to the brig. The Commander would need to be prepped for his full-honors funeral.

After seeing the medics off, the Warden headed back to the bridge. Along the way, a signal came in on a private, encrypted channel to his chrono. It was Dr. Gamela.

"Is everything ready?"

The Master of Biology's lined green face frowned on the tiny screen. "Your friend Quantum has had the devices in production since his return. We can have about a thousand distributed to those within the city in the next hour or so."

The Warden inhaled sharply. "I don't think that will be enough. Thargrimm has a crew of some four or five thousand, and they *know* their technology. You need more people."

Gamela clucked her tongue. "There are no more people, Warden. Unless we try to round up more of the jungle inhabitants and convince them, and that could take considerably more time than we have."

"What about the prisoners? Jones's people?"

Gamela blinked, but said nothing.

"You're going to have to start trusting them at some point, Doctor. And there's no time like the present."

"...Very well. I will authorize it, but I do not think Thede will be too happy about it."

"He'll be ecstatic if it works."

"And if it doesn't," she added with a sigh, "he'll be dead along with the rest of us."

vii.

"How in hell did they do that?" Bohr asked. The *Silverheels* had just materialized in an enormous, cavern-like hangar bay inside the *Bellicose*. The Star Cav destroyer was surrounded by what appeared to be an entire battalion of armored troops with support weapons.

The Warden shrugged as he placed his gun belt and Comet blasters into the bridge's safe. "I suppose we can ask them, but don't count on any answers unless Thargrimm is still in a mood to show off his superiority."

A raspy voice came over the coms. "Silverheels, *prepare to be boarded. Please note that any resistance will be met with extreme prejudice.*"

Commander Morris straightened his tunic. "Ambassador, gentlemen, shall we make our way to the boarding hatch and greet our captors?"

The Warden nodded, gave Castille a reassuring smile as Morris led his command staff from the bridge. By the time the small group reached the hatch, a squad of Hrothshaar marines had crowded into the corridor. The tall warriors had to hunch to keep their crested helms from scraping the PlaSteel ceiling tiles.

General Bohr stepped to meet them. Standing tall, he spoke in a deep baritone. "I am General Leonidas Bohr of the United Planetary Council Star Cavalry. As senior officer aboard this vessel, and in this theater of operations, I hereby surrender myself and my command into the hands of Admiral Thargrimm and the Hrothshaar Empire. I expect all officers and crew to be treated with the due respect owed them."

A soldier in red-trimmed black armor, apparently the detachment's leader, stepped forward and scanned the human captives with a device in his left gauntlet. "Is this the entirety of your command, sir?"

"It is."

The Hrothshaar squad leader checked his device. "You will accompany my team to temporary quarters. The one called Warden will come with me."

"Very well." The Warden nodded. He had expected Thargrimm would want to speak with Bohr or Morris, but then the Warden had previously met the alien admiral. Perhaps Thargrimm thought he could "pick his brain" more easily owing to that sense of familiarity.

Castille spoke up, the strength of her voice belying any unease she might have felt. "I am the duly appointed ambassador to this system. I demand to speak with your commanding officer in order to open a channel of communication with your empire on behalf of the United Planetary Council."

The Hrothshaar soldier ignored her. "Please follow us."

As the squad led them from the *Silverheels*, a company of armored troops boarded the captive ship behind them. The Warden doubted Thargrimm would order his men to massacre the ship's crew while they were confined to quarters, but he knew there was not a blessed thing to be done about it if he did. The Warden could only pray that cooler heads would prevail, and this encounter would not result in a galaxy-spanning war that could leave countless worlds decimated for centuries.

Bohr leaned close to him as they crossed the hangar. "I hope you know what you're doing, Warden. Even if this works, they are gaining priceless intelligence concerning our military spacecraft as we speak."

The Warden frowned at the apparently older man. "Loose lips sink ships, General."

While the rest of the squad led Morris and his command staff, the general and the ambassador aboard one of the nanotech "elevators," the leader stepped back against the hangar wall and stood to attention.

The Warden looked at the armored warrior with curiosity. "We waiting for the next ride?"

"No, Warden. You are waiting for me… That will be all sergeant."

The Warden turned as Thargrimm stepped from the shadows of the immense room. The squad leader departed, leaving the admiral and the Warden alone in a vacant space half a kilometer from the nearest body of armored troops. The Warden was keenly aware that he had left his pistols aboard the *Silverheels* so as not to provoke an altercation with the boarding party. He questioned that decision when the much larger Hrothshaar officer slowly circled him like a predator sizing up its prey.

"I do not trust you, Warden. In fact, I do not trust any of your kind. Most reasonable people would have seen that there was no way to win a confrontation with my forces and taken advantage of my offer to withdraw in peace some time ago. However, you lot have stubbornly remained here in this system, cut off from any hope of reinforcements. I want to know why."

The Warden slowly turned to keep his eyes on the circling admiral. "I have lived among the people of Un Quan for a little time and have grown fond of them. Even if the Star Cav ships had taken their troops and their officials back to U.P.C. space, I would have remained to prevent you from destroying this world. I have friends down there. Loved ones. Does your culture understand the concept, Admiral?"

Thargrimm's saurian face split into a sly grin. "We understand honor and family bonds, Warden. So, to a certain extent I suppose I can empathize—that is your word, isn't it—I can empathize with you in this matter… But you still haven't answered my question. Why has your U.P.C. not withdrawn? Are they hoping that I will start a war that will justify their expansion into our territory? Or are you secretly allied to the Malcontents? Are you waiting for them to trigger some secret plot in hope of turning the tables in this encounter?"

The Warden raised his chin. Thargrimm had just given something away, a hint of uncertainty, a hint of fear. He did not yet know what K'Luk had told Quantum, and his suspicions had amplified that uncertainty into a legion of possible surprising dooms. "The U.P.C. delegation came here to find a peaceful means of opening channels with the people of Un Quan. When you arrived and informed them that the system lay within the borders of your empire, they quite naturally hoped to open those same peaceful channels with your government."

Thargrimm hissed. "You talk a great deal about 'peaceful' channels and 'peaceful' negotiations, Warden. And yet it is your people who are forcing my hand to wage war."

"Only because war is apparently all you understand, Admiral. You are a tool of conflict, not of peace. You are simply not the right man for this job, sir."

"Oh, but I am." Thargrimm moved like a striking cobra.

The Warden gasped for air as he found the admiral's massive, claw-like hand encircling his neck, lifting him off his feet. Before he could lash out in self-defense, the Warden had already left his body somewhere very far behind.

Thargrimm had not been sure that the Warden's human mind could be drawn into the Hrothshaar collective consciousness, but no great military career was ever made without taking risks.

Here, in the higher dimensions, the man's psyche had no shape, no form. It was simply a multifaceted smear of scintillating colors and cacophonous sounds, unlike Thargrimm's own solid psychic construct or the artificial region he had created in the collective consciousness. Sealed off from the rest of his species' thoughts and knowledge, Thargrimm's private sanctum manifested as a high windswept aerie beneath a starry sky. Scudding clouds drifted across a plane of ice and fire far below.

Thargrimm studied the alien mind, appraising it for a moment. He had expected the shock, fear, and pain radiating from the Warden's persona, but the man's sense of wonder and inner resilience genuinely surprised him.

"Where are we? What have you done to me?" The Warden's thoughts boomed and whispered in weird echoes, assaulting Thargrimm's mind with the power of his emotions.

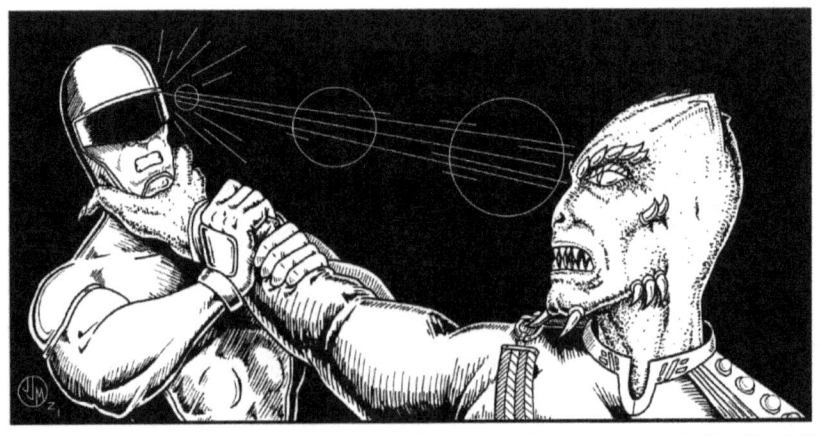

"Be still, Warden." The admiral would have to exert some of his own will to stabilize the human personality if he was to achieve his goal. "Calm yourself. I have brought your mind into the collective consciousness of the Hrothshaar. We now occupy a constructed psychic space within what you would call the tenth dimension. Were I to expose you to all the thought and knowledge of my people at once, your mind would be obliterated, and that would not serve my purposes at all."

The amorphous shadow of color and sound shimmered and growled, seemed to take on a human-like outline for a moment before recoiling again into chaos. "Amazing…"

Thargrimm felt the human's pain and disorientation, but he had long become inured to the weakness of lesser minds within the collective consciousness. "Your psyche cannot long withstand this state of being, Warden. Tell me what I wish to know and I will return you to your body. Done quickly, there may be no long-term effects. Other aliens who have experienced this condition have suffered psychoses and incurable madness. Some have even died."

The Warden's misshapen avatar pulsed and writhed while making low growling sounds. The human's will was strong, but uneducated and undisciplined.

"What did the traitor K'Luk say to you? What are you really planning?"

The Warden's thoughts remained obstinately silent.

Thargrimm placed the construct of his hand inside the Warden's cloud. Blue bolts of lightning rippled through the human's mind, eliciting wails of agony. "You are completely at my mercy here, Warden. Answer my questions."

"She… said your government… was a cruel dictatorship!"

Thargrimm sensed the interpretation as being true from the Warden's point of view. It was an honest answer, if not particularly helpful. "What else? What was she planning? What are the Malcontents playing at in this system?"

The Warden's mind battled Thargrimm's will ferociously, but to no avail. The admiral was reminded of the games he would play as a child, when he and his clutch-mates would pit captured *shenga*, the tiny arboreal mammals common on Hrothsha, against their *valuk*, the six-legged carnivorous lizards kept as household pets. For all his strength of will and courage, the Warden was as doomed as any shenga in this match.

"She... wanted the U.P.C. to help... her freedom fighters..."

The Warden's mind cloud lost color, wisps of energy trailing off and vanishing into the ether. The man wouldn't last much longer. "How? What are you trying to do with this surrender? What is your plan, Warden?"

"...Barycenter..."

Thargrimm frowned at the unexpected answer. He was prepared for "bomb" or "secret fleet" or "surprise attack" or some other military jargon. It took him a moment to orient himself to the scientific word.

"Admiral." A voice reached him within his private partition of the collective consciousness. It was the lieutenant commander who had taken K'Luk's place. "Admiral Thargrimm, sir. We have a problem."

The Warden had never experienced such pain and loss in his entire life. His body had been broken, battered, and put back together several times, but his mind had never suffered such a vicious assault. Every personal loss, every secret shame, every moment of guilt, of sorrow, of defeat he had ever known had been gathered up and forged into a mighty weapon and unleashed upon his soul. Painful memories long forgotten, hurts long healed, and griefs long mourned now joined with those of recent days, amplifying them, feeding them, and feeding upon them to tear at his confidence, his personality, his strength of will.

In the darkness of encroaching madness and despair, as his howling, hungry personal demons crowded and swarmed the shadows of his thoughts, he felt a moment's reprieve as Thargrimm's focus was diverted. In that moment, he saw a light in his mind's eye, a soft blue light. He heard a voice, calling his name as if from very far away.

"Quantum?"

"Warden." The voice was nearer. It was Quantum's and yet not Quantum's. "Warden, can you hear me?" It was the strange voice of the Hrothshaar spy, K'Luk, as it had sounded coming from Quantum's lips. "We are here for you, Warden. Quantum and I are here."

The Warden felt so weak, so worthless, so useless, so pathetic. "Help… me. Please…" Maximo Ryan's accusing eyes and Marajin's dead face filled his mind, and his grief and guilt were overwhelming.

"Star Warden!" The sharpness of the voice thundered through his mind, refocusing his will. The use of his title, his occupation, his purpose reaffirmed his identity. "You must fight. Thargrimm has ordered the assault force to attack Un Quan. You must hurry!"

The Warden gathered his wits, pulled himself back together. He imagined Quantum's hands lifting him back to his feet, and with that mental image firmly in place, he manifested himself fully in Thargrimm's psychic construct. He put all of his private woes back in place, again understanding that they were not his weakness, but rather his strength. Every psychic wound, every personal pain, every setback and defeat, had been a hammer blow on the anvil of his life, forging him into the man he had become.

The Warden stood as an embodied soul upon the high promontory overlooking the psychic valley of fire and ice. He stood and faced the dragon of Thargrimm's will.

Now fully aware in this strange new dimension, the Warden sensed the Hrothshaar admiral's thoughts. Thargrimm had learned that a battle for control of the *Bellicose* was taking place, the people on Un Quan having successfully put Quantum's plan into action.

Instinctively, the admiral had lashed out with his fighters—countermanding the order to attack the orbiting ships before targeting Un Quan—while his flagship inched ever closer to the twin suns. However, the planet's rotation had carried Quan City and the surrounding inhabitants to the opposite side of the world from the Hrothshaar attack craft, giving the Warden just a little more time.

"Thargrimm." The Warden felt his avatar grow stronger. He knocked the distracted admiral's constructed hand from his personal manifestation. "I think it's time we had a talk on even footing, man to man."

The alien psychic projection shimmered as Thargrimm's focus again returned to him. The saurian avatar snarled. "Impressive. I see that K'Luk has implanted part of herself on you, helping you to function in the collective consciousness. However, your mind is not strong enough to endure this place for long, Warden. I am much more powerful than you here. I can destroy you upon a whim."

"Maybe so. But that won't help your ship escape destruction between those two stars. At present, several thousand souls on Un Quan are using technology given us by K'Luk to wrest control of the *Bellicose* from your crew. Once they have it, this ship will be destroyed in the barycenter."

There was a ripple of energy and the Warden again found himself standing face-to-face with Thargrimm in the empty hangar bay. Blood trickled from the Warden's nostrils and ears and the taste of burning metal filled his mouth. A pain behind his eyes felt like someone was trying to punch their way out of his skull. With brass knuckles.

The admiral had released him from the higher dimension and appeared to search the collective consciousness for information. "That is an act of war."

"That is an act of self-defense, Admiral. Now, unless you call off your attack ships and agree to open channels of negotiations with your superiors and the U.P.C. delegation, you will likely succeed in your mission to eradicate all life in this system. But it will be your final mission. I'm guessing your people may even name that sort of 'victory' after you. Whenever a force wins at the cost of its entire command will forever be known as a *Thargrimm Victory* in the Hrothshaar Empire."

For a moment, the huge officer glared at the Warden, the shrewd intellect in his platinum eyes flickering toward primal bloodlust. Then, with a smile of grudging appreciation, Thargrimm said, "Very well, Warden... This is Admiral Thargrimm. All assault wings, abort attack operations and return to the *Bellicose*."

The Warden kept his eyes on Thargrimm as he raised his chrono. "Quantum, what's happening out there?"

"The Hrothshaar ships are leaving orbit and appear to be heading toward the center of the system. We are slowly gaining control of the *Bellicose*'s position. Shall we continue to direct it into the suns?"

The Warden looked to Thargrimm for confirmation. The admiral bowed his head and spread his arms wide in a display of surrender. "No. Let her crew regain control. For now."

Thargrimm shook his head. "You have destroyed me, Warden."

"On the contrary, Admiral. By avoiding bloodshed here, we may have averted a war that could have led to the ultimate destruction of one, if not both our peoples. If the diplomats do their jobs, in time, you'll be remembered as a hero."

Thargrimm narrowed his eyes, revealing his doubts about that, and turned to leave. "I will release your ship and its crew as soon as *peaceful negotiations* are underway between your delegates and representatives of the Radiant Council. Until then, make yourself at home as my personal guest aboard the *Bellicose*."

"Thanks for being here. I know this isn't your sort of thing." The Warden smiled at Quantum as he welcomed him into his penthouse suite in Quan City. Soft music played from the wall speakers, complementing the soft overhead lighting and the starlight filtering in from the opened balcony. The other guests milled about the spacious room in elegant dress, sipping wine and spirits, nibbling at the hors d'oeuvres served by domestic robots.

Quantum's antennae twirled as he looked the Warden up and down, taking in his silver and blue robes, specially tailored for the occasion. "My pleasure. I know it is not your 'sort of thing,' either. I believed you might need my support."

The Warden clapped Quantum on the shoulder, remembering how his friend had bonded with the alien psyche of K'Luk in order to rescue him in Thargrimm's psychic arena. "Always."

The two were leaving Un Quan and "Uncharted Space" on the morrow. A week had passed since the confrontation with Admiral Thargrimm, and the *Bellicose* had been recalled to deal with other threats along the Hrothshaar Empire's borders. The massive warship had been replaced by the *Halcion*, a heavy cruiser by Star Cav standards but which the Hrothshaar called a "diplomatic escort."

Similarly, the *Silverheels* had been joined by another U.P.C. transport carrying a much more experienced delegation. And, in light of this First Contact being "relatively peaceful," the United Planetary Council had begun facilitating Solomon Jones's request concerning his soldiers. Privately and through back channels, of course.

But this night was not about any of that. The Warden had gathered his closest friends and acquaintances on the eve of his departure in order to celebrate and remember the love he had found on this planet. Tonight was about Queen Marajin XVI.

In attendance were the Masters Thede, Dr. Gamela, and Dr. Hydrax, the jungle royals, King Mascos, Prince Andres, and Queen Jynnessa, and their trusted captains, Hurm and Sappoc. As the evening unfolded, they shared stories about the late warrior queen, they laughed and they cried, and they toasted her memory. The Warden feared he might have to make a speech, though he knew he had no words to share with others about his feelings for Marajin, as he could hardly explain those feelings to himself.

He was spared this dilemma when King Mascos called for everyone's attention. The one-armed warrior raised a goblet when all eyes were on him. "I would like to announce that I am abdicating my throne in favor of my son, Andres. May he and Queen Jynnessa reign in peace and happiness, founding a dynasty that will last for a hundred-thousand lifetimes!"

The announcement was greeted with polite applause. The Warden raised a questioning eyebrow to his friends, Andres and Jynnessa. In answer, the couple took their place beside the aging king. Jynnessa and Andres flashed radiant smiles as they held hands, and the young queen said, "I am with child."

The applause was more pronounced this time.

As the noise quieted, Andres said, "This is the beginning of a new age for Un Quan. We shall rule a united kingdom of men and women, governed with justice and wisdom under the guidance of the Masters of Quan City. And with this unification, we shall safeguard an ongoing peace between the United Planetary Council and the Hrothshaar Empire."

The Warden embraced the young couple, congratulating them. He smiled as he looked at the two rulers, unable to forget how they had been at one-another's throats like children on their trek through the jungle to find this city. "That is a bold statement. How did you come to such an accord so suddenly?"

Jynnessa kissed him lightly on the cheek. "Did you really think we sat on our hands down here while you played with your rocket-ships up there?"

The Warden congratulated them again and moved aside as Thede and Dr. Hydrax stepped up to offer their remarks. He had spotted Captain Sappoc standing alone beside the framed portrait of Marajin. The powerful warrior cradled a tumbler in her hand, her blue eyes sparkling in the soft light.

"How are you doing?" The Warden stepped as close as he dared.

Sappoc sniffed and finished her drink without looking at him. "I… I just wonder what she would have thought of all this… Her daughter mated to a male…" She shook her head, then finally faced him. Narrowing her eyes, a tear escaped and trickled down her blue cheek. Without showing it any notice, Sappoc said, "Thank you for this, Spaceman."

She placed the empty glass on a table and left the party.

The Warden sighed, experiencing something of what Sappoc must have felt. How would Marajin have taken all this in? He wondered what she might have said upon hearing the news of becoming a grandmother. That thought brought a lump to his throat, and he stepped to the balcony for a breath of fresh air. He stared in wonder at the beauty of Quan City at night, a city that was reawakening from centuries of hibernation, a city on the verge of becoming an important crossroads in interstellar commerce and politics.

"Is it customary on Earth for a host to abandon his own party?"

The Warden smiled at Dr. Gamela's deadpan voice. He turned from leaning on the balcony. "I suppose congratulations are in order, Doctor. Your experiment to encourage the natural reproduction of your species appears to be a complete success."

Gamela joined him at the rail, her green eyes scanning the lights of the city. "You jump to too many conclusions, Warden. I have noticed that about you. There are still many hurtles we must cross before the words 'complete success' can be used. But your sentiments are welcome, all the same."

"Still, you don't seem as happy as I thought you would be at the Queen's announcement."

"You see this, Warden? This city, this world, its people? These are the things I have dedicated my life to preserving. Not just the life on Un Quan, but the way of life, our culture… Since I was a small child, it has always been my dream to one day see the Un Quan of my ancestors—our civilization at its zenith—be reborn. I have worked hard for that dream every day of my life."

She turned to face him, a sadness in her eyes he had never seen before. "But now, with the U.P.C. and the Hrothshaar Empire turning this city and this world into their bargaining table, the ships will come, bringing new people, new commodities, and new ideas. And those naïve young savages in there will never rule over a *real* Un Quan, not the Un Quan that should have arisen. Our world will become a mishmash of interstellar ideologies, technologies, and ways of life, and our own cultural identity will die before ever being reborn."

The Warden tried to encourage her with a smile. "Maybe. Maybe not. And even if that does happen, it isn't always a bad thing. You know, once upon a time, my ancestors thought it was a good idea to burn other people alive in giant wicker men. Then, one day a stranger came, and after running all the snakes out, he convinced them this wasn't a very nice thing to do…"

He added with a wink, "Who knows? Maybe one of those ships will bring a stranger to Un Quan that just might convince you not to look down your nose at the folks who grew up in the jungle."

Dr. Gamela almost smiled.

END

Author's Note:
The Origin of Un Quan

Before the wheels came off *our* planet in 2020, I had started creating this sci-fi world around The Last Star Warden and looking to the future. I'll be honest, I was thinking that the Warden could be my Conan or my Sherlock Holmes, my literary legacy for future generations. And then 2020 happened and everything seemed like there might not *be* a future where people actually read and enjoyed books about space adventurers. But rather than swallowing the black pill and descending into the depression which haunts most writers like an ancestral ghost, I sat down and got to work.

I had been toying with the idea of a sword-and-planet tale in the vein of the great Edgar Rice Burroughs, maybe dusting off my childhood creations *The Space Crusaders* (possibly a project for another day, but probably not). Then it occurred to me, why not use the Star Warden to tell a sword-and-planet adventure, and why not deal with some of the real-world issues that were plaguing my mind at the time? Why not, indeed?

Initially, I thought this would be a single short story, "The Forbidden City of Un Quan." (And I'll admit the primary inspiration for the tale as well as the formidable character of Marajin was a rather racy illustration by one of my personal icons, Frank Frazetta, entitled *Tarzan Meets La of Opar.*) But as I got into the story, it occurred to me that I could explore not only the world of Un Quan but also the Warden himself. I had recently asked my editor, Andrea Thomas, what she thought was my biggest weakness as a writer. Andrea has read more of my stories than anyone else on Planet Earth aside from my wife, who is "contractually obligated." Andrea told me that I hadn't delved very deeply into the Warden's character, his personality, and his motivations. So Un Quan was my chance to do so.

And, as the story unfolded and things continued to spiral out of control in the real world, I realized this story could not be wrapped up with a "The Bad Guy Gets His" bow and everything-goes-back-to-normal happy ending. Plus, I'd left a whopper of a dangling plot thread in that Einstein-Rosen bridge which had initiated the Warden's sojourn into Uncharted Space. So, who had built that thing and why?

Well, if you have a Last Star Warden, it only makes sense to have a First. Here was my chance to shed a little more light on the Warden's origins and personality without giving too much away in one go. And again, Commander Jones, his small army of castoff veterans, and the cybernetic master program allowed me to work through some concerns I have with what is going on in my world right now. And again the story couldn't have a simple ending where everything goes back to the way it was. Un Quan, like Earth, had been changed forever.

Which brings us to "The Fate of Un Quan" wherein we find that there are forces at work in the galaxy of which we are not even aware. As above, so below, as the old adage goes. Though the Warden reconnects with Quantum and his part of the Galaxy (alleviating the sense of isolation which we all shared in 2020), he now has to deal with the consequences of what has happened since his arrival on Un Quan. And not just the socio-political ramifications, but also the personal ones. In the end, the Warden is as changed as is Un Quan.

It is my fervent hope that we, like the people of Un Quan, can come out the other side of 2020-21 a better people and make our planet a better world. I hope we learn to heal the wounds that have divided us. I hope we start to see one-another not as members of a race or gender or sexual persuasion or political slant or philosophical creed or what-have-you, but as individuals, as fellow human beings. I hope we stop listening to those who tell us otherwise, and start questioning their motives. Why do they want us divided? What's in it for them? How does that make the world a better place?

In the end, there really are terrible things out there in the forever night of space—comets, asteroids, solar flares, cosmic radiation, possibly even alien invaders—that don't care about us or our petty squabbles. So it behooves us to realize that we are one people, one world, alone against the dark. Alone unless we learn to start working together.

Jason McCuiston
March 2021

About the Author

Jason J. McCuiston was born in the wilds of southeast Tennessee, where he was raised on a carnivorous diet of old monster movies, westerns, comic books, horror magazines, sci-fi and fantasy novels, and, of course, Dungeons & Dragons. He attended the finest state school that would have him with the intention of becoming a comic-book artist. This did not pan out, so following his matriculation and a brief and unprofitable stint as an illustrator of tabletop RPGs, he embarked upon a whirlwind tour of spectacularly underpaid and uninspired careers. Half a lifetime later, he came to his senses, realizing he was meant to be a professional storyteller.

Publishing his first story about zombies, kung fu, and family ties in Parsec Ink's 2017 *Triangulation: Appetites* anthology, Jason has been a semi-finalist in the Writers of the Future contest and has studied under the tutelage of bestselling author Philip Athans. His stories of fantasy, horror, and science fiction have appeared in numerous anthologies, periodicals, websites, and podcasts.

Project Notebook, his first novel, was published in the summer of 2020 to critical acclaim, and Volume I of *The Last Star Warden* was released by Dark Owl Publishing in the spring of 2021. You can find these and most of his other publications on his Amazon page at https://www.amazon.com/-/e/ B07RN8HT98.

Jason lives in South Carolina, USA with his college-professor wife and their four-legged child. Connect with him on the internet at: https://www.facebook.com/ ShadowCrusade.

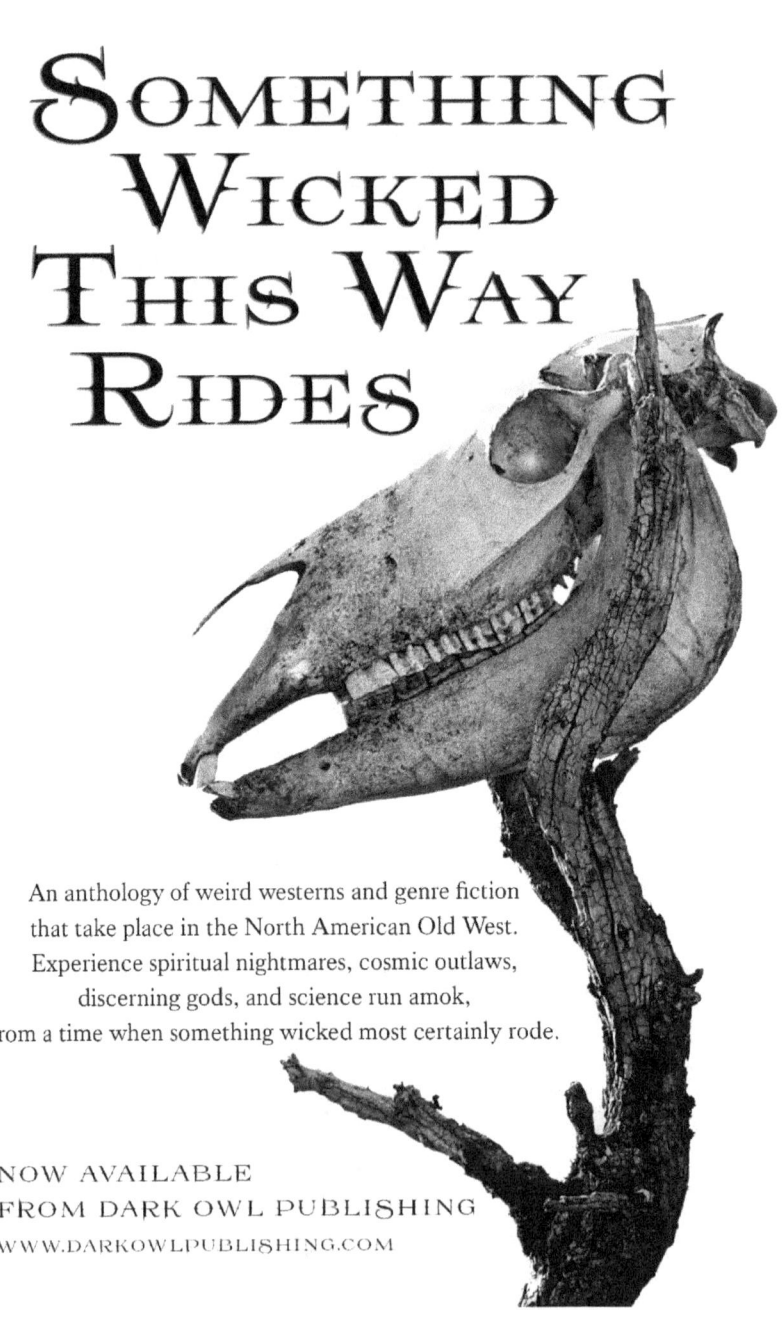

From Dark Owl Publishing

A Celebration of Storytelling

This is the Gathering. This is the Festival of Stories.

Editing by GD Deckard

The Anthological Festival of Tales

58 stories by 39 authors designed to honor the art of writing
by including a fair, festival, or celebration in each telling.
From fantasy to sci-fi, from thrillers to mysteries,
we know readers will truly enjoy this feast of fables.

Now Available from  Dark Owl Publishing, LLC

www.darkowlpublishing.com

In the summer of 1947 – months before something fell to Earth near Roswell, New Mexico – the skies above the Pacific Northwest were filled with mysterious lights and strange phenomena. Members of a top secret organization are dispatched to investigate the Maury Island Incident in Washington. The team of elite WWII veterans must uncover the truth behind these extraordinary occurrences... even if it means facing their own self-destruction.

PROJECT NOTEBOOK

BY JASON J. MCCUISTON

Available in paperback and on Kindle
via Amazon

www.ingramcontent.com/pod-product-compliance
Lightning Source LLC
Chambersburg PA
CBHW051502170626
46811CB00002B/600